Bucking
the
Rules

MORE FROM KAT MURRAY

Taking the Reins

Bucking
the
Rules

KAT MURRAY

BRAVA

KENSINGTON PUBLISHING CORP.

www.kensingtonbooks.com

BRAVA BOOKS are published by

Kensington Publishing Corp.
119 West 40th Street
New York, NY 10018

All Kensington titles, imprints, and distributed lines are available at special quantity discounts for bulk purchases for sales promotions, premiums, fund-raising, educational, or institutional use.

Special book excerpts or customized printings can also be created to fit specific needs. For details, write or phone the office of the Kensington special sales manager: Kensington Publishing Corp., 119 West 40th Street, New York, NY 10018, attn: Special Sales Department; phone: 1-800-221-2647.

BRAVA and the B logo are Reg. U.S. Pat. & TM Off.

ISBN-13: 978-0-7582-8106-7
ISBN-10: 0-7582-8106-4

First Kensington Trade Paperback Printing: July 2013

10 9 8 7 6 5 4 3 2 1

Printed in the United States of America

First electronic edition: July 2013

ISBN-13: 978-0-7582-8107-4
ISBN-10: 0-7582-8107-2

Chapter One

Trace Muldoon danced out of the way of the elegant-but-deadly female legs threatening to break his foot. One wrong move, one moment of lost concentration, and he could kiss his toes good-bye.

"Easy, sugar," he crooned. "Come on, now. You don't want to hurt me, do you?" He brushed a hand down her back, watching her eyes close in delight even as she tried to get in another bite to his shoulder.

Females. Prickly even when they were getting something they wanted. Trace continued to stroke and speak softly until she swayed on her feet, under some sort of hedonistic spell.

"You do have a way with the girls."

Trace turned to see Red Callahan at the door, amusement tilting the corners of his mouth.

"Jealous of my superior skills?" Trace joked back.

Just then, teeth clicked around his shoulder in a not-so-playful bite. He yelped and skidded to the corner of the stall while the six-hundred-pound mare swished her tail and tossed her head in some sort of female satisfaction at getting the upper hand.

Red chuckled. "Yep, jealous. You pegged me. Can't get enough of those bites."

Trace flipped him off, but laughed and shrugged the

sore shoulder. Working with horses, you expected to get a few kicks and bites for your trouble. He slipped out the stall door and closed it behind him gently. With one last glance behind him at the mare, who looked quite pleased with herself, he fell into step with Red and headed out to the hot walk area.

"Where's my sister?"

"Still asleep, I believe." Red checked the clock on the rough plank walls of the barn by the entrance, showing 6:15 in the morning. "She'll probably be up soon."

Trace shook his head. "She never used to sleep so late. Not that she was ever a morning person, but she'd get up and get started before anyone else thanks to sheer grit and caffeine."

Red smirked. "Now she's got a reason to stay in bed a little longer."

Trace grimaced in return. "Really don't want to think about my sister in bed with a guy, but thanks for that."

"Plus," Red went on, as if Trace hadn't said a word, "I shut her alarm clock off and asked Emma to let her sleep as long as she could. I try it about once a week, but it rarely works."

"Good." Trace nodded and stepped up on the rusted bottom rung of the metal fencing that surrounded the hot walk area, folding his arms over the top for balance. "She needs a little management from time to time. Peyton works too hard, like she's afraid to let Bea and me take on the responsibility. She's going to kill you for it, though."

"I can handle your sister," Red said confidently with a cocky-ass smile to go along with it. "All it takes is—"

"La, la, la, I can't hear you." Trace watched a ranch hand walk a colt new to his halter around and around in circles. It was an apt metaphor for his current life: one big circle.

"Maybe she's going off experience," Red said, hopping up next to him. "You and Bea weren't exactly there for her in the past when she was battling your mama for control of the ranch."

Memories, one worse than the other, flooded him before Trace could shut them down. But much like slamming the barn door closed after the horse was out in the pasture, too little too late. "Yeah, well, I can't speak for Bea, but I had reasons for staying gone. Though I can easily guess leaving was just as much survival for her as it was for me."

Sensing the topic was closed, Red wisely moved on. "Steve!" The hand turned to look at him, calming the skittish horse with a few murmured words and a rub on the neck. "I want to see some figure eights with that one. He's eager to learn, so give him something to do."

Always the trainer. Trace took a moment to sit back and watch the man his prickly sister had gone and fallen in love with. A couple years older than he, Red was well-respected in the horse world. How a trainer of his level had landed at M-Star, a still-struggling breeding operation, was a question most people scratched their heads over.

Of course, once news of Red's relationship with Peyton went public, some assumed they understood the score. Red was there for easy sex.

The thought had Trace laughing quietly. Nothing with Peyton was easy. Red had fought hard for every inch of gained ground there. But he also knew the man was just as crazy for his sister as she was for him. So Trace figured he wasn't obligated to break the guy's nose for taking advantage of his sister. She was a big girl.

Though it was getting a little tight in the house, with all three siblings back at home, and one shacked up. As kids, the house had been plenty big. As adults . . . they all needed some more space.

Not to mention, though Trace appreciated the help with his young son, he'd like to gain a little more independence. Stand on his own two feet, without worrying he was overstaying his welcome.

"Switch him up." Red pointed and circled his hand in a signal for Steve.

"Say," Trace started, warming up to the idea now circling his head like the colt in the warm-up ring. "You're spending most nights at the big house now, aren't you?"

Red's eyes never left the horse's legs. "Yeah."

"And I saw a few of your boxes migrate up to Peyton's room." What used to be their parents' master bedroom, though they'd almost never used it together. "I guess that's pretty settled now, isn't it?"

"Hmm. I think he's done for the day, Steve. Let's switch him out for his neighbor, see what she's got to show us this morning." He turned to Trace. "Back up a few steps. What's settled?"

"You living with Peyton."

Red's mouth thinned a little. "Look, I understand you're protective, but you know I'm not playing her. So if you're going to get all butt-hurt over me moving in, then you can just—"

"I want your place."

Red stopped and his eyes widened. "My place?"

Trace nodded to the large garage, over which the trainer's apartment sat. "Yeah. You're not using it, so it's just sitting there. Someone might as well, right?"

The corner of Red's mouth twitched. "But where will I sleep when Peyton's mad at me?"

"The couch, like all good husbands." He chuckled as his friend's face whitened a little. "Calm down. It's just an expression. If you need some alone time, you can take Seth's room. Without a crib in there, I think a futon would fit nicely."

"It's only a one-bedroom place," Red reminded him.

"We can make do. Two guys don't need much room. Plus, one of us can't even walk yet, so it's not like he's gonna take up that much space. I'll find a nook for his crib and put one of those ugly silk screens Ma used to spread all over the house in front so he's got a little mini-bedroom. Done deal." The idea grew in his mind, and he could already taste freedom.

As much freedom as a single father with a not-quite-one-year-old son could have.

Red shrugged and smiled a little. "Well, it was a nice dream, but you're too late."

"Too late? What, did you rent it out to someone?" The thought had him laughing. They were in the middle of nowhere, with Marshall—the small town they used as a home base—over ten miles away. And nobody was going to rent an apartment out here.

"Rent, not quite. But your sister got to it before you did."

Bea? His sweet little sister Bea—Bea had swiped his apartment from him? Well, not quite his . . . yet.

"Damn."

"Yeah, sorry about that. Guess you'll have to suck it up and hang around the big house a little longer."

"I'll live."

They watched in silence as Steve brought out another horse and started the slow warmup.

"There's good news about this though," Red said after a stretch.

"What's that?"

"With Bea and all her clothes gone—that's like clearing up room for three."

Josephine unlocked the door to her bar and walked in with a satisfied sigh. Sure, the place smelled the way you might expect a bar to smell like the morning after a weekend. But it was her bar. And she knew tomorrow she'd be doing the exact same thing. And she loved it.

Two feet in, her feet hit a sticky spot. She made a mental note to have her afternoon staff go over the floors again with a mop, and get on the night crew to do a better job cleaning up. Though even with one sticky spot, the place was a vast improvement over what she'd walked into when she'd bought the place.

She surveyed the room, looking for anything out of place. Missing chairs, broken tabletops, knocked over wall decor . . . you never knew. The place had been transformed from a rough honky-tonk that appealed to cowboys alone to a more civilized—though still fun—bar where both men and women felt at home. Her goal had been to make a haven for both genders, and to appeal to both the cowboys and the non-ranchers. A delicate balance, but one she thought she'd managed to find. Rather than the dark, oppressive, barely-lit cavern it had been, she'd brought in funky light fixtures and painted the paneling a cream tone. She'd updated from a crappy-ass juke box to a real sound system, though she kept the juke in the corner for the sake of nostalgia. And even though she still played country, she kept it to country from this decade, with some good oldies tossed in for variety. And she'd updated the drink menu to include more choices than bottle or draft, and the kitchen menu to more than pretzels or peanuts.

"Mornin', Jo."

Her day cook, and currently her only friend, stuck his head out the kitchen door.

"Hey, Stu. What are you in for so early?" She walked around the bar and opened the cash register, reaching for the receipts she knew would be there from the night before.

"Wanted to double-check my order before the produce guy got here. Something wasn't adding up, but I found the problem."

"Always good." She hopped up onto a bar stool, rather than taking the paperwork into the back, to her rarely-used office. One of the main reasons she'd moved to such a small town after so many big cities was so she could become part of the fabric of the place. Become someone everyone knew, the community could point to and recognize. She couldn't do that if she hid in the back all the time.

"What'd you do with your night off?" Stu walked in from the kitchen, wiping his hands with a towel. Though they didn't open for the lunch crowd for another two hours, his apron was already on, the strings wrapped twice around his impressive girth and tied into a neat bow right under his belly. A belly that was considerably larger than the rest of him. Middle-age spread had hit Stu hard, but he didn't seem to have a care in the world. His motto was "Diets are for quitters," and he stuck to it with a tenacity that made Jo smile, even as she mentally winced at the potential side effects of that extra weight.

"Watched some TV, gave myself a pedicure, went to bed early."

"Boring as hell."

"It was amazing."

He sneered. "If you think that's amazing, you need more than one night off a year."

Silently, she agreed. But when you owned a business, when your name was on the deed and it all fell to you, nights off were a precious commodity. "Maybe."

"Maybe you should get a place elsewhere, instead of living above the damn bar. Then you'd at least have some sort of separation from work. How can you take a break if you're living above the dang place?"

"The rent's cheap." She smiled and went back to the receipts, double-checking her night manager's calculations. She liked the guy, and trusted him . . . mostly. But her name, her business, her final calculations.

"Rent schment. Like you aren't making out like a bandit. You could afford better."

"I don't want better. I want what I have. Go stir something."

Stu walked off, muttering not so quietly about stubborn women and the problems they bring on themselves. She grinned and went back to her figures. Nothing started her day off quite like a quick spar with Stu. Though he probably knew it, she liked to think of their verbal duels as a better, more healthy version of the morning cup of coffee.

Twenty minutes later, employees started filing in.

"Hey, Amanda." She waved over one of the waitresses she'd inherited with the bar. Most hadn't wanted to stay and work for someone they didn't know, and that'd been fine with Jo. Can't embrace change? Probably wasn't meant to be. But Amanda had stayed, and proven herself worthy enough to start making decisions on whom to hire for wait staff. If she kept it up, Jo would be ready to move her into an assistant manager position . . . when Jo was ready to loosen the reins a little herself.

"Hey, Jo." The perky brunette slid onto the stool next to her. "Good night last night. Had a reunion in here, they closed the place down. Good tippers, when all was said and done."

"Good for the till." She shifted a pile of receipts to the left, and moved another stack in front of her.

Amanda leaned back against the bar, elbows bent, legs propped out. "A crowd like that never would have stepped foot in here five years ago. You've really taken this place and run with it in your own way, haven't you?"

Jo raised a brow and punched in another number, writing down the calculation. "Did this place look like something I'd bother with five years ago?"

"Nope. But I have to say, you didn't stray too far off the mark." Amanda's eyes wandered over the décor. Exposed beams, decent lighting, classic Western-style art mixed with simple contemporary photos. "Most people got one look at you and decided you'd turn the place into some sort of gallery style. All slick glass and steel. Cold. City."

Jo had the distinct impression she'd just been gently insulted. She smiled, amused at the assessment, and fingered the fourth piercing in her right ear. "Well, you know me. I hate gossip and don't bother with it."

"Your city's showing," Amanda said with a smile. "Everyone here listens to gossip. It's like a professional sport. Everyone wants to make the first round draft."

"Have at it. More power to 'em. Gossip away . . . just do it with a drink in your hand and ordering off my menu." Jo gathered up the receipts and stuffed them in a vinyl zippered pouch. "I don't care what people think, as long as they're paying their tab at the end of the night."

"Is that how it is in Chicago?"

Jo smiled. "Chicago, New York City, L.A., San Fran . . . you name it. Big cities are about as likely to change as small towns."

"Which is to say, not at all." Amanda grinned.

"Exactly." Jo swatted at her shoulder with the bag and hopped down from the bar stool. "Now get to work. I'm not paying you to sit around and talk."

Amanda gave her a cheeky salute and hurried off to prep her station for the afternoon lunch crowd.

Jo headed into her office to drop off the bag and pick up the night's cash from the safe. Then, after a quick debate, she left her car keys behind and headed out the front door. The walk would do her some good. Being in the same building day after day—upstairs or downstairs—started to get stuffy and boring.

It still amazed her how quiet things were in Marshall. She passed the tack shop and peered in. The owner, Mr. Hollins, saw her and held up a hand in a tentative wave. She did the same, adding a smile for effect.

She made people nervous still, despite having been there for almost a year. Change was hard for people in Marshall. The town embraced the changes to the bar much faster than accepting her. But then again, the bar served a purpose to folks. So naturally, it was in their best interest to be grateful.

Her, on the other hand . . . Well. She'd just wait and see. Eventually, they'd come around.

She'd just make them.

"Name the last time you went out."

Trace shoveled another bite of breakfast in and chewed longer than necessary to give himself a moment to think.

Peyton wasn't fooled. That was the problem with working with your sister. She saw straight through your bullshit before you had a chance to even use it. "Put down the fork and answer, Muldoon."

"But how could I possibly ignore this culinary master-piece Emma slaved for hours to create?" He gave the woman in question a sly smile as she walked by the table and refilled Peyton's coffee mug.

Emma snorted, completely unamused and immune to the sibling squabble. She should be; she'd been hearing it for over twenty years. "What a crock. It's scrambled eggs. Don't drag my breakfast into your little talk, or you'll be eating toaster waffles for a week."

The horror of missing out on a week of Emma's home-

made breakfasts had him putting down the fork and staring at his sister. "It's none of your business. I don't ask
about you and Red." He cringed at the thought.

"That's self-serving. You don't *want* to know about my
relationship with Red." Peyton took a moment to look
toward a babbling Seth and nudge a Cheerio closer to him
on his high chair tray.

"No, no, I really don't. And it's still none of your business what I do with my life, just because you *do* want to
know."

Emma set a pitcher of OJ down on the table with a
heavy thump. "Well, it's my business, and I wanna know
why you're holed up in here like a hermit." Before he could
reply with a joke, she narrowed her eyes. "And don't even
try turning that into some sort of perverse joke."

Damn. Emma had all but raised the three Muldoon kids
from diapers. And when she did that narrowed-eye thing,
none of them was safe. "Come on, Emma. It's not exactly
like there's much to do around here. Besides, I've got
Seth." He rubbed one knuckle over his son's soft cheek.

"You know I'll babysit anytime." Peyton grabbed a ba-
nana out of the bowl on the table and began to peel. "So
that's not a good excuse at all."

"It's good enough for me. I hate asking you to watch
him if I'm not out at a gig for M-Star. It's not fair. You're
not his nanny."

"I'm his aunt, which is even better. Isn't it, little man?
Yes, it is." She tickled him under his chin and grinned
when he squirmed and giggled in delight. "And on that
note, I've got some work to do." She passed by Emma and
gave her a quick kiss on the cheek. "Thanks for the eggs.
I'm out!"

"That girl works too hard," Emma said with a sigh and
set a platter of bacon in front of him.

Score. One of Trace's favorite things about Emma—besides her unconditional love and unwavering support of the Muldoon siblings—happened to be her old-fashioned view of men and food. If there was a man in front of her, she was positive he was half starved, and it was her job to fix it.

"You never say I work too hard," he pointed out, crunching into the first bite of bliss. Seth—seeming to sense his father's pleasure—reached for the strip of bacon. His little face contorted with concentration and one chubby arm waved frantically.

"Sorry, little man. You're a way's off from the good stuff. Stick to Cheerios. You'll graduate to the goods in a bit."

Bea, the youngest of the three siblings, breezed into the dining room with a swish of a silk robe. Though she probably intended to convey that *just out of bed* look, Trace would have bet his favorite boots she'd spent at least ten minutes fixing her hair and makeup to achieve the look. Waste of time.

"Speaking of not working too hard," he muttered.

"Hmm?" Bea slid into the seat across from him. "Did you say something?"

"Morning, Bea-Bea." He gave her a smile. Fighting in front of Emma at the table was a surefire way to get his breakfast yanked out of his hands. "You're out of bed ridiculously early. Sleep well?"

His sister yawned and patted her mouth with one perfectly manicured hand. "It's too quiet. I miss the sound of traffic. I swear, the dead silence woke me up faster than a garbage truck ever would have."

"Music to sleep by."

"You know it." She stared for a moment at the platter of bacon in the middle of the table. Trace knew that look. It was the same look his old dog used to give a treat in his hand just before he got the command to take it. But Bea had more willpower. "Emma, do we have any grapefruit?"

Emma rolled her eyes and set a glass of juice in front of Bea. "Do I look like a woman who has grapefruit in her kitchen?"

Bea pouted prettily and leaned into Emma's side. "But you know I love grapefruit."

"And I love Hugh Jackman. I don't see him on the table for breakfast." With a wistful sigh, Emma waltzed back into the kitchen.

Bea stared once more at the bacon, then shook her head. "We might have very different views on cholesterol, but at least I can say our taste in men is a little closer to matching."

"I did not hear that." A thought occurred to him. "You know, it's not going to be much fun walking here every morning for breakfast."

"Hmm?" Bea looked up from her juice.

"From the apartment. The trainer's apartment? Red said you asked for it, and you were moving in."

"Oh, yes." She smiled widely. "Rather genius, I thought. Of course, it needs paint badly. And hopefully I can find some covers for that ugly furniture. A new bedspread would liven things up. Maybe Emma would let me take some dishes." Bea's eyes started to glaze over.

Trace could practically see color wheels dancing in her head. He snapped his fingers once in front of her to get her attention. "Focus, please. I wanted the apartment for me and Seth."

"Aw, that's a cute idea. The two of you out there, baching it up." Her lips twitched as she sipped her juice.

"So you'll let me trade? You can take my bedroom here—it's bigger than the one you've got."

"No."

No? "Bea, come on. A guy needs his space."

"So does a girl, and I got there first. Plus, you have Seth. Isn't it nice that Emma's right here every morning? She watches him, after all."

He took a moment to evaluate his baby sister and see if he could find any weakness in her. A softness to poke at, a loose thread to pull. But her mouth set in that straight, mulish line that was so much like Peyton's—though she'd hate to hear it—and he knew without a doubt, there was no budging her. Not now, anyway.

"Damn," he muttered into his plate. Trace shoveled the last bite of egg into his mouth and reached for Seth's bib. "Ready for your day, little man? What's on the agenda? A little crawling, maybe some scooting? Maybe Emma will take a blanket out and let you play in the grass. That'd be fun, yeah?" He lifted the wriggling boy from his seat and frowned at the waterfall of crumbs spilling to the scrubbed wood floor. "Shit."

Seth giggled and clapped, as if realizing this was a word he normally shouldn't be hearing.

Bea raised a brow. "Problem?"

"Yeah. Here, hold him a sec while I go get a dust pan and sweep this up. Otherwise, Emma will skin me alive."

As he held out Seth under the armpits, she backed up into her chair, arching away from the offering. "Thanks, but no. I don't do babies. We talked about this."

"I'm not asking you to change a diaper. Just hold him for a minute. It won't kill you." He waited a beat. "Unless you want to do the crumb sweeping."

"Give him to me." Bea held out her arms and took the bundle onto her lap. "Can't he just, like, crawl around on his own?"

"He could, but he wants to be held right now. He's still waking up. It's early."

"You're telling me."

Trace headed toward the supply closet, smiling as he

heard Bea yelp and scold, "Don't pull those, they're attached to my ears."

True, Peyton took to aunthood much easier than Bea. But he didn't worry. His youngest sister had a heart of gold under all that makeup and perfume. She might play the cold-hearted bitch on that soap opera thing she was in—or was that her evil twin? Who could keep up?—but in reality, she just needed a chance to get her feet under her again. He had a feeling her extended stay at the M-Star had nothing to do with contract negotiations and "career readjustment" like she'd claimed. But he wasn't going to push it. She'd share, in her own sweet time, what was going on.

Just like he'd take his own sweet time finding a social life in this place. But damn, could they not give a guy five minutes to get settled?

Okay, yeah, it'd been well over six months. But still. He'd get around to it when he was good and comfortable. He finally felt like he had a handle on the whole single dad thing. Slowly but surely, he could add in a chance to meet pretty ladies and have a good time.

Eventually.

Chapter Two

Jo watched two hotheads start revving their engines for a fight. Damn. She checked the corner of the bar and made sure her favorite bat was still handy. Not that she ever used it—hardly ever—but at times, it was the visual reality check men needed to take her seriously when she kicked them out. Something about a pissed-off woman didn't always register. But a pissed-off woman holding a bat? Always a big score.

"Want me to step in?" Stu popped his head in from the kitchen. "Or I could send one of my guys."

"No, I've got it. They're about to receive an invitation to the parking lot." Jo pulled her hair back at the nape of her neck and walked through the passway to the spot where the two idiots were riling each other up.

"Call if you need me!"

Amanda raced up behind her as Jo approached the two men. "Shouldn't you let Stu—"

"Nope. You know me. I've got it." How often did she repeat that phrase in any given day? *I've got it. No, I've got it. Really, I've got it.* Was it so hard to believe one woman could handle her own business without a man stepping in every time things got a bit sticky?

Luckily, brawls here didn't seem to happen nearly as much as they did in a larger, more crowded bar. She'd never imagined being able to run a bar without a bouncer. But in Marshall, it just wasn't necessary.

"It's bullshit, that's what it is." The first man shrugged a hand off his shoulder. It belonged to a buddy wanting to calm him down.

Good luck with that.

"And I say it's not." The second man's friends cheered him on. Clearly his friends were just as stupid as he was.

Though he was about five inches shorter, and at least twenty pounds lighter, the first man stepped forward, chest pressing against his opponent. "The Vikings don't have a shot at the Super Bowl in this decade, and you know it. Stop while you're behind, dipshit."

Fueled by righteous anger, the Vikings fan took this as a personal attack and pushed the shorter man back a step. "You gonna make me stop?"

"I'm going to make you both stop." Jo stepped between them, knowing she had to grab the chance to intervene while she could. "If you want to be assholes, I've got no problem with it. But be an asshole somewhere else. People are drinking and eating and having fun in here."

The first man actually looked a little contrite, his head hanging slightly. "Whatever. I'm already cashed out." He nodded to his buddy, the one whose commonsense had been evident before, and they started heading toward the door.

Jo breathed a sigh of relief. Easier than expected. Almost too—

"Pussy!"

And there it was. The big guy just couldn't resist a parting shot. But when the other man didn't respond, he jumped forward to grab him by the collar of his jacket. *His* friends, it seemed, were not only pleased, but encouraged him by pushing against his back.

Unfortunately for them all, Jo was still in his way. She

managed to twist enough so when she fell, she only smacked her elbow on the cocktail table, rather than her face. But it was enough to enrage her. Drunks, she could handle. Assholes, sure. But the minute someone hurt something in her bar—including her own body—she got nasty. With a quick spin on the floor, she shot one foot out to connect with the man's knee. His leg buckled and he went down hard, face-first. But he didn't have the same grace and experience as Jo, and his face planted on a chair.

Bull's-eye. Jo was never a super fan of retaliation, but she couldn't be anything but honest . . . that one felt good.

A few male patrons nearby stepped in and asked if she needed assistance. Nice timing, of course. Couldn't have been bothered ten minutes ago, but now that the guy was flat on his face, they were all eager beavers and concerned citizens. She asked two to help scoot the man out the door and into his friend's truck.

"Did he pay?" she asked Amanda as they trailed behind the prone customer.

"Yeah, they cashed out about ten minutes ago. I made sure to keep up with their bill."

"Nice work." After the ever-so-helpful patrons shoved the half-conscious man into his truck, she offered them each a free round. "Who's driving this guy home?"

One of his cheering squad mumbled he'd do it. She took a moment to gauge the way he walked, the look in his eye, then asked, "How many beers?"

"Two."

She looked at Amanda, who nodded in agreement. But Jo still paid attention as they walked to the truck. Not a hiccup or falter to his step.

"Need us to call the cops?"

She watched from the doorway of the bar. When the friend got behind the wheel and took off, she shook her head. "He's on his way. No point."

The other man nodded at her arm. "Already starting some color there. Should be assault, if you ask me."

And yet they'd hung back until she was finished dealing with the belligerent drunk. Typical. Jo had learned early in life to never count on a man to do anything. One of the few useful things her mother passed on. "I'll be fine. A little ice and it'll be good as new."

They both shrugged and headed to the bar to claim their free drink.

"Jerks."

"Eh, give 'em a break. It's hard getting your hands dirty after a long week of work." When Amanda gave her a confused look, Jo rolled her eyes and threw an arm around her shoulder. "That's sarcasm. Remember how we talked about that?"

"Right, right." But Jo could tell she was still mulling it over in her mind. "Still, a real man would have stepped up, regardless."

"Possibly. Or maybe the real man would see that a real woman can handle herself."

"No real man out here would dare let a woman step into a fight. It falls under the same category as opening doors and carrying boxes."

"How nineteen-fifties." Jo joked often about how ass-backwards everything seemed in Marshall after living in large cities her whole life, but the truth was . . . she loved it. Not the part where men still thought women couldn't handle themselves. But the more simple way of thinking, overall. It was one of the reasons she'd come to a small town, rather than striking out on her own in another big city.

"I've got an order to deliver."

"Off you go, then. Otherwise, the boss might fire you." She grinned as Amanda stuck out her tongue and hurried off to the table. After seeing Amanda wasn't too frazzled to keep working the rest of the shift, she headed back to her spot behind the bar. There were enough drink orders to keep her busy until closing time, when she managed to drag her tired ass up the stairs to her above-bar apartment. Not quite the Ritz, but perfectly adequate.

She stripped off her black polo with Jo's Place stitched over the breast pocket and dumped it into a hamper full of identical shirts. Time for laundry. She'd have to run a load while doing the books tomorrow morning. After a quick debate between sleep and a shower, sleep won. Who did she have to impress in bed? Nobody, that's who. So she'd grab the extra twenty minutes of shut-eye any day.

Another depressing thought, she realized as she changed into a sleep tank and some ugly shorts with a rip in one hem. One of the major drawbacks to small town life . . . no pool of single, available men looking for a night of fun. Not that she'd been a total slut or anything in Chicago. Or New York, or San Fran. . . . She just enjoyed a man from time to time, and working in a bar, she had her pick.

Now it was all cowboys who went to bed before the sun was fully set and married men who loved their wives. And good for them, she added, getting into bed and sighing at the glorious feeling of being off her feet.

Well, she'd known getting the bar up and running was priority number one. Now that the first year was nearly complete, she felt more confident. Maybe it was time to start watching for a man to slip into her bed now and again. Who wouldn't like a little extra company to come home to after a long night?

With thoughts of sexy, faceless cowboys in tight chambray shirts dancing through her head, she fell asleep.

Trace laid on his back on the carpet of the upstairs family room, his son crawling on the floor beside him. Though the living room downstairs was more spacious, it was a little too perfect for any of the Muldoon siblings. Sylvia, their mother, had taken it into her mind to turn the big house from comfortably lived in to a show palace. Something about looking rich if you wanted to be rich. Not that it worked.

Trace thought it was just another excuse to do whatever she wanted with the family money. And as usual, their father had gone right along with it. The man was brilliant in so many ways, but a businessman and a husband with a backbone—those were two things he'd never managed in his lifetime.

Peyton walked over and flopped down on the couch. "So. Are you going to tell me who his mother is?"

"Nope."

"Okay. I'll just ask again next week."

"I know."

Seth's mom. A weekly conversation topic. Trace had known when he'd showed up at the ranch with a three-month-old baby and no woman in tow, he'd get questioned. He hadn't realized, months and months later, Peyton would still be picking at it. But he should have. Peyton was a bulldog with a bone when she wanted something. But she wasn't heartless. She'd use manipulation to get it out of him if she could.

But it wouldn't work. Who his son's mother was didn't matter. She wasn't in his life, wouldn't be in his life, and that's what was important. Besides, the odds were the story would bore her to tears anyway.

"Come here, little man." She rolled and reached over with one arm, scooping him up just before he started to pull himself up on the coffee table to cruise. Plopping him on her stomach, she grinned and started messing with his still-bald head. "When are you gonna grow some hair? Is there some sort of baby Rogaine we can give the kid?"

"Doubt it. Plus, being bald is cool. How many athletes shave their heads these days?"

"Hmm." She rubbed his back through the footie pajama top for a moment. "I'm thinking this guy and I need to start a new tradition."

"What's that?"

"Movie night."

"Movie night?" Trace lifted his head a little from the floor. "He's not even one. He can't focus on anything for more than two minutes. Plus, all the books say introducing screen time early can ruin babies' eyesight and lower their attention span, plus the added consequences of—"

"Were you this boring when we were kids, or is this a recent development?" Peyton asked mildly.

"I'd say it's about nine months old. Movie night, Peyton?" He snorted. "What kind of bullsh—crap is that all about?"

"Earmuffs, Daddy." She grinned and covered Seth's ears with her palms for a moment until he started shaking his head in annoyance. "Okay, okay. So maybe I'm leading into this badly. I have a favor to ask. . . ."

"No. I absolutely will not help Bea move out. She wants the apartment? She can do it herself."

"Agreed there, though for different reasons. Mostly, I just want to see her actually break a sweat." Peyton snickered at the thought.

"Like she'd do it herself. She'll just get a few of the hands to come up here after work and do it for her."

She thought about that a moment. "Damn. You're right."

"Earmuffs, Auntie Peyton."

She shot him the finger. "Fine. I want you to go out with Red."

Of all the favors he'd been imagining, that was the last he'd expected. "Go out where? Out of town? I don't have anything this weekend on my schedule." Did he miss something? He glanced at Seth. Already he regretted missing another weekend of his son's life.

"No, no. Not out of town." Peyton stood, shifting and supporting Seth carefully as she maneuvered. With the child on her hip, she started walking slowly back and forth around the room. The swaying motion of her hips lulled Seth enough that he let his head drop to her shoulder. Thank God. "Red's got it in his mind to head for a night out on the town. I think he needs some company, but you know how he is. He's not going to ask one of the guys here. Something about muddying up the trainer–work hand relationship. Balance of power and yadda-yadda."

"I think you two yadda-yadda'ed the balance of power last year when the trainer and owner started boinking."

Peyton rolled her eyes. "I'm choosing to ignore that."

"Choose away," he permitted.

"The fact is, he's itching to get out. I know he likes staying here in the big house, since he's with me. In my bed," she added with a smirk.

"Jesus, TMI, Peyton. You two can't let a guy pretend to not know, can you?" Trace rolled over and buried his face in the carpet, arms covering his ears.

"I'm sorry. I forgot what a boring prude you are these days. Didn't you know Red and I host midnight Scrabble matches every evening? I'm currently ahead in the ranking, thanks to his horrible spelling."

"Better. Continue."

"But I think he needs a little separation. We work together, we're shacking up—I mean, *playing Scrabble*—together." She used air quotes around Seth's head for that little tidbit. "He eats all his meals here or in the barn, where he's likely to run into me during the day. And we travel together more times than not. He needs a breather. I can see it."

Trace watched as Peyton took another lap with his son

on her hip. He focused on her eyes, then her hands. They were the two places he knew she showed stress the most. Even as a child, she'd managed to face their bitch of a mother stone-faced. But her hands would clench into fists or widen into stiff boards, and her eyes would shoot daggers when Sylvia's back was turned.

He didn't see anything like that now.

"Does that bother you?"

"Bother me?" She turned to look at him, eyebrows raised in confusion. "How so?"

"That he needs space from you. I mean, you love the guy. Does it bug you that he needs to get away?"

"Hell, no." She winced and stroked Seth's head. "Sorry. That's still hard to curb."

"I'm calling 'hell' a free pass. It's a location as much as a curse, so it's a freebie."

"Good. But no, it doesn't bother me. I love him, he loves me. I don't think he's going to run out and find the first available woman to lie on her back and roll in the hay. He needs some space. It's natural. And frankly, if he is getting space, so am I." She grinned at him. "Between you and me, I wouldn't mind a night off from the girlfriend routine either. I get to do whatever I want while he's gone for the evening, like play with my favorite nephew. And tomorrow, back to being the sexy gir—uh, great speller." She jiggled Seth a little and he smiled back at her. "So. Help a gal out?"

Trace searched his mind for plot holes. "I don't want you to babysit."

"You didn't hear me, did you? This is movie night for us. Not babysitting. We're bonding. Now, go change into something a little less icky, and let my man take you out for a drink."

"That sounded so wrong."

"Go be wrong elsewhere. I've got a DVD to watch."

"It better be PG."

Red opened the door and motioned for Trace to step through first.

"Jesus. First Peyton tells me to let you take me out for a drink. Now you're opening the door for me like I'm a chick."

"And you look extra purdy in your finest shirt, darlin'." Red grinned when Trace elbowed him in the stomach. "Relax. It's just a guys' night out. No harm."

"Last guys' night we had, someone ended up trying to break into the big house." He regretted the words immediately when Red winced. Since the guy breaking in had been in cahoots with Red's father, he wasn't a fan of the memory. "Sorry."

"Yeah, well, let's not repeat that, shall we?" Red headed to a table near the pool tables and positioned himself to watch a poker game on one of the TV screens.

Trace sat down and debated asking. But then he decided, if the guy was going to deck him, he'd at least wait until they got back to M-Star to do it. Red was classy like that. "Are you getting ready to break up with my sister? Or maybe quit the ranch?"

Red set the drink menu back down on the table slowly and looked over at him. "What?"

"Because if you are, you know it's going to kill her." Shouldn't have said that part. "I mean, you know, because of all the crap she had to deal with to get over dating her trainer. You know, mentally . . ." Shit. Hole was halfway to China now, might as well keep shoveling. "I'm just saying—"

Red held up a hand. "Don't 'just say.' I appreciate the big brother routine, which is why I'm not telling you we're going to draw blood in the parking lot. But Jesus, dude, you know I'm crazy about her. Why would you think that?"

Trace shrugged. "Forget it."

"Hard to, when you toss a conversation starter like that at a guy." Red smiled as the waitress, a cute redhead, strolled up. "Bud, bottle."

"Same," Trace said, and waited until she sauntered off. Because it would have been unnatural not to, he took a second glance at her butt. Not bad. Cute, good butt, nice smile. And yet, his self-imposed celibacy continued.

"If it's about Peyton shoving me out of the house for the night—"

"Peyton? She said you were dying to get out of the house."

Red smiled. "Uh-huh. Of course, she did."

Trace had the distinct feeling of being on the losing end of a fight he didn't even know he was in. "So, you didn't tell her you wanted to go get drinks."

"Nope." He smiled again as the redhead delivered the drinks, and took a sip. "Not that I don't appreciate a good beer and some time out watching poker. Maybe shoot a little pool in a bit."

"But it wasn't your idea."

Red shrugged. "I'd be just as happy at home with your sister. Happier, probably. No offense meant," he added easily.

"Playing Scrabble," Trace muttered. Red shot him a confused look, but he shook his head. "Never mind."

"Fact is, variety is the spice of life. Not variety in women," he added, as if he realized Trace wasn't entirely following. "But variety in experiences. I got so used to following my dad around the country, from one barn to the next, that I just fell into doing the same thing myself as an adult. One ranch after another, whichever one wanted to hire me next, there I went. But now that I'm static, and happy to be so, I can always use something new to do with my days to throw off the normal a little. No harm."

"Yeah." Trace sipped his own beer, wondering why it always seemed to taste a little better when it came from a bar rather than the fridge at home. "I got it. So overall, this whole plot was to get me out of the house."

Red lifted a brow. "Mind me asking why you think that?"

"Peyton's been up my ass about getting a social life for months. I'm happy at home. Is that a crime?"

"Not at all. But there's also nothing wrong with taking some time to get out. Nobody back home minds watching Seth. Except maybe Bea . . . It's not a big deal. It's not," he added when Trace started to protest. "I know you want to do it all, and you hate imposing. You're just like Peyton that way. You feel it's bad enough Emma takes him on during the day. But she got a raise out of it, didn't she? And did Peyton look like she was suffering, keeping him for the night?"

"No."

"Exactly. We all love that little guy. And we mostly tolerate your ass, too. So in the end, it all works out. Now, enjoy your beer and shake off your mad, because if you ruin my own night out, I'll kick your ass when we get home."

Trace grinned, despite himself, and saluted Red with his bottle. "Yes, sir."

Chapter Three

"**N**ow there's a real man."

Amanda nudged Jo and nodded toward a back table.

Jo looked up from the pint she was pouring and tried to focus. "The entire back of the bar is full of guys."

"Guys, sure. But a real man? Come on, Jo. Don't tell me you can't see him." Amanda took the glass from Jo's hand and switched places. "See him now? Red shirt, brown hair, sitting in the back with Red Callahan? That's Trace Muldoon."

Jo struggled to remember who Red Callahan was. The name was familiar, but no mental picture was springing up. Despite her years and years as a bartender, server, manager, and sometimes bouncer, she'd never quite picked up the habit of being great with names and faces. "Still batting zero, here."

"Oh, my God. You are hopeless." Amanda slid the beer three seats down into waiting hands. She finally squared Jo's shoulders and pointed straight ahead. "See?"

Jo squinted, and finally saw what Amanda wanted her to. A good-looking man. Two of them, in fact. Though Jo struggled to remember which one was the guy she supposedly knew. "And Callahan would be . . . ?"

"The other one. The unavailable one. He's with Peyton Muldoon now."

"Oh, Peyton. Right." Peyton, Jo knew. She always appreciated another female making it in a man's world, doing the unexpected. Though they were opposites in many ways, Jo enjoyed Peyton's company on the infrequent times she stopped in. "Muldoon. So is he Peyton's brother? Cousin? Other random relation?"

"Brother." Amanda snorted. "Seriously, how do you live in this town and not know everything? This place runs on red meat and gossip. It's been a year. Get with the program."

"I live where I work, and I hate listening to gossip." Jo hauled a bus tub full of empties and kicked the kitchen door open. "Full tub!"

The dishwasher of the evening came and grabbed the tub from her.

"Thank you." She let the door swing back closed and headed to wash her hands.

"I thought you loved gossip."

"Right, well, you hear enough. . . ." Her mother loved to gossip, about everyone. Since Jo moved, that was the only thing their conversations seemed to consist of. Months of gossip-heavy phone calls with her mother had sort of killed any love of that particular form of conversation.

"So, what do you think?"

"Well, I'm a dozen yards away from the guy, and I still don't even know if I'm looking at the right one. But overall, I'd say he's obviously cute, or else he wouldn't have gotten your attention."

Amanda smiled. "He's cute, all right. He used to compete on the pro rodeo circuit; then he came home when their mama died. He was always a cutie in school, but he's really filled out. Of course, there's always the matter of his—"

"Amanda."

"Yeah?"

Jo picked up another drink ticket from the printer and started finding the bottles listed. "You know I adore you. And you're my best server."

"Yup."

"But if you don't get your cute little ass from behind my bar and out serving drinks and stop filling my head with gossip I didn't ask for, I will seriously consider docking your pay."

Amanda just smiled at the empty threat and filled a tray with the bottles from the order. "Well, don't mind me. I'm going to go scout out the playing field, see if there are any other contenders."

"Have fun," Jo said with a laugh.

Twenty minutes later, a new face settled down in front of her at the bar.

Or, rather, a surprising face. New? Not so much. Not since Amanda made a big-ass deal over him.

"Changing scenery?" Jo leaned over the bar, as much as she could at her height, and smiled.

Trace Muldoon smiled easily. "Change the scenery, change the experience."

"And exactly what kind of experience are you looking for?"

He shrugged, as if he hadn't intentionally gotten up and moved to come sit at the bar. "Right now, just a bottle of Bud and some PBR on the screen." He looked to his left, then his right, and leaned in close as if imparting a secret. "I can't take watching poker on TV. Boring as hell."

"Only thing more boring is watching golf," Jo agreed, pleased when he laughed. Flirting was a part of the job.

She'd learned that one early. Flirt, be agreeable and pleasant, and appear attainable, and your tips will soar. Give the
Fuck Off vibe and eat ramen. Of course, that didn't mean
flirting ever had to lead anywhere. Not unless she wanted
it to. But her friend had already pinned all her hopes on
this one, so he was off limits.

And suddenly, it clicked. He'd been in here once before,
hitting on her. He'd come in with Red last time as well.
Hit on her—an abysmal strikeout, despite the serious at-
traction. It had been like he'd been out of practice or
something. The moves were right, but they hadn't felt
natural. Tonight seemed to be a much different story.

"Where'd your friend go?" She twisted the top off with
her bar towel and set the bottle in front of him. "Did he
abandon you?"

"Oh, Red. He caught a ride home with one of our guys
he saw here. Running home to the little woman." He
winked. "If the little woman weren't my sister, I'd say
more about that. But she could kick my ass if she caught
me by surprise, so I'll just leave it there."

"A wise man. I like that. I like your sister, too. Peyton."
He nodded. "I admire her." She propped a hip against the
cooler under the bar and watched him a moment. "You
used to do the cowboy thing, right?"

"Used to?" He looked mortally offended and placed a
hand over his heart. "Sweetheart, 'cowboy' is a state of being. Not just a profession."

"Is that right?"

"Cowboy born," he said solemnly, as if repeating something serious. "Cowboy bred. I'll be a cowboy still as I'm
buried dead."

"Ha. Cute. Let's try that again. You did the whole *professional rodeo* thing, right?" This time she used air quotes.

"That a city thing?"

"What?"

He mimicked her air quotes. Only on him, they looked ridiculous. Was that how it looked when she did it?

"It's just a . . . I don't know. Never mind, just answer the question." She swatted at him with her towel and grabbed the next drink ticket.

"I did the rodeo circuit for a while."

"Bustin' those broncs?"

He tilted his head back and laughed. "Worst accent ever. Never try to pass for a native. Nobody is ever going to buy it."

"No problem there."

"And no, I didn't often bust the broncs, as you so cutely put it. But that's in the past anyway. Now I'm at the ranch."

She wanted to ask another question—completely violating her MYOB policy—but three tickets came in together, followed by a steady stream of orders and issues to handle at once. At one point, she glanced back to see if he was waiting for her to return and finish the conversation, but he seemed intent on the TV screen above the bar. Just as well, since she didn't have the time to stand around chatting with an off-limits man.

An hour later, things slowed down. But when she returned, she found only money in Trace's spot, well more than would cover the bill. She passed the tip off to Lori, since he'd started at her table, and worked on autopilot, prepping the bar for shutdown. But stupidly, she kept looking over her shoulder to see if he was around the bar somewhere. He wasn't. He'd left without saying good-bye. And why should he? She was just the bartender, and he was just a customer. Besides that, Amanda had her eyes on him, and Amanda was a friend, as well as an employee. She had no business looking for the man in a crowd.

Didn't mean, when she pulled on her pajamas that night, he didn't float through her mind. The faceless fantasy cowboy had features now, and they were too close to Trace Muldoon's for comfort.

"Oh, good, you're in here already," Red said as he walked up beside Trace.

Trace stood beside his equipment, staring at it. "Something's off with my stuff."

Red glanced toward the tack. "Looks fine to me."

"Yeah, but I don't put it away in this order. Has someone been messing with my stuff?"

Red shrugged, unconcerned. That annoyed the hell out of Trace, since he knew Red would be the first to boil over if he thought someone had been jacking around with his tack. "Nobody should be using my stuff but me."

"Well, I didn't use it. I've got my own stuff, and you know it. If you're so sure someone did, feel free to question the hands. But don't say I didn't warn you if it turns out you were a paranoid bastard."

He started to reply, then just shook his head. No point. Red hadn't used it, that much he was sure of. And he'd look like an idiot questioning people about using his stuff, when none was missing or damaged. He'd just keep an eye on it. "What'd you want?"

"I need you up on Lad. We've got two weeks before you head out again and we could really use some good PR at the next event."

Trace grinned and grabbed his stirrups. "And when have I ever given bad PR?"

Red opened his mouth, then shut it again. After rolling his eyes, he pointed to the tack. "Just get your 'messed with' stuff and saddle up. And get your head in the game. I'm not putting up with a shitty practice."

Trace waited until Red walked away, then kicked dust after him, just on principle. He liked the guy, tolerated him with his sister, and knew he was good for the ranch.

But still . . . he cast one more glance at his tack. Someone had definitely touched his stuff. He gave everything an extra look over before using it, just in case. But as he'd thought, it was all in perfect working order. Almost as if someone had merely knocked it over and put it back in the wrong order. Maybe it was as simple as that. Maybe he really was a paranoid bastard.

On the road, when he'd traveled solo for years, barely making enough to feed both him and his horse, he'd learned keeping his tack safe was a matter of whether they both got to eat that night or just the horse. Some cowboys were as petty and vindictive as a bunch of sore losers backstage at a beauty pageant. Loosened buckles, ripped nylon, weakened straps, they would stop at nothing to give themselves the upper hand. His tack never left his side if he could help it, and if he couldn't, it was locked up in his truck. End of story.

He didn't want to go back to that place, where he felt so alone, like he was fending for himself constantly. His son didn't deserve that existence.

So he'd brush it off. As he walked over to where Steve had Lad waiting to be saddled, he told himself, time to move on. He had a permanent place at the family ranch as long as he wanted it. And he did, for his son's sake.

"You have fun at Jo's the other night?" Steve rubbed a hand over Lad's neck while Trace adjusted the saddle blanket. "I saw you at the bar before I left."

"Not bad." His mind wandered to Jo and their conversation. One he'd had to walk away from before he wanted to. "Nights out always have a way of ending early now. Must mean I'm getting old."

"No doubt. Monday always comes too soon." Steve waited until Trace was up in the saddle before stepping back. "Need anything else?"

"We're good. Thanks."

"In that case, I'm gonna, uh, take my lunch." He glanced around quickly, then nodded. "Yeah. I'll be back after lunch."

Trace shrugged as Steve hurried off. Barely ten in the morning and the man was all gung ho for a break. He led Lad over to the practice arena, where Red had set up an obstacle course in the middle.

Red waved him over to the side where he was sitting on the top of the metal gate, his boot heels hooked into the second bar. "Finally. Get done playing detective?"

"Fuck off," Trace said good-naturedly. He had a horse under him and he was getting paid to ride. Nothing could kill his mood now.

More serious, Red asked, "You checked the tack out, right?"

"Yeah. It's fine." He gave Red a long look. "I'm not crazy."

"Didn't say you were. Least, not this time. Take a few laps outside, then we'll get to work. And don't make me yell—I'm not in the mood."

Trace flipped him the bird, but a smile curved his mouth as he and Lad started their warm-up lap. The guy could be a Grade A dick sometimes, but he knew his horses like nobody else in the business.

Lad was in a spirited mood, no shocker there, and Trace had his hands full keeping the horse on task. But that was the beauty of his chosen mount. When called on to stand perfectly still, those in the arena would recognize both the training and the talent. Keeping a docile mare who walked into the ring half asleep in a hold was no big feat. But a gelding with energy to kill and a desire to run free? The ability to harness that power and attention into the task at hand was what people had paid Red big bucks for in the past.

And if Peyton had her way, they'd pay the M-Star handsomely for the privilege to work with Red now. Or to buy a horse trained by the M-Star staff, overseen by Redford Callahan.

Brilliant.

"You're slacking, Muldoon! He's about to—"

Red's words were drowned out by the buzz in his ears as Lad bucked and sent him flying. He forced himself to relax a moment before his body hit the ground; the impact was jarring but not bone-breaking. A novice would try to gulp in air, gasping harder and harder when he couldn't catch his breath until he passed out from the effort. Trace knew better. He stared at a pinpoint in the sky and waited quietly for the roaring of his blood to stop and his nerves to return to normal before taking a slow, steady breath.

He was almost back to normal when Red's mug appeared above him. "Nice work, Ace."

Trace said nothing. Breathe in, breathe out. Deep and steady.

Red sat down beside him and waited silently, knowing the drill. When Trace finally shifted to his stomach, resting one cheek in the dirt, Red spoke.

"What the fuck were you thinking? You can't just let your mind wander with a horse like that. This isn't a kid's pony ride."

"Bite me," Trace wheezed. Though his breathing had returned to normal, residual adrenaline and the physical beating he'd taken kept his voice hoarse.

"I think the ground already did that. Anything feel off?"

Trace slowly flexed and relaxed the muscles in his arms and legs. "Nothing so far. Let me stand up." Red held out a hand, but Trace ignored it. After dusting off the worst of the dirt, he twisted his torso and stretched his arms back. "Feels okay. Is Lad fine?"

"Yeah. He definitely won that round. You know the

deal. Back up." Red waved a hand and Steve walked by with Lad.

Trace took hold of the halter and gave Lad a long look. "Son? Not okay."

Lad's eyes half-closed, as if ashamed of his behavior. Trace wasn't fooled. He'd do it again in a heartbeat if he could get away with it. Lad didn't mind a rider, but he needed one with a stronger head, stronger will than his own. Otherwise, he'd take the rider to Canada and back for fun, just because he could.

"If that's how you're gonna handle yourself in two weeks, my reputation is screwed."

Trace rolled his eyes and settled one boot in the stirrup, hauling himself up and settling down to the comfortable sounds of creaking leather. "I think your reputation can take the hit."

"Can yours? How about Peyton's?"

Instantly, Trace regretted the comments. "Sorry."

"I know." Red stroked a hand down Lad's neck, calming his excitement a little. "It's just too important to Peyton for me to not care. Everyone expects me to up and leave soon. But Peyton can't just take off. This isn't just a business you three own together. It's her home. Always will be. You're transient, Bea's here for who knows how long before she goes back to California."

Trace snorted. "She said she would only be here a week. It's been months."

Red smiled. "Yeah, well, as I'm coming to learn . . . that's Bea. But the fact is, this matters too much to Peyton. She's so used to going it alone. After you left—"

"I'm not talking about that." Trace had enough guilt about having left home as soon after high school graduation as physically possible, leaving Peyton and Bea to handle their mother alone. But it hadn't been possible for him to stay. He just wasn't able to.

"Fine. Less talking, more working. I like it that way." Red gave a final pat to Lad's flank and motioned. "Let's run him around the ring a few times, then we'll get back into it for the obstacle course."

This time, as the horse circled the ring, Trace blocked all thoughts from his mind but becoming one with his animal and walking away from a great workout.

Trace was walking down the stairs, still rubbing at his damp hair with a towel, when he bumped into Bea.

"Hey, you. Coming out to admire my new place?" She grabbed his bicep and tugged, fluttering her lashes. "I've got a few more boxes if you want to help me carry them out while we walk."

He knew her brand of "help." He'd carry all of them while she walked beside him as an accessory. No thanks. "Nope. I'm going out."

"Out?" She pouted a little, then scrunched up her nose. "Again? You just went out a few days ago."

He had, and the reminder was eating at him a little. But still . . . "Yes, again. How often do you go out back in California?"

She waved that off. "Beside the point. In Hollywood, there are actually things to do when you go out. What are you up to tonight, cow tipping?"

"Exactly. Care to join?"

The look on his sister's face was comical, at best. "No. Absolutely not. That is beyond disgusting, Trace Muldoon."

"Good thing I'm not actually going cow tipping. You're too easy, city girl." He kissed her cheek and left her standing on the bottom step.

"So where are you going?"

"Probably just hit a bar a little later," he hedged, heading to the kitchen for a bottle of water.

"Dressed like that?" Bea shrieked behind him. Her heels clicked a staccato across the tile as she raced to catch up with him, making him wince at the sound. It reminded him too much of their mother. "Absolutely not, I forbid it."

He glanced down at his outfit: a clean button-down flannel shirt, a clean—if a little worn—pair of jeans, and his nicer pair of boots. The ones that weren't constantly covered in grime and shit. "What's wrong with this? I'm clean. I showered ten minutes ago, and none of this stuff was sitting on my bedroom floor or in the dirty hamper."

"Well, isn't that encouraging." Bea gave him a pitying look. "I don't have enough time to tell you what's wrong with the look. I mean, it's cute and all for the barn, but—"

"Listen up, Fashion Fanny. This isn't Hollywood, in case you didn't notice. I'm heading out for a drink. I'm not trying to land a modeling gig."

Bea crossed her arms over her chest and huffed. "Listen up, big brother. In case you didn't notice, your social life sucks. And I'm just trying to help."

God preserve him from sisters who wanted to improve his social life. "Yours is any better?" he shot back. He walked to the utility room beside the kitchen, opened the door and tossed the towel into the hamper situated there. Emma would thank him later for remembering and not leaving it on the floor like an animal. She'd raised him better. "You're always here. Or, well, not here, but now you're always in your little apartment looking at paint chips. You almost never go out. You leave once a month to do God knows what in whatever big city you head to."

"Shop for things that don't have snaps and denim," she said dryly.

"Fine. That. But it's not a social life, any more than me hanging out in the barn is a social life. So don't kid yourself. I'm not sure what crawled up your butt and decided it was Bug Trace Day, but it's not. Check your calendar. It's officially MYOB month."

Bea's mouth fell open. "I'm not sure which is more disturbing. The fact that you think my social life is pathetic, or that you just used the term 'MYOB.' It's 2013, in case you didn't notice."

He ignored that and walked around her. Then an idea popped into his mind. "You want me to have a social life?"

"Yes. Because I love you. Though right now I'm wracking my brain trying to remember why."

"And you want to help me."

"Yes." She smiled patiently at him.

"Then this is how you help." He unhooked the baby monitor from his back pocket and thrust it at her. "Babysit."

She stared at the monitor like it was a remote detonator to a bomb. "What the hell do I do with this?"

He sighed and reached over to turn it on. The green light lit up and the soft sounds of his son's snoring rasped through the speaker. "You just keep it with you. Go up and surf the Internet on the computer. Read a magazine. Watch TV. Cook a meal. I don't care, it doesn't matter. Just do something in the big house, and have that with you. And don't leave to go back to your new apartment."

She started to hand it back, but he stepped out of the way. "I can't babysit. You know I don't do the kid thing."

"He's asleep. He's been sleeping through the night for months now. There's no reason to think he won't do it again. So all you have to do is be in the house. That's it. If he doesn't make a sound, then you do nothing but stay in the house and do whatever it is you want to."

She stared at the monitor again and he could see her starting to mentally draft an excuse.

"Bea, I need this."

She watched him, and he could see her softening.

"I spent almost a whole year not leaving this house except for work. I hate relying on Emma—it's not her job after hours. And Peyton already watched him recently."

She hesitated, and then her shoulders drooped.

And he knew he'd won a hard-earned battle for a night out.

"Fine." She narrowed her eyes and pointed a finger at him. "But those boxes? You're moving every single one of them when you get back."

"Done," he agreed quickly, in case she changed her mind. "Every one." He leaned over and brushed a kiss on her cheek. "Thanks, Bea."

As he headed out the door, she called out, "Don't be shocked if you come home and Seth's dressed in a sweater vest!"

Trace shuddered and wisely kept walking.

Chapter Four

Jo sat down at the bar. The nonworking side, for once. She had a night off, and where did she go? Right back where she'd started. Her own bar. She'd be annoyed and disgusted with herself, if she wasn't so sure there was literally nothing else to do.

No movies to see. Nothing on TV. The nearest town had promise, but it wasn't like she was going to drive out there by herself, only to drive back in the morning. Waste of time and gas.

So she resigned herself to playing where she worked. It could be worse, though. Most people seemed to give her a decent berth. No married men hitting on her, hoping for an easy lay before they went home to their sweet wives. No weird underage kids hoping to score some beer. No CEO assholes who thought she'd be impressed by the size of their portfolio.

Nobody. She was still alone in the small town. Still an outsider. And it was starting to piss her off.

"Hey."

She turned at the familiar voice, and before she could help it, she smiled. "Back for more?"

Trace gave her a friendly grin. "Can't resist your . . . selection." He gave Jenna, the bartender of the night, his order and sat back. So fluid and easy in his skin. His hair was a little damp, like he'd just taken a shower. Because he was coming to the bar? Or because it was a long work day . . . ?

Didn't matter. She shouldn't be thinking about him like that. *Amanda, Amanda, Amanda.* Amanda has dibs, she mentally reminded herself.

Her sexual nerve endings were apparently not receiving the memo, because they were getting all fidgety just looking at him.

"Night off for you?"

She held up her almost-empty bottle. "Yeah, I get one of those every so often. Though when you're the owner . . ."

"You're never really off," he finished. "Yeah, I'm coming to learn that myself with the ranch. Though it's Peyton's thing more than mine."

He settled back a moment and watched the screen above the bar, breaking his silence only to thank the bartender when she set the bottle in front of him on a napkin. Jo watched from the corner of her eye, but his line of vision never wandered from the bartender's face, despite her low V-neck shirt.

Interesting. Maybe he wasn't there for women. Maybe he had a woman at home. The thought had Jo taking another mental step back. Shit. Did he? No ring, she could see that easily enough with his hand wrapped around the bottle. And no tan line or indents from a recently-removed band. But not all men wore wedding rings, especially if they worked with their hands all day.

This was one of the few times not listening to gossip would get her into trouble.

And why did she care? No. She didn't care at all. That was Amanda's problem, not hers. She finished off her beer and headed around the bar to dispose of the bottle.

"Working even when you're off."

She smiled at Trace as she got a rag to wipe her place down. "I'm not one to leave a mess for others when I'm capable of handling it myself."

"I'm capable of handling this." He held up the empty bottle. "Should I go back there and toss it myself?"

She laughed and shook her head, holding out a hand for the empty. "No, but thanks for the offer."

"My Emma raised me right," he said with a smile.

"Your Emma?"

"Housekeeper when we were growing up. Mama was . . . not quite into the whole motherhood thing. Emma stepped in and did her best for us. Which was pretty good."

But not the same as having a mom there. Jo understood. Hadn't she spent much of her life growing up wishing for a father? A real one, not the constant "new stepdaddy" types her mom brought around who seemed to change as often as the seasons.

"So, Jo from Jo's Place." Trace balanced his elbows on the bar and gave her a focused look. "Tell me about yourself."

She rolled her eyes. "Bad. Really bad, cowboy."

He shrugged. "Wasn't a line."

"Oh." She busied herself with the rag, wiping down the already-pristine stainless-steel bar sink. "Not much to tell. I own a bar, I work in it, and I live above it."

"Sounds tidy."

"Easy," she corrected. "Bars are rarely tidy."

"Oh, I don't know." He looked around. "This one's pretty good. And trust me, I've seen some shithole bars in my time."

So had she, which was one of the reasons she prided herself on keeping a clean place.

"Where were you before here?"

"New Orleans."

"Never been. Did you like it?"

She shrugged and tossed the rag into the hamper below the ledge. "It was a place to live and work. Nothing to get too attached to."

"Before that?"

"L.A., Chicago, New York, Houston . . . I could go on. Should I?"

Jenna walked by and offered Trace another beer. He hesitated a moment, then nodded. After taking the bottle, he waited for her to elaborate.

Instead, she found something to do with her hands. She got out a cutting board and a knife and started slicing fruit for garnishes. He said nothing, just watched her. And, when she peeked from the corner of her eye, she was amused to see he watched her hands more than her face, or down her shirt.

"Got a hankering to be a bartender?"

"Nah. Tried it once, when I needed some cash. Didn't have the knack."

She settled a sliced lemon in a container and closed the lid. "And what is the knack, exactly? Short pours and steady hands?"

"That helps. But a lot of it's got nothing to do with liquor. Good listening skills, or the ability to fake it. Pleasant personality. The ability to upsell."

She smiled. Observant. "Am I really listening, or faking it?"

He looked her dead in the eyes. "I hope it's the real thing."

The moment sent shivers down her spine, and she used finding a towel to wipe her hands on as an excuse to break the eye contact. There was nothing more keeping her behind the bar. Tuesdays were slow evenings. She had two choices. Either head to her apartment upstairs, or sit back down next to Trace.

The apartment was a safer choice.

She sat down and settled in for danger.

"Why a bar?"

Jo took her eyes off the screen and glanced at him a moment. "Why not? Every town needs a bar, right?"

"We have a few." Not nearly as nice as this, granted. But the town did have two other bars, ones that did an okay business on the weekends. Probably did better before Jo came into town.

"I know bars. I practically grew up in them, and I'm good at the business. Some people have an eye for retail, others for selling insurance. I know my beer, and I know how to sell it."

"No argument there." He took another sip of the beer, reminding himself to nurse this one. It was his last for the night. "But some people might want to escape the family business."

"Family business?" Her long black ponytail whipped him in the shoulder as she turned her head.

"You said you grew up in them."

"Oh, right." One hand lifted to rub her ear, the one with four studs in it. Damn, why was that hot? He'd never noticed piercings on a woman before. Never cared. But for whatever reason, the reminder she wasn't quite country revved his blood. "We never owned bars, really. My mom just worked in them my whole life. Once I was old enough, it was a natural progression to get a job there. It stuck."

"But you didn't stick. You've moved around a lot."

"Where Mother went, so did I. At least until I felt like I could strike out on my own. But even when I tried to go it alone, I wasn't finding anywhere that felt permanent."

He shouldn't ask, but he did anyway. "Are you planning on sticking here?"

Her eyes grew hot. "Yes. I'm here to stay. And if anyone has a problem with it, they can—"

"Whoa, now. Easy." He rubbed her shoulder in soft circles. "I wasn't asking you to pack up and get out of town. Just making conversation."

She blinked, as if not even realizing she'd been so fired up. "Sorry. I'm just tired of people around here thinking I'm a flash in the pan. That I'm too city to stick."

It hurt her, he could tell. To be thought so little of. To be thought less because she wasn't a native. "Who said that to you?" He'd kick their ass.

Wait. He'd what? No, no, he would not. He wasn't a hot-blooded teenager with raging hormones anymore. She wasn't the star cheerleader he wanted to impress more than anything. This wasn't high school. He was a father, for the love of God.

"Nobody." She smiled a little and took a sip of the water she'd given herself before sitting back down. "You know people are too polite for that. But I have my ways of hearing things. Though I do try to ignore gossip. It can be ugly," she added.

Definitely a story behind that one.

"Small town. Gossip is the course between dinner and dessert."

She snorted. "I'm learning that. It's getting harder and harder to avoid it."

He liked that. That she at least made the attempt to avoid it, even though it might make it harder for her to acclimate. Plus, he didn't have to wonder what she'd heard about him. A true blank slate.

A pretty brunette waitress walked by at that moment and cozied up to the bar next to Jo. "Hey. Shouldn't you be out doing something other than this?"

"Probably, but this is what I'm doing, isn't it?" Jo shifted ever so slightly away from him in her chair. Maybe it was just his imagination, or she was only getting comfortable. But it felt to him like she purposely drew away from him.

The waitress looked over, as if just noticing him. "Oh, hey, Trace."

"Hi. How're things?" He wracked his brain for the name. He probably should know it. It was an A-something. April, Ashley . . .

"Things are good. You've been in town awhile. Planning to make it a permanent move?" Was it his imagination or did she really just jut her breasts out a little farther in that tight uniform shirt?

And did Jo scoot farther away?

"Amanda!" another server called from behind her. "Table nineteen is ready to cash out."

Amanda. Right. He thanked his lucky stars he was saved from having to remember it himself. He sucked at names . . . which only made it more awkward when he would run into a woman on the rodeo circuit he'd slept with once, thinking he'd never see her again.

That only happened . . . always.

Amanda rolled her eyes in response, but she smiled brightly enough that he knew it was only for effect.

Jo swatted her arm. "Go make me some money."

"Yes, ma'am." She gave a demure nod of her head, which contradicted the twinkle in her eye. Then she scurried off to do whatever it was waitresses did behind the scenes.

Jo smiled as she watched Amanda hustle off. "She's one of the best. Despite the attitude," she added with a laugh. "She's cheeky, but it's always in good fun."

"The best kind of cheeky." It wasn't his imagination. Jo's attitude toward him had definitely cooled off. What the hell had he done wrong?

After a minute, Jo stood and brushed her hands off. "Well, thanks for the company."

"Yeah . . ." What could he say to keep her longer? "How about sometime we—"

She shook her head, the small hoops in her bottom piercings wiggling enticingly. "I think I know where you're going with that, and it's best we just not take that trip."

He stared for a moment. "Why the hell not? You married or something?"

She snorted. "No. Not at all. But just because two people are single doesn't mean it's a good idea. There are other factors."

"What other factors?"

Jo just shook her head again, maddeningly. "Thanks for thinking of me though, cowboy." She said it lightly, almost mockingly, and it stung.

As she walked away, he wanted to just shrug. He'd been turned down before. But never when he'd felt so strongly about the woman. New territory for him, and he didn't care for it.

Not because of the rejection itself, but because it meant he didn't get Jo.

Not tonight, anyway.

Jo's night off, and she was closing up shop. Figured.

Her manager had pleaded an early night because of a migraine, and she'd relented. Though she was pretty sure "migraine" was code for "wanna have sweaty sex with my boyfriend," she couldn't really argue. If she had a man in her bed, she'd want to be having hot, sweaty sex, too.

No, no, no. No thinking about sex. Or sweaty sex. Or

Trace Muldoon . . . damn it! Did it again. Now her mind was mentally stripping him, one article of clothing at a time.

She'd have to start with the shirt. Snaps were so much easier than buttons. How convenient that cowboy fashion lent itself to the sweaty sex. The man had to be ripped, working with large animals all day. Plus, the loose shirts couldn't hide everything. Maybe he had a hint of a farmer's tan. Now that she could get into. She'd dealt too long with Big City assholes who thought dual manicures was a good way to spend quality time on a Saturday. Something about the thought of a man with a tan from working outside all day, using his hands, getting dirty, really dirty . . .

Glancing down, she laughed at herself. Instead of gripping the soft cotton of Trace's shirt to rip it off, she'd been squeezing the life out of a bar rag. Not quite the same. Definitely less satisfying results.

"I'm heading out!" Amanda breezed by and set her apron on the counter with the others to be laundered in the morning.

"You're in a cheerful mood," Jo commented, tossing the mangled bar rag in with the aprons.

"Got myself a hot date." She grinned and checked her watch. "Not that there's much of the night left for dating. I'm just looking forward to the part where we tear each other's—"

"Point taken!" Jo smiled and covered her ears with her hands. "Shoo. Go, have fun, be safe."

"Yes, Mommy." Amanda blew her a kiss and sailed out the front door. Jo watched as she took three steps, then sprinted to the parking lot and jumped into the arms of a man waiting by a pickup truck.

She walked to the front door and watched as the man spun her in a quick circle while Amanda wrapped her legs around him like a tree monkey. From a distance, it was difficult to pick up any details on the man. His hat shaded his face in the darkness, though she could imagine he was smiling. With a cutie like Amanda in his arms, most men would be.

But the jeans and boots, she recognized.

Jo scolded herself as she caught a sigh forming. Another nonstarter, as far as she was concerned. She'd known from the beginning that Trace Muldoon was off limits, and she'd behaved accordingly. Now it was official, and she just needed to get the hell over it. She barely even knew the guy. It wasn't as if she'd lost her great love or anything.

Maybe the loneliness was seeping in deeper than she imagined. Time to get a man. Or a pet . . . pets were easier.

Too bad she hated most animals. The only thing she could tolerate were fish. And that wasn't really the way to handle loneliness. Five days after buying her companion, she'd have to flush him.

She finished quickly and closed up shop, locking the door behind her. The stairs to her apartment were around the corner of the building, slightly hidden from the street. She liked the privacy, even though most would have thought she didn't have any. The separate entrance was enough for her though, and she started to head in that direction, glad once again she had made installing outside lighting along the path to her stairs a main priority when she'd first bought the place.

"Hey."

She yelped and covered her mouth with her hand. Jesus, Mary, and Joseph. Turning, she saw Mr. Jeans and Boots himself leaning against a truck parked along the street. At first glance, it looked like the same truck from the parking lot, but in the dark she couldn't tell dark blue from black or another deep color.

"Sorry, didn't mean to scare you."

"I wasn't scared," she lied.

The twitch of his lips said he wasn't buying the BS, but he let it slide. "Good. I didn't know what time you would close up, since you don't close the same time every night."

She hefted her large tote more securely over her shoulder. "If people are still paying, I'll stay open."

"Right. Well, luckily I had a book in my truck." He took one step forward, and then stopped.

She waited, but he didn't say anything. "Where's Amanda?"

"Amanda?" His brow furrowed in confusion. "Why would I know?"

"You picked her up like half an hour ago. I thought you two had a date." She wanted to use air quotes around the word "date" but refrained.

"No," he said slowly. "I didn't, actually."

Jo blinked. "But I saw you. She met you in the parking lot."

"Did I wave and say hi?" He was starting to smile.

"You were wearing jeans and boots," she said with a look down. Then she wished she hadn't, since it drew her eyes to the long lines of his legs, the worn-out places in the denim reminding her what kind of hard work he did on a regular basis. She shivered a little and blinked to clear the images that wanted to start up again.

"Well, hell. Every guy in the bar tonight was wearing jeans and boots. That hardly means it was me. Plus, I hate to sound like a jerk, but if it was Amanda I wanted, I'd be with her, not here with you."

"So why are you here with me?"

The teasing light died in his eyes, replaced by something Jo could easily recognize. Easy to relate to, because she'd felt it, too.

Hunger. Desire. Deep need.

"I think you know." His voice was quiet, but it carried perfectly to her. "I thought things were going well, and then suddenly I got the cold shoulder. What'd I do wrong, and how do I take it back?"

A man who could admit he was wrong, even if he wasn't sure yet why. Interesting. "You didn't do anything wrong. I just thought you and Amanda . . ." Well. They weren't, so there was no point in going in that direction.

"You thought Amanda and I were meeting tonight instead and didn't want to poach."

"Basically." It sounded stupid when he said it.

He smiled and walked to her. "I can respect that. But just to cover the bases, I'm not with Amanda."

"I see that."

"I'm not with another woman. I'm with you, and it's where I want to be. If you feel the same, then I'd say we were on to something good."

Chapter Five

She waited until he was close enough to touch, then let her bag drop from her shoulder. Hot man in front of her, all but telling her he wanted her? No contest.

He took those final steps forward and she reached up to grab his shirt. Just like in her daydream, and she pulled him in. His mouth was on hers before she could adjust to the closeness of him. God, he tasted good. He felt even better, his hard body pressing against hers, gently maneuvering her until her back butted up against the brick of the bar.

"Damn," he whispered against her lips. "I've been wanting to do that for months."

"Since the first time you hit on me and I shot you down?" she asked with a smile.

"Busted. You remembered that, huh?"

"I did."

"Not my finest moment. But I'm hoping to erase that particular memory." He kissed her again, blazing hot. "Have I mentioned I've been dying to do this?"

She smiled and kissed him again. "And now you are."

"Now I am," he agreed and let one hand wander down to the hem of her tank top. If she'd been scheduled to work, she'd have worn the black polo uniform shirt. But she was glad she wasn't when he tugged down until the scoop-neck of her tank slipped past her breast, exposing her lacy bra.

"Hard, tough woman on the outside, lace underneath, huh." He looked amused, but no less turned on. One big hand covered her breast, squeezing gently, massaging, learning the shape and playing. Through the lace, he plucked at her nipple.

She sucked in a breath. God, she'd all but forgotten this was what it felt like to be with a man. To be completely wanted, desired. She turned her head until she could run her lips along his bristly jaw.

"Sorry, forgot to shave tonight." He pulled back a little, but she made a sound and tugged him back.

"I like it. Different textures, they work for me."

He traced the edge of lace where it lay against the swell of her breast. The skin under his touch rose in awareness. "I'll agree to that. I'm enjoying the new discoveries myself."

She nibbled at his ear. "Should we go upstairs and keep finding new ones?"

"I think that's a—damn." He muttered another curse and pulled back, reaching for his cell phone. "Sorry, normally I wouldn't do this but—"

"It's fine. Check it." The sooner he answered that call or text message, the sooner they could head upstairs and pick up where they'd left off. She shivered again, this time from a chill, and looked down. Right. Her tank was still down and her bra was completely out in the open. She huffed out a laugh and readjusted the shirt so she was decently covered.

He could always start over in a minute.

"Shit. You've got to be kidding me."

His tone caught her attention more than the curse and she turned to him. "What's wrong?"

"I have to head home." He tucked his phone back in his pocket and frowned. "They need me."

"Horse emergency?" she joked. But he didn't smile. "Oh." Disappointment swelled in her, knocking loose the wall of lust and hope she'd started to build up block by block. "Okay." She smiled, though it felt tight at the edges. "Drive safe."

He stared at her a moment. "You think I'm lying."

"I didn't say that." Didn't believe it, either. Trace was man enough to say he wasn't interested if he wasn't. And if he wasn't interested, hc wouldn't have been waiting for her after closing.

He grabbed for her wrist and molded her hand over his zipper. Beneath her hand, his hardened erection twitched at the pressure. "That's no lie. I want you, Jo. I want you like I haven't wanted anything in a long time."

"All right."

His brows rose. "All right? That's it?"

She smiled. "Not all city girls are complicated, Muldoon." She patted his cheek and pushed his shoulder. "All right just means what it sounds like. Come on by next time you've got a night off. I'll buy you a round."

He stood rooted to the spot for a moment, searching her face as if waiting for the "Gotcha" or a hint of sarcasm or something to indicate it was a trick.

She shrugged a shoulder and bent down to pick up her bag. He got there first, their hands crashing together as they both reached for the strap.

"I've got it."

"No, here." He lifted the heavy tote with ease and helped her adjust it over her shoulder.

"Thanks, big guy." She patted him again, determined to leave with her dignity—and pride—intact. "Guess I'll see you around."

She started to walk toward the stairs, but he caught her

and pulled her in for one more long, indecently delicious kiss. When he was finished, they were both fighting to catch their breath.

"Damn," he muttered once more, his forehead dropping to hers.

"You can say that again." She pressed a more innocent kiss to his lips and gently pushed him toward the truck. "See ya around, cowboy."

He shook his head, as if reluctant to go, but go he did. After the truck pulled into the deserted street, she kicked the front step of the stairs.

Not how she wanted the evening to end up. She was no better off than when she'd started the day. Still no man to curl up with and get dirty with between the sheets. But at least now she had something to look forward to. Jo touched her lips with the back of one hand while she dug through her tote for keys with the other.

Now she had a hint of what was to come.

So maybe she was a little better off.

Trace thundered up the steps, not taking the ten seconds to remove his boots by the front door like Emma taught all the kids. Some things were more important.

"Bea?" he called halfway up.

"We're up here."

She sounded remarkably calm for someone who'd texted an SOS while babysitting his son. He forced his breathing to reach a normal level and walked the last few steps to the top landing. When he got there, he stopped short at the sight.

Bea, in a pair of ripped shorts and an oversized stained sweatshirt that looked like something of his she'd stolen from his hamper, walked the floor with Seth over her shoulder. He was quiet, but looked as miserable as Bea. Her cropped hair stuck out in different directions, and she was missing an earring. He prayed to God that wasn't the reason she'd called him back home. If she'd let his son swallow a piece of jewelry, so help him . . .

She caught him from the corner of her eye and turned, her face a bland mask. No panic, no confusion, no worry. It was as if she was zoned out in front of the TV.

"I don't understand why you left him with me."

Trace walked over and gently removed Seth from her grasp. Her arms went limp at her sides.

"I'm not maternal. I don't even own a pet. I don't think I like animals. Or babies." She stared in disgust at the sweatshirt. "Do you know what comes out of that kid?"

"Yeah. I've changed a diaper or two myself," Trace said dryly, inspecting his son for damage. Now that he was being held by someone he recognized and trusted, Seth relaxed considerably, his face morphing from wary concern to a big smile. "Hey, little man. You scaring your Auntie Bea-Bea?"

"Scare. Yeah." She blew out a puff of breath that ruffled her hair and flopped to the overstuffed armchair. "He has a rash."

"A rash?" Trace looked once more at Seth's arms and legs, his neck, his face, even his bald head. "Like, an allergy? Did you feed him something other than his bottle?"

"No. On his butt."

Trace stared at his sister for a full ten seconds. "You sent me an SOS because of diaper rash?"

She threw up her hands and rocked back. "I don't know! I've never babysat before! He woke up crying and so I got one of the bottles Emma left me in the fridge and I fed him. And that wasn't too hard, but then he spit up on me when I burped him." The disgust in her voice had him choking back a smile. "So I put on your sweatshirt in case he did it again. I figured it was too ugly for anyone to care if it got nasty."

"Thanks."

"You're welcome. But then he started stinking so I checked his diaper and . . ." Bea turned a little green at the memory. "And it was disgusting, too. Did you know how gross your son is?" She didn't wait for an answer. "And when I changed him, I noticed the rash. It looked painful and I wasn't sure if I would hurt him if I put something on it, but then he started freaking out anyway because kids don't like me—especially that one—and then I was afraid it was because I was hurting him and I didn't know and Peyton's in there with Red and I didn't want to bother them—"

"So you bothered me." He jostled Seth a little to settle him down. "You're nervous and he's reacting to it. Calm down a bit."

Bea closed her eyes and started humming something nonsensical.

"What are you doing?"

"Meditating," she said without moving her lips. "Try it sometime."

"Yeah. Okay then. Let's go to bed, little man. I think you've pushed Auntie Bea-Bea over the edge."

Seth found this vastly amusing and clapped his hands in delight. Trace smiled and tapped his son's little nose. "That shouldn't be funny. It's not nice to drive people crazy." He lowered his voice and stage whispered, "Even if it's Bea."

"I heard that."

"Go meditate something."

He walked a few laps around Seth's room in the dark and sang a country lullaby in a low tone, barely mouthing the words. Seth's eyes drooped enough to put him down in his crib easily. After closing the door and waiting a few moments to see if he woke back up, Trace walked over and stretched out on the couch.

"Did I ruin something for you?"

"Maybe."

Bea sniffed. "Good. Don't you dare pull a stunt like that again, Trace Muldoon."

"Oh, I don't know. Seth seemed to have fun torturing you." He laughed when Bea threw a pillow at him. "Come on, it wasn't that bad. You get better the more you do it."

"Pass, thanks." Bea was quiet for a moment. "Do you wish his mom was around?"

"No." Easy answer. "We're a duo."

"Who was she?"

"Nobody you'd know."

"Where is she?"

"Nowhere important."

"Wow, big brother. Don't talk my ear off. Please, stop with the oversharing."

Trace smiled at Bea's dramatic tone. She was destined to be an actress, even at an early age. "Don't worry about his mother. We're doing fine on our own."

"I know you are."

The softness of her voice had him looking up. She smiled. "Hey, I tease, but you're good with him. Way better than I would ever be. It's cute, the two of you. Two boys hanging out. Dad would have loved him."

Trace settled back down and stared at the ceiling. "Think so?"

"Oh, yeah. Another male to carry on the Muldoon tradition of roping and riding? Right up his alley."

The bitterness took him by surprise. "What's up?"

"Nothing." She stood and flopped one long sleeve at him. "I'll throw this in your hamper in the morning. Though, if you ask me, you should burn it."

"I didn't."

"Sadly, I know." She stared at his jeans. "Still can't be-

lieve you managed to find a woman who would be attracted to you dressed like that."

He raised a brow. "And you think I was with a woman,
why?"

"You were too annoyed at being called back to have
been alone." She smiled knowingly, aware she had him
there. "I'm too tired to hoof it back to my own place. I'm
crashing in my old room. 'Night, big brother."

"'Night, Bea-Bea."

Her door closed, and a few moments later the light
went out from under the door frame.

Trace stared up at the ceiling once more. Yeah, he was
annoyed, though less so than he thought he might have
been. Seth was safe, Bea was going to survive, and that's
what mattered.

But damn, why tonight? He'd been so close. Since the
first night he'd caught sight of Jo, he'd wanted her. That
curvy body packed into jeans and those polo shirts everyone at the bar wore haunted his dreams. Her long hair,
that thick rope of black silk, begged for his hands to wrap
themselves in it. And though he'd never have guessed it
before, the piercings even intrigued him.

Where else was she sporting some metal?

He needed to investigate. He smiled a little at that. Ah,
the mysteries of women. Kept a man happy and healthy.

He'd have another chance. Though he had no clue
when, since he'd gone out twice in a short time, and
wasn't comfortable just leaving Seth with either of his sisters again. They weren't last-minute nannies, and he tried
hard to remember that whenever he got the itch to do
something or go somewhere.

So he'd bide his time and wait. Hopefully, when he got
the chance, Jo would be ready.

*   *   *

Jo grabbed her shoes and started lacing up. She was running way too late to count, thanks to sleeping late. At least, late in Jo's world, which was really about half an hour early. But was it her fault restless dreams kept her up most of the night?

No, it most certainly was not. The blame there would rest solely on the shoulders of one Trace Muldoon, and whatever it was that had pulled him away the night before.

After both shoes were ready to go, she stood and grabbed her cell phone, shoving it in her back pocket. But as she was grabbing her keys to lock up the apartment and open the bar, her apartment phone rang. She debated for two seconds, then answered.

"Hello?"

"Josephine, how are you?"

Resigned, she sat back down and mentally deleted at least three tasks she normally completed before the lunch crowd came through. "Hey, Mom."

"Oh, no, no, no. What did we talk about?"

Jo sighed. "Hey, Regina."

"Ah, that's better. So much more mature, don't you think?"

No. She didn't think. Mature would be a woman of her mother's age realizing it was okay to be called "mom" by her own daughter, rather than wanting to pretend they were sisters and BFFs. But then again, when one was constantly between meal tickets—oh, sorry, *husbands*—one couldn't stand to appear one's real age. "What's up? I've got to open the bar soon."

"Oh, sweetheart. I just needed to let you know I've moved."

"Moved, past tense? As in, already happened?" Most kids might be shocked to hear about such a thing after the fact. Jo was just asking for clarification.

"Yes, about a month ago. I met the nicest man from Oklahoma City and . . ."

Jo tuned Regina out. What was the point? Same song and dance. In fact, Jo could probably tell it better than Regina herself. Met a nice guy, who just happened to be rich—how shocking!—and was willing to move her in with him. Or, even better, find her a sweet apartment just around the corner where she could do whatever she wanted. Of course, this meant uprooting her sweet daughter, but that's okay. A new city was a great place to start over. Again. And cities were just full of educational opportunities, weren't they?

"Don't you think?"

"Hmm?"

Regina blew out a harsh breath. "Honestly, Josephine, were you even listening?"

Not really. "Sorry, Mo—Regina. Something distracted me. What were you saying?"

Her mother gave a long-suffering sigh, as if mentally asking *why was I saddled with such an ungrateful child?* "I was simply saying that I think Rich will make a wonderful husband. He's got all the qualifications."

Wealthy, not hideous looking, wealthy . . .

Actually, Rich was a perfect name for someone her mother would target.

Regina laughed, a well-practiced little trill that sounded something close to a cross between a nightingale singing and angel wings fluttering. Well-practiced, indeed. "After all, fifth time's the charm!"

"Seventh," Jo muttered, looking for something to throw without damaging property.

"That's not right."

"I guess if you choose to not count those two annulments, then, hey—your math works."

"What has gotten into you?" Regina snapped. "Your attitude is horrible."

"Sorry." Jo rubbed between her eyes with her thumb. "I didn't get much sleep last night."

"Oh, dear." Regina *tsked*. "You need sleep if you want to look your best. No man wants to deal with a woman who has bags under her eyes."

"Right, well, owning a bar doesn't always lend itself to restful nights." Nor do lusty dreams about unfulfilled promises from damn sexy cowboys.

"You could just work at a bar. Owning something is so complicated." Regina's goal in life was to avoid complication.

"I manage, somehow."

"Is that sarcasm?"

"Nope," she lied without a second thought. Lying had become a way of life with her mother. If Regina hated complications, then really, Jo was just giving her mother what she needed. She never felt guilty about it. Regina would just stop contacting her altogether if Jo took a hard line.

"Did I tell you the story about that horrible woman who worked at that bar with us in Dallas?" Regina's disgust was telegraphed loud and clear. "You must remember her. She was the one with all that hair like that snake woman from those stories. Anyway, I heard through the grapevine—"

"Mom?" Jo said loudly. "Regina? Can you hear me?"

"Josephine?" her mother called back. "What in the world—"

"Regina? Reg—damn," she muttered, as if to herself.

"Must be a poor connection. If you can hear me, I'll let you go now so you can go back and get to your . . . *work*." Regina said the word "work" the same way some people might say "spiders" or "taxes."

"Okay then. Let me know if I should be looking for a wedding invitation." Which she would RSVP a big fat *no* to, but would send a nice gift. Just as she had the last four times.

Oh, sorry. The last two. Apparently two of those four weddings didn't count in Regina math. Funny how those gifts never got returned though. Regina math was very one-sided.

"Will do. Love you, baby!" Regina blew noisy air kisses and hung up without waiting for a response. The only thing Regina was truly interested in was her next season's wardrobe, and whatever adoration she could scrape out of the current cash cow.

Whoops. Husband.

Jo set the phone back down and made her way to the door. No point in dwelling on the Cleaver-esque mother-daughter relationship she would have killed for as a kid. The hand she was dealt would suffice. Besides. She was thirty years old. Did she really need her mommy's approval and unconditional love at this point?

No. But it would have been nice. . . .

Jo walked down the stairs with heavy steps. Sometimes, life was just too complicated to even think about.

No wonder people drank.

Trace checked his watch, sighed, then stared out the window behind Peyton's desk. The desk—and the office it graced—had once belonged to their father. Though their father had been less of a businessman and more of a horseman himself, which explained a lot of why the ranch had been in such dire straits when it was passed to the three Muldoon siblings in equal shares. He'd tended the stock, not the books, which gave their mother free rein to run the numbers into the ground.

By the time their father was gone and Sylvia had full

control, the debt had been impressive. After she'd had her way, it had become monumental.

But Peyton had definitely put her stamp on the place since. The dark wood would have seemed masculine if not for the touches of Peyton everywhere. More pictures than before. Books on animal husbandry and genomes dotted the shelves next to tomes of business marketing, capped by a few fiction best sellers.

And a pretty little figurine of a young girl with two braids riding a horse sat in a place of honor next to the computer. Trace knew Red had given the silly thing to her for Christmas. A year ago, Peyton would have scoffed at it and hidden it in some dark corner of a bookshelf. Instead, she'd gotten all teary and kissed the guy.

Figured.

"Where's your sister?"

Peyton rolled her eyes. "I thought she was *your* sister this week."

"Please. I can't keep track of her for five seconds. Why does she have to be mine?"

Peyton kept typing an e-mail, using the time wisely. Trace couldn't say the same for himself, but then again what was he supposed to do? He was a figurehead for the company, not involved in the business end. Nobody wanted him answering e-mails, not if they wanted to sound professional.

"Hello, little people." Bea breezed in on a swirl of fabric. The skirt she wore was an impractical number—as usual—with strands that looked like silk scarves hanging all over it. Her top was gauzy and almost see-through, though she wore a tank top under it, thank God.

Why couldn't she just dress like a normal person?

"You're late," he said flatly.

"I am? Oh." Zero remorse. She sat down and gave Peyton a hurry up look, as if she were the one who'd been kept waiting, rather than the other way around.

Peyton merely kept typing, holding up one finger for a moment to indicate she'd be done in a second.

"Do you know what this meeting is about?" Bea asked in a loud whisper, leaning over toward him.

"I'm assuming it's where Peyton kicks you off the ranch."

Trace expected her to smile and say that was fine with her, she was done with the place anyway. But Bea's eyes widened for a moment, and he could almost see the wheels turning in her mind as she calculated the possibility of that being a real threat.

Interesting. For a woman who claimed almost daily to miss Hollywood and her soap star friends and the fast life and who couldn't stop ranting about how much Marshall and the state of South Dakota sucked . . . she looked rather frightened to be kicked out.

Something to think of later.

Peyton slammed the laptop closed and shoved it back by the desktop. "Sorry, finishing up an e-mail I started waiting for Tardy Pants here."

"I resent that."

"Then stop being late," Peyton said simply. "The meeting is to discuss the business of the ranch. I know neither of you particularly enjoy that topic, but it's got to be dealt with."

Bea rolled her eyes and inspected her nails. "As I've said before, you may simply cut me a check for the price of my portion."

"And as I've told you, currently that's going to be squat. You want a check made out to squat?" Peyton smiled. "Plus, I'd like to remind you we have this nifty thing these days called the mail service. It carries letters all over the world. I could easily slip a check into the mail when it's ready. Nothing is keeping you here."

Bea simply sighed, her chest heaving with the effort. "I'd hate to think what my leaving would do to this family. The damage it might inflict. Emotional trauma, and all that."

"Yeah. Heartbroken." Peyton turned to him, sensing he was the only one bothering to listen. "We've made some serious ground since last year, thanks to both you and Red. But that doesn't even put us back at even. Mama screwed us badly when she ignored the business side of the M-Star." Her face ticked. "No, actually I wish she had ignored it. That would have been better than her thinking she knew a damn thing about horses and just randomly throwing money all over the place and losing it hand over foot."

"But we're heading in the right direction."

"Nowhere to go but up," Peyton said cheerfully. But he could see the strain in her eyes.

"Peyton," Trace said, and her smile slipped. "Just give it to us straight."

Chapter Six

Bea was silent, but from the corner of his eye, he could see she'd dropped her hand in her lap and was watching rather than inspecting her manicure for chips.

"We've still got outstanding bills to pay. People have been generous, and I appreciate it. But that generosity can only go on for so long. People want their money, and I can't blame them. Plus . . ." She looked at the large computer monitor.

"Plus?" Bea asked anxiously.

"Back taxes."

Ouch. Trace winced. Uncle Sam wasn't known for his generosity on excusing taxes. "Sylvia really was a peach."

Bea bit her bottom lip, finally looking enough disturbed by the conversation to pay attention. "So now what?"

"We're on a payment schedule. But between the taxes, which I didn't see coming, and the catch-up we're still playing in other areas . . . it's tight." Peyton laid her hands on the desk. "I'll be honest . . . we need something more. Something new."

"Something new? Like what, new horses? A new trainer?" Trace's mind spun, trying to follow his sister.

She shook her head. "Those are band-aids. We need to branch out a little more. Find a new clientele."

"Wasn't that my job, with my old rodeo buddies?" Was he really tanking that badly? Was this his fault?

"You're doing great. Your friends and their word of mouth . . . it's what's keeping us going right now. Without it, we would have handed our keys over to Uncle Sam months ago. But we need to reach even higher." Peyton tapped one finger on the desk and stared meaningfully at Bea.

She looked blank for a moment, then Bea's head snapped back. "Me? What the hell do you think I'm going to add to this mess?"

More mess, was Trace's guess.

"You have a ton of skills you haven't tapped into yet," Peyton said, all warmth now. "We just need to think outside the box and use your own personal brand of . . . individuality to our mutual benefit."

Wow, clearly Peyton's skills in diplomacy had improved in the last year.

"I'm not a rancher." Bea crossed her arms over her chest. Trace recognized that stance.

"I didn't ask you to be." Peyton flattened her hands on the desk and leaned forward.

Yup, he recognized that stance, too. It was from every fight his sisters had as teenagers, all over again. Trace settled back in his chair and prepared to watch the fur fly.

"Then there's nothing I can do."

"You could start by getting your ass out of bed before ten in the morning," Peyton snapped.

Trace watched diplomacy take a flying leap right out the window.

"My ass and its time schedule are none of your concern."

"They are when you're sleeping in my house."

"I have my own apartment now."

"Which is actually the trainer's apartment. Which is a part of the ranch."

Bea smiled smugly. "Which, I'll remind you, I own a third of!"

Oh, Jesus. The death blow. Peyton's face flushed and she slammed one fist down on the desk, standing. "You arrogant little—"

"Who are you calling little, you hobbit!"

"Hobbit this!"

"Ladies?" Trace tried once, quickly, to intervene before Peyton jumped over the desk and mauled their baby sister where she sat. She might have been shorter than Bea, but she had more muscle and endurance.

Though Bea did have those nails . . .

Not his problem.

"This is doing nobody any good," Trace said. "Can we get back to that whole 'mutual benefit' thing? I was interested in that."

Peyton took a few calming breaths, though they didn't do much to improve the flush still covering her face. Some of her hair had escaped her braid and curled crazily around her temple, and her jaw looked clenched hard enough to break ice. Bea, for her part, still looked completely unruffled, as if she went through screaming matches like this daily.

"Fine." Peyton spoke through the clenched jaw. "Beatrice—"

"Don't you dare."

"Bea," she corrected with emphasis. "I know you have friends in higher places. People who own land out there in California. Friends who might be interested in horses trained by the best in the business. People who are willing to shell out six figures for a horse."

Bea stared at her as if she were speaking Greek. "You're sure I have friends like that?"

Peyton blinked. "I'm hoping."

"Time to let that hope die, sis. None of my friends ride."

"But maybe they've thought about it. Or they have friends who might. Don't all movie producers have little ranches just outside the city limits? It's a cliché for a reason, right?"

Bea scoffed. "In case you didn't realize this, we lowly soap stars aren't exactly all that high up the food chain. I was second string, if that. I don't have a list of movie producers I can just call up to chat with."

Trace cocked his head to the side. Interesting. This was the first time Bea had mentioned her career in anything but glowing terms. She'd led them all to believe she was only in South Dakota to give herself some distance from the life, and reevaluate her direction for the next acting gig.

"Can you make friends? Use connections? Something?" Peyton's eyes started to develop a hint of desperation. "Anything?"

Bea shook her head, and for once Trace believed her remorse in telling Peyton no. "I just don't have the connections you think I do."

Peyton stared for a moment over their shoulders. He would have turned around to see what she was looking at, but he knew that glazed-over expression. It was the same one he'd had when the woman he'd been sleeping with told him she was pregnant. A look of recalculation, of reconsideration, of rejiggering your entire life to fit around whatever new card you were just dealt.

She nodded once, firmly. "Okay then. Sorry I wasted your time, both of you. I'll just . . . figure something else out. I haven't looked hard enough, I guess. There's another way."

Trace didn't believe her. But there was no point in talking more. She was beaten, and she wanted them to leave the office so she could privately grieve for the failed plan she'd so obviously hung her hopes on.

He stood and waited for Bea to exit before speaking. "You've done good, Peyton."

She gave him a sad smile. "I think we both know that's a crock."

"You can't fix everything. Sylvia did her damnedest to drive this place into the ground before she crashed into that pole. That's not on your shoulders. If you were starting from scratch, there'd be no contest. You'd be unstoppable."

She stood and walked around the desk, stepping easily into his arms for a hug. Her ear rested against his chest and she sighed. "I wanted to save it for Daddy."

"How about for yourself, too?"

"Oh, yeah. That was obvious." He chuckled. "But I just had this image of Daddy watching us, cheering us on like he used to when we'd be out in the arena learning a new trick."

"Sittin' on a barrel or draped over the top rung of the gate, yelling at us to keep pushing harder, not give up," he said, the image clear as crystal in his mind. In a few years, he could substitute himself for his father, Seth for a younger Trace. That made him smile.

"It's over, isn't it?" Peyton leaned back and looked at him. "I need someone to tell me the truth."

"Do you still have the keys to the front door?"

She grinned. "Yeah."

"Then it's not over."

Trace twisted his back around and moaned when he found the pulled muscle. Something hadn't felt right the entire day, and now he knew why. Damn. He needed a masseuse and a heating pad.

Too bad all he had was lukewarm bottled water and a horse trailer.

Actually, he stood and watched as Steve drove away the

M-Star vehicle with the trailer attached. Now all he had was his own pickup.

The thought of a three-hour drive with his back aching so badly was enough to bring a grown man close to tears. After a quick debate, he realized he needed to suck it up and drive. His back would only be worse in the morning; he knew that much from experience.

Damn Lad and his desire to throw him off whenever the animal damn well felt like it. And damn that kid for screaming and scaring the piss out of his horse. Who the hell taught that kid barn etiquette, a pack of wolves?

An hour into the drive, his cell phone rang. He picked it up out of the dusty cup holder and flipped it open, hitting the speaker button at the same time. "Yeah?"

"Well, hey there, Daddy. Someone wanted to say goodnight."

"Da!" Seth's shrill scream pierced his skull and sent shards of glass rattling through his brain.

Trace gritted his teeth and fought back the rough edges of pain to keep his eyes on the empty road. "Hey, little man. You being a good boy for Peyton and Emma?"

"Da! Bah bah. Da!"

"Sure, uh-huh. Sounds like fun," he said, wanting to smile. He would have, if it wouldn't have hurt. Man, he missed his son. Two days away and the kid picked up new syllables.

"He's reaching for a ball. I'm pretty sure full words are right around the corner." Peyton's voice was strong again and it was clear she'd taken the phone back from Seth. "So how'd it go?"

"Not shabby, until the end."

"Define 'not shabby' and then what happened at the end?"

"Second overall in my division, and a few guys who are

gonna be popping by this week to check the place out. And one guy who was interested in Lad."

"Huh. Not a bad idea."

"Lad's my horse, Peyton."

"Technically, he's an M–Star horse. Besides, I thought you never wanted a horse of your own. Something about responsibilities and how you had too many of them already."

Yeah, he'd said it. And meant it, too. Trying to travel everywhere with a horse of his own while towing Seth along for the ride had proven too much. And Trace never got in the habit of attaching any sentiment to his animals anyway. They were livestock, end of story.

But the thought of watching some other man drive away with Lad in his trailer, riding Lad on his own land . . .

It left a sour taste in his mouth. Maybe he was changing his tune.

"Forget Lad. The end part was basically something spooked him after we were done with the day and he threw me like a sack of potatoes. I think I pulled a muscle in my back."

"Are you out of commission?"

"Thank you for your concern, Peyton," he said dryly. "No, I don't think I need a doctor. Yes, I'll live. Your worry is overwhelming."

"Can it, big bro. You're talking and you're alive. If it was worse you'd have told me and made me feel all sympathetic. It's how men work. 'Oh, poor me, I'm near death's door. I have a cold. It's like the plague, but worse.' "

She had him there.

"Should you be driving if it hurts that badly?"

"Steve took Lad back with him. I'm on my own so I can pull over when I need to stretch it out. But I'm probably not going to get back tonight, just a warning. I'll need to pull over and rest for a while."

"No problem. Little man here's about to hit the hay and then he's out for the night. I'm not going anywhere, so we're set. Just be careful on the road."

"Yeah . . ." He thought about it a little and wondered if maybe he should push all the way home. "Just don't expect me tonight."

"You got it. We'll see you tomorrow, and don't push yourself."

She hung up without a good-bye. So like Peyton.

Don't push himself. Well, Peyton had ordered. And if Seth was going down for the night . . .

Trace ran some calculations and wondered if he could really make it back to Marshall tonight. Maybe, but it might not feel great.

He'd try. And if he made it, he might see about stopping in and asking a certain bartender to work a kink out in his back.

He could only try.

Jo watched the young man pound back his third beer in an hour. If he ordered another, she'd have to call him a cab or refuse service. She always hated playing hardball, so it was time to be a little diplomatic instead. She walked up and leaned over the bar, elbows resting on the polished wood.

"Have you been in here before?"

The younger man—she knew he was twenty-two, as she'd checked his ID herself—predictably let his eyes wander from her face down to the cleavage the polo shirt provided. She couldn't even bring herself to be annoyed about it. The reaction was too expected to rate annoyance. "I've been here. Just hang out in the back, usually."

"And I'm always up front." She took his empty away

and started to fill a tumbler with ice. "Mind keeping me company while I take a quick breather?"

He nodded, then shook his head. "Sure. I mean, I don't mind."

He was cute, in an awkward, still finding his feet sort of way. She poured him some water as well, and as she hoped, he took a sip to match her own. Years and years behind the bar provided enough tricks to get a patron to slow down without being blunt. Lucky for her, her new young friend was easily led.

"So you work on one of the ranches around here?" She pulled the hair from her ponytail off her flushed neck and fanned the skin a little.

"Hell, no." He looked offended. "I'm just home on break. I'm heading to law school next semester in Vermillion."

"A smarty. I like a guy with brains." The quick, teasing comment made him flush. Cute. "What's your name again?"

"J. J. Jeff," he corrected. "Jeff Junior, but everyone called me J. J. growing up. I'm trying to get rid of it."

"Well, Jeff, it's nice to meet you." She held out a hand and he quickly shook it. She flashed him an apologetic smile as she stood to fill an order quickly, and then came back. "Excited about law school?"

"Sure. Family business. Can't beat what you already know."

She could relate, so she nodded. "Leaving any girls back here with broken hearts while you run off to school?"

"No," he answered fast. "No girls."

"Just as well for them, then. No need to leave a trail of crumbled souls behind you, right?" Jo winked, then glanced up as Stu motioned for her to follow him into the kitchen. "Looks like my break's over. Thanks for keeping me company."

He saluted her with his ice water, and she was relieved to see it didn't appear as though he would order another drink. With any luck, he'd finish off that glass before heading out the door. And as she watched from a distance while he cashed out with her secondary bartender, leaving a healthy tip behind, she was glad to see he walked straight and without a hitch. She took her business seriously, and over-serving was never an option.

Three hours later, Jo stretched and watched the last of her servers clock out for the evening. Amanda hung back and waited while the rest walked across the street to the parking lot as a group.

"How was your date?" Jo asked, swiping her manager's card to bring up the day's receipts.

Amanda gave her a knowing smile. "Can't complain."

"Who was the lucky cowboy?"

"Oh, some guy passing through. I think he's already gone." Amanda shrugged and folded her apron before tossing it into a bin to be laundered. "I wasn't looking for forever. For now is good enough. Know what I mean?"

"Yeah." She did. She'd always had for now. Sometimes she wondered what forever looked like. God knew, she didn't have a solid example from her mother. Her father? Never seen him. But even her friends had a similar outlook to Amanda's. There were no wedding invitations— Regina excluded—no calls to be a bridesmaid, no gushing e-mails about being the love of someone's life. Her friends all sat on the same side of the line with regard to soul mates and true love.

Bunk it. Give me a good drink and a good orgasm and I'm satisfied.

"I saw Trace Muldoon hanging around a long while the other night." Amanda stalled by starting to roll silverware for the next day's lunch shift. "He have anything interesting to say?"

"Not a word," Jo lied. "Just another cowboy. You know how that goes."

"Yeah." Her friend sighed lustily. "But God, what a sexy one. And there's something to be said for the quiet types who know what to do in bed and don't ruin it with a lot of chatter."

Jo couldn't disagree, so she simply kept her mouth shut.

"You know, it's interesting about him. He—"

"Amanda. For the love of God. I'm—"

"Not listening to gossip. Yeah, yeah, yeah." Amanda rolled her eyes and let the last silverware roll drop into a bin. "No fun, that's what you are."

"Says so on my name tag." Jo patted the embroidered pocket of her polo saying it was Jo's Place.

Amanda snorted in disgust. "Fine. Stay here in your little bubble of solitude. When you want to know the good shit, come find me."

Amanda left, and Jo watched her walk across the street and get safely into her car before turning away from the door. Now that she was alone, she hauled ass to get through the last of her duties and locked up. Walking around the corner toward her steps, she slowed, and then stopped as a feeling of déjà vu came over her.

"Hey, stranger."

"Hey, yourself." Trace leaned against the side of his truck, but didn't approach. Just like last time. "It's a little late, but I took a chance you wouldn't kick me out on my ass."

Jo shrugged. "I'm more inclined to get pissed over an early wake-up call than a late night visit."

His smile was slow and easy. "That's encouraging."

Jo waited a beat, then swept her arm toward the stairs. Why pretend they didn't both want it? That was self-defeating, and she made it a point to not be. "Well, if you're coming, then let's go."

He followed her, then held out a hand when they reached her front door.

She eyed it. "What?"

"Keys."

"I'm not giving you my keys. I can open the damn door myself. Country boys," she muttered as she wrestled with the key ring and the fifty thousand keys on it. Seriously, did they make babies while the lights were out? When did she ever get this many keys? After trial and error, she found the one she wanted and unlocked her door.

"Maybe it's just a polite thing, not a country thing. What, no city guys open your door for you?"

"They knew modern, twenty-first century gals like to do some heavy lifting ourselves," she shot back. Clearly, she would have to lay down a few rules or else the man would be running over her life like a freight train. "I'm fully capable of carrying my own packages and opening doors and paying for dinner."

"Of course you are." He said it so easily, it took her a moment to figure out if he was joking or not. "But why do it, if you don't have to?"

Jo opened her mouth, then closed it again. He'd asked a legit question. One she didn't have a smartass answer to. She'd save that for later. "Whatever. Are you staying?"

"Are you inviting me?"

"You're in my home and it's one in the morning. I think if I didn't want you to stay, it would have been foolish to let you in." It was probably foolish, regardless. Something about Trace Muldoon screamed danger, and not in the *bad boy biker dude* sort of way. But in the *you could so get burned* way.

"Well, since you're struggling to issue the invitation, I'll do the hard work myself." Trace took his hat off and ran a hand through his hair, fluffing it a little. The hat dropped to her entry table and his boots thudded softly over her scarred hardwood floors. "Jo, I'd like to stay with you tonight."

Jo dug for some sort of snappy remark, but she came up empty. When his body closed in on hers, she breathed, "All right."

His own sigh matched hers. Jo almost laughed. Was he relieved she'd said yes? Like she'd be able to resist him.

Trace reached out with one hand and cupped the back of her head, just below her ponytail, and tipped her face up to look at him. "I'm planning to stay all night."

"If I get sick of you, I know how to bounce you."

Trace chuckled low, and she wanted to hear more. It sounded rusty, as if he didn't make the sound often. But she'd be willing to bet Trace was a guy who found humor in life frequently. He just seemed to have that kind of personality.

"Let's hope you don't have to bounce me, period." It was the last thing either of them said before he bent to kiss her.

Chapter Seven

She could taste the salty sweetness of his lips, and a hint of coffee, as if he'd been drinking it on the road. His tongue invaded her mouth without waiting for an invitation, though he likely assumed her moan was one.

Close enough.

He wrapped his hand around her ponytail and tugged so her neck was arched back, exposing her throat. "God, you are sweet," he murmured against her skin. "I don't think I've tasted anything better."

Sweet was so not a word used to describe Jo Tallen. At least not usually. Sassy, sometimes sexy, if she played it right, sarcastic for sure. But sweet? New territory.

"Okay, cowboy. Take me to bed."

"I thought you'd never ask." He shifted and put his arms under her knees, as if he were about to lift her up. Everything girly and completely illogical in her sighed with delight . . . though she would go to her grave denying it. But then he stood again and winced. "Sorry, darling. I had these big dreams of sweeping you off your feet and carrying you in there, all movie-style like."

"I can get behind that."

"Except I sort of wrenched my back at the event this weekend and the only thing worse than not being able to carry out this little fantasy of mine is the thought that I might drop you."

"Oh." Hmm. "Good point. Well then." Lemons into lemonade. She stepped to the side, out of reach, and pulled her polo top over her head, letting it drop to the floor. She crooked one finger and walked backwards toward the bedroom. "Follow me, if you please. No heavy lifting required."

He snorted. "Like you'd be heavy."

As a woman who would never be thin, Jo appreciated the comment. "You can try the he-man thing another time, when you're less broken." Suddenly, she stopped. "Should you even be . . ."

He waited for her to continue, but she just jerked a thumb to the bed instead of saying it. "Oh, hell no. There is no way I'm about to miss out on this again." He growled and pounced on her, half-pushing, half-pulling her over the threshold of her bedroom. "Hell if I'm letting you escape."

Before she could say a word or crack another joke, he had her bra off. How did he do that? The practical, beige number designed to keep her too-ample breasts in place while running her ass off behind the bar dropped to the floor unnoticed.

At least he didn't dwell on the industrial strength underwire. So not sexy.

Trace's hands were cupping her breasts, pushing them together, testing the weight of each one individually. Learning her body, her shape. Would he be a total breast man, or more interested in her legs? In her experience, men tended to be one or the other.

She had her answer when he leaned down to kiss the swell of one breast. "These are definitely being hidden beneath that black shirt you wear every day."

"The health inspector warned me to stop serving drinks with my shirt off," she said, biting back a moan when he took one nipple in his mouth and sucked. "Something about health code violations or whatever."

"I won't argue. If no other man knows what he's missing, then I don't have to share."

"I don't share, period." Might as well get that out of the way now. "When I go to bed with a man, he's it . . . until he's not."

He looked at her, warm mouth abandoning her breast. The now-wet skin peaked and tightened in the cooler air until she wanted to beg him to go back at it.

"I'm not looking to just fuck and run, Jo. I'm not starting a harem."

He looked so offended at the thought, she had to laugh. "I didn't say you were. Just telling you how I play. I'm a one-on-one kind of girl. And I expect the same from whoever I'm with."

"I'll try to keep my horny pants at home, unless I'm with you," he said dryly. He started to head for her other breast, but she needed to get it out of the way now.

"And you have to wear a condom. Always."

One brow raised. "Okay . . . any other rules?"

"I don't like gossip." Not anymore.

"Not a fan of it myself," he agreed easily.

"Just saying, I don't want to get into work tomorrow and have everyone I serve a beer to ask how you were in bed the night before. I don't want people thinking we're, like, together or whatever. . . ." she finished, wondering how she could have screwed that up so badly.

A thundercloud of anger crossed over his face. "So, I'm good enough to fuck in secret. Just as long as nobody knows, right?"

"No!" She replayed what he'd said. "Yes? Hold on, I'm

confused." She stepped back, out of his reach, so his touch couldn't distract her more. "It's not you. It's anyone I'm with. I just don't like the thought of anyone talking about who I'm with, or not with, or what I'm doing with my personal life." She took a breath.

"I'm not used to the small-town thing yet. I'm used to nobody caring what everyone does with everyone else, and being anonymous. Now that that's not an option, I want to keep things private."

He nodded slowly. "All right. Since I feel likewise, I don't see a problem. Now, can we pick up where we left off?" He stared at her chest meaningfully.

"Good enough for me," she chirped, and was rewarded with a long, possessive kiss. When he broke free, she could barely open her eyes again. "God, you're good at that."

"Let's see how many times we can get you to say that exact same sentence tonight."

The prospect had her shivering.

Perfect. She was perfect. Every dream of the ideal woman was plowed over by the sight of Jo standing there, defiant as she casually laid out the rules of their affair, her chin jutting out like she was prepared to take on the world. Without a shirt on.

Her breasts were a handful, maybe more. That torture device she wore clearly kept those babies under wraps at work, and he couldn't blame her. But now they hung free, heavy, red wine-colored nipples puckered, waiting for his touch. And he was more than willing to give them all the attention they desired.

"You have the prettiest breasts I think I've ever seen." He said it softly, then mentally winced. Probably not what a woman wanted to hear.

But Jo smiled brightly. "Why thanks. I grew them myself." She cupped one breast in each hand, the soft flesh spilling up invitingly. "You should come back here and tell them yourself."

"Gladly." She was short enough—or he was tall enough—that standing while attending to her home-grown breasts was difficult. After a split-second decision, he went down to one knee, biting back a wince at the soreness from his fall. Like hell would he let Lad's bad attitude ruin this for him.

The pain subsided quickly when he nuzzled against the soft skin of her cleavage. She moaned and gripped the back of his head, guiding him to one rosy, gathered tip. He sucked it into his mouth, smiling as she tightened her hold at the back of his head. Her breasts were responsive, just as he'd hoped. And Jo wasn't intent on letting him just run the show himself. No, when she felt she'd had enough on one side, she cupped her other breast and rubbed it along the side of his jaw, silently directing him.

He wasn't averse to a woman leading things in bed. Not if it got them both to where they wanted. And if Jo was ready to show him what she needed? He'd give it to her without hesitation. He moved to the other breast, nibbling the skin around her pointed tip, drawing it out before finally taking her into his mouth to use his tongue and teeth to tease more.

"You're good at this," she said on a breath. Her fingers ran through his hair, scratching his scalp a little.

"No use in being bad." He kissed his way down to her stomach, pausing a moment to examine the little silver bar with a dangling star hanging from her belly button. "This makes seven."

"Seven what?"

"Piercings. Four in one ear, two in the other, and this little guy here." He traced the bar with his tongue, wiggling it a little with his teeth. "Any more to find?"

She looked down at him and grinned. "There's only one way to find out."

"Guess I've got some exploring to do." With hands that nearly shook with anticipation, he started to undo the button of her jeans. "Why a star?"

"Would you believe it's a reminder to always shoot for the stars?"

The wry tone in her voice made him laugh. "For you? Not a chance in hell."

"You're right. Too cliché. Really, it was a gift from a friend. I have another one around here somewhere, a plainer one that I like better. I lost the bottom ball so I can't wear it. And Marshall isn't exactly teeming with body piercing stores to get a replacement."

"That it's not." He finally managed to slip the button from its hole, then went after the zipper. It rasped down slowly and he wondered for just a moment what kind of underwear she would be wearing.

Would her panties match her bra, simple and serviceable? Maybe she went wild on the bottom and had something completely sexy.

He wasn't expecting to find smiley faces grinning at him when he parted the denim and pulled it down.

"Don't worry, be happy?"

She laughed. "I'm not really into lace or G-strings. So I like to have fun with them."

"I'm all for it." He pulled down her jeans to her knees, then realized his own knee was starting to ache like a son of a bitch. If he didn't change positions soon, he'd struggle to get up. Nothing was sexier than stiff joints. "How about we shift this program to the bed?"

"Luckily, I happen to have one mere steps away." She shuffle-slid over until she could sit on the edge of the queen-size mattress and started to take her simple black shoes off. Shoes she probably wore because they were easier to stand in for eight hours than anything else. When those came off, she started peeling the jeans down. "Hey, cowboy, make tracks. You're losing steam."

He realized she meant his clothes, and stood without groaning—barely. He toed off his boots and looked for a good place to put them.

"Under the bed will work." She grinned when he smirked. "Hey, if I'm going to be taking a cowboy lover, I might as well go for the whole country-western song appeal, right?"

"You have a twisted mind, Jo Tallen."

Taking that as a compliment, she beamed. "Pants off, cowboy."

He wasn't sure if he liked the way she used the word "cowboy," as if she were checking this one off her list of types of lovers. Fireman, police officer, cowboy, athlete . . .

Not his concern. He unsnapped his shirt and shrugged out of it, trying his best to not mess his back up in the process. All the night needed was him half naked, locked up on the floor in agony. After that, the pants took seconds and he was completely naked.

He turned to the bed and his eyes nearly rolled back in his head in visual pleasure. She was a pagan goddess, brought down just for his enjoyment. She'd taken her ponytail out, so her long black hair spread out over the pillow around her. Her breasts were full and waiting for his touch once more. One hand rested lightly over her stomach. And the panties were gone, revealing . . . everything.

He raised a brow and stroked his cock once. He couldn't help it. From this distance, he couldn't tell if she was pierced below the belt. But he did see she was waxed. And holy hell, he nearly had to squeeze the base of his cock to head off an early end to the evening.

"I'm impressed." She rubbed the heel of her hand over her stomach, silver bar glinting in the low light of the one lamp she'd turned on by her bed. "I mean, one always hopes for a decent treat once you get the wrapping off, but . . ." She crooked a finger to him. "You're exceeding expectations so far."

"Let's see if I can keep that up." He climbed on the bed next to her, taking his time. He didn't want to just mount her and go. This wasn't a horse trailer and they didn't have ten minutes before his next event. He had all the time in the world, and he was going to take it.

Jo shivered in anticipation. The way Trace watched her, waited for her, stared at her body made her feel beautiful. Sexy. She hadn't hurt for partners in the past, but half the time she'd felt like they were just taking what was in front of them, rather than pursuing her for her. Bartender at the end of a night at the bar. Convenient. If she got her bell rung in the process, who cared? End goal achieved.

But with Trace's attention spent all directly on her, she knew what she'd been missing out on. The intensity of the experience when you wanted each other, and nobody else . . . the need for the other person, because nobody else would do. There were no substitutions. He stared at her like he would have chased after her even if she'd been a bank teller, an accountant, or a stripper.

Well, the stripper was probably a given.

His thick cock brushed against her hip as he moved over her, kissing her shoulder, her breast, the tip of her nipple. He moved down more and once again found the belly button ring she'd gotten at nineteen, and regretted by twenty.

Who knew why she kept it.

Oh, right. Because her mother hated it. Jo wasn't above being petty when it suited her.

She wondered just for a moment if he cared that her hips had a little more padding than she'd like, if she was a little more round than what was considered sexy. But he said not a word as he found his way down to the crease between her thighs, nudging them open with his elbow.

And then making her moan as his tongue found her center with deadly accuracy. He got right to the heart of it—to the heart of her—as he licked and worked his tongue expertly. Alternating between deep, penetrating licks and quick flicks of the tongue directly on her clit, he had her biting back moans she knew would come out closer to sobs. Once he added in a finger, she couldn't keep her hips still. She bucked and swerved and tried to keep up with his thrusts, his sliding licks, his quick sucks until she couldn't even keep track anymore and relented to the oncoming orgasm.

A freight train might have been a softer blow. She screamed, turning her mouth into the pillow to muffle the sound, even though nobody lived near her. Some habits were hard to break.

He kissed his way back up, nuzzling into her neck. "Don't go anywhere."

And then he was gone. She sat up quickly. Where the hell was he?

But in the dark she could barely make out his form heading for the pile of clothes he'd left by the door. He picked up his jeans and rummaged through the pockets until he came up with a wallet.

Condom. Right. She smiled and waited until he was properly suited up before patting the top of the nightstand. "Just for future reference, I keep a stash in here."

"Do you now?" The bed dipped as he joined her once more.

"Modern woman, and all that." She looped her arms around his neck. "All I need is a kid clinging to my leg while I'm trying to sling drinks downstairs."

He froze for a second, and she wondered if he'd misunderstood her. His face, what she could see of it in the dim light, gave away nothing. She'd meant it as a joke, but did he think she was serious? Time to smooth that over. "I mean, kids are cute and all, but they sort of don't mesh with my lifestyle."

He relaxed a little, one muscle at a time, and then he kissed her once more. Crisis averted. The tip of his penis nudged against her clit, and the little extra post-orgasmic zing made her squeal against his mouth.

Embarrassing.

But he didn't seem to mind, or maybe he didn't even notice. He was too intent on kissing her blind. And God, it'd be a fair tradeoff to go blind if she could have a kiss like this every night. He was methodically persistent, not leaving any centimeter of her lips untouched, unkissed. One hand found hers and linked their fingers together, raising their arms over her head. The intimate link that had nothing to do with sex was momentarily startling. His warm, roughened palm over her smaller hand felt so . . . trusting. Safe. So natural.

Back to physically gratifying sex before she started getting stupid ideas.

Her hips rose and she moved a little until she positioned him right where she wanted him. But he had to be the one to push in.

"Come on, cowboy. Let's giddy up." She grinned at the stupid double entendre. But Trace didn't catch the joke. Or at least, if he did, he wasn't amused by it.

"Say my name."

"What?"

He pushed in, just a little, before pulling out again. "Just say my name."

She had nothing against a little bedroom talk, but that was a first. "Trace?"

"No. Say it like you want me. Use it."

Ah. Now she was catching on. She used her free hand to stroke down his cheek, the beard stubble catching on her own calluses. "Trace. I want you, Trace."

With fierce pleasure, he drove into her, their hips bumping together. She arched back, finding a more comfortable angle while he pulled out and did it again, repeating the movement until she nodded and moaned. God, was she really going to come again? After already having one turn on the Ferris wheel? She never came from sex alone. What the hell?

Oh, who was she to look a gift orgasm in the mouth?

Trace's rhythm built her up until she was ready to cry for him to end it before she combusted. Then he reached down with his free hand and found her clit once more with precision and gave her that final boost into her second orgasm of the evening.

Trace followed quickly, jerking above her until he let out a hoarse cry and then collapsed over her before shifting quickly to the side to keep her from bearing all his weight.

"Yee haw," she whispered.

"You have this obsession with cowboys, don't you?" His words were slurred, as if he were drunk on sexual excitement.

"When in Rome . . . or South Dakota. I forget how the saying goes."

Trace stood and headed to her small bathroom. She waited to see what his next move would be. Damn if she would ask him to stay all night. Not her style, even if she wanted to. Would he just come back to bed? Or pick up his things and be on his way.

She got her answer quickly after that, when he shuffled back into the room and to the bed. After lifting the sheets, he crawled in and pulled her against him.

"I don't do the cuddle thing," she warned.

"Then don't cuddle. Just be a prop." His words were fading, like he was almost asleep.

She thought about arguing. Cuddling was too touchy-feely for her taste. It fostered ideas that they didn't have any business thinking about. But the warmth his body gave off lulled her, calmed her still-fizzing nerves, made her want to stretch and curl into him like a kitten with a basket of dryer-fresh laundry.

"I can be a prop," she said quietly. "Just this once."

"Just this once," he agreed, though she couldn't tell if he was being serious or not.

Chapter Eight

Trace was basking. The completely foreign concept had him smiling. He'd never basked after sex in his life. He'd gotten in, gotten them both off, and gotten out. And he wasn't ashamed of it, either. No woman who was willing to roll around in a horse trailer or in the back of his truck cab should be expecting much else.

But this? He sighed a little as Jo's small hand brushed up and down his back. This was something he could get used to very easily. The comfort of lying still after a good ride. The feel of his woman's soft skin against him. Her hands roaming his body, as if memorizing the lines and hollows. And maybe, after a little recovery time, another turn around the sheets . . .

"Oh, my God!"

His head snapped up at her exclamation. What, was she a mind reader now? He didn't think it was that bad an idea. . . .

"What happened to you?" Jo crawled away from him, and the movement made him face plant in the mattress. She maneuvered and rolled. Trace bit back a groan of pain, but then she was straddling his thighs. It would have been a sexy position, if he'd been facing up. But with him positioned on his stomach, it wasn't doing much for him.

"I told you. I fell off a horse."

Her fingers traced over one of the more tender areas, and he imagined she was following the lines of a large bruise with her fingertips. "You didn't say the horse nearly killed you."

"Because he didn't. Horses throw riders every day. It's a hazard of the job. I fixed it."

"By shooting the horse?"

He laughed, then realized she wasn't kidding. "Hell, no. I got back up there and finished my job."

"You got back on the same animal that did this to you?" Her voice conveyed something . . . either awe or shock. He couldn't see her face to tell which.

"Well, yeah. Animal goes too long after bucking someone off and they start thinking they're running the show. If you get right back on 'em, show 'em who's boss, they learn bucking isn't going to answer any of their problems. That you won't let it keep happening, and that that's not the way to behave."

"I'll just stick to driving a car and walking."

"Never ridden a horse?"

"Does a carousel count?"

"Uh, no." He couldn't believe it. He'd never met someone who hadn't been on a horse at least once. Even a simple pony ride at a local fair. "Maybe I could take you sometime."

"That's a big pass. I don't do the horse thing." Her hands started to massage. "Now, the cowboy thing? That's a hobby I could definitely dedicate myself to."

He smiled into the pillow as her hands started working out some of the kinks in his lower back. Slow and sure, those fingers massaged deep into his muscles, getting to the root of the soreness. "God, woman, you've got good hands."

"Years and years of opening bottles and carrying trays. They're small, but strong."

He couldn't disagree. If she kept this up, he might be almost back to normal by morning. But soon enough her hands weren't massaging so much as caressing his back, fingertips trailing over him so lightly they brought chill bumps to his skin.

"Cold?"

"Opposite." He ignored the pain in his back and did a quick roll, grabbing her before she could fall off the bed and depositing her on his thighs. "I'm a little hot, to be honest."

She started the same finger-trailing thing over his chest, scratching lightly beneath his chest hair and massaging when she went over his biceps.

"Hot, huh?" She rolled her hips until her exposed center nudged against his erection. "I'll accept that."

Jo flexed and rolled her hips until he felt her moisture spread over his hardening cock. But she focused her attention on the massage, rubbing his shoulders, arms, and chest. Every so often, she would discover another bruise and trace the perimeter with one soft finger, a frown marring her brow.

"Is it always so dangerous?"

"Riding?" He fought to keep his voice normal and not embarrass himself. God, what was wrong with him? Whenever he actually had the time for it, he loved foreplay. Why was he so goddamn eager to get back inside her? "Hardly ever."

She didn't look convinced. "I still think I'll pass on that form of entertainment. I wasn't meant to ride a horse."

"How about a cowboy?" He gripped her hips and slid her along his shaft. "Think you could take on riding one of those? I think there's a song that encourages such practices."

"Sounds promising." She sighed heavily. "If only I knew a willing cowboy."

He reached out blindly and rummaged through the nightstand she'd pointed out earlier and luckily came up with a condom in short order. "I think you might have found one. Why don't I saddle up and we'll take a test ride?"

She grinned and snatched the foil packet out of his hands. "I'm capable of this kind of saddle, I assure you." She was efficient and quick, not fumbling, but sure and easy with the task. Watching her fingers roll the rubber down his cock had him swelling bigger than he might have ever been before.

Slow down, cowboy. She doesn't need you to be a rough bronc. Not this go-round. Take your time and show her you've got some finesse to you.

Jo wasted no time in holding herself up so she could slide down over him. As her body clamped around him, Trace gritted his teeth. Finesse would be hard won this time around, too.

She picked a rhythm quickly, one that kept him on his toes every step of the way. Just when he thought he had the pace down, she changed it. And each time, he knew she picked up on his frustration because that damn cocky grin would spread over her gorgeous lips and she'd laugh, low and throaty.

"You're enjoying this."

"It's sex. What's not to enjoy?" She bent down and brushed a kiss to his jaw, changing the angle once more. "If you're not enjoying it, you're doing something wrong."

"I'll have that one stitched on a pillow." He tried to take control by thrusting up, but she evaded him and laughed hard and loud.

"Stitched on a pillow." She looked down at him, her raven black hair spreading around her shoulders like a cape. "I'm going to remember that one. I like a man who's witty in bed. So much more fun."

He wasn't sure he liked being compared to other men. But then again, he was coming out on top, so he shrugged it off and thrust once more into her wet heat. This time she stayed put, letting him, before taking charge another moment later.

"One of us is going to have to stay in the driver's seat."

She bit her lip. "Eventually. But the whole back-and-forth is doing it for me." She swiveled her hips instead of pumping up and down, making a circular motion over his pelvis. Trace's eyes wanted to roll back in his head at the feeling. God, she was something.

He loved a little bed play, but he was going to lose his fucking mind if she kept that up. And then he'd embarrass himself and shit knew he didn't need that. Proactivity time.

Reaching down, he found the bare, silken skin of her mons and massaged with his thumbs. The way her eyes widened, then drooped a little, he knew he'd hit a winner. Soon, she was rhythmically seeking his hands and their touch, which meant she was thrusting down on his cock at a speed he definitely wanted.

But she would never come like that. To add some fuel to the fire, one thumb slid down into her wetness and found her clit. He massaged in slow—achingly slow—circles. Jo's eyes closed and she leaned back on her hands, back arching like a dancer's to accommodate the position.

"Oh, my God," she moaned. "That feels so . . . so good."

"If it doesn't feel good, you're doing it wrong," he said, tossing her words back at her.

She grinned in acknowledgment at the hit, but didn't open her eyes.

She was a goddess, he decided. No, not quite. A nymph. A city nymph who landed in the country with too much polish and nerves of steel to match. His own personal nymph.

And he wanted her to be his. Over and over again . . .

Whoa. Too much, too soon. He slowed down, both mentally and physically. Time to slam on the brakes with that theory.

Jo raised herself back up. "Problem?"

"I can't see your face." He motioned with his head and she came down over him, breasts pushing into his chest, face inches away from his. "I want to see your face when you come."

"Here I am." She kissed him hard, tongue tangling with his. And she moved against his hand, along his shaft, until he was mentally cursing again.

But this time, he didn't have to worry. Jo throbbed around him, clenching uncontrollably and he knew she was close, so close. . . .

"I'm coming, cowboy," she whispered.

"Name." He needed to hear her say it again as she went over the edge.

"Trace," she said easily, then again louder as she climaxed and buried her face in the crook of his neck.

He surged up one last time, holding onto her slender hips and driving into her until he collapsed back on the bed, spent. Content to hold a boneless Jo over his chest as long as she wanted.

"Morning." Trace walked into the kitchen after dumping his boots by the front door and headed straight for Seth in his high chair. "Hey, little man. Were you good for your Aunt Peyton and Miss Emma?"

"Wild one, that Seth." Emma set a platter of hash browns on the table. "Had to stop all the crazy parties he was trying to throw."

"That's my boy." He rubbed over Seth's still bald head and gave him a quick kiss on the top of his fuzz before sitting down next to him.

Peyton watched him for a minute. "You feeling okay?"

"Yeah, good. Great." Trace scooped some hash browns onto his plate and grabbed the ketchup to squirt a little red river over them. As he grabbed his fork and picked up a bite, he caught his sister's look. "What?"

Peyton shrugged. "I just thought you would be back later. If you stayed somewhere overnight, then—"

"I made it most of the way." He shoveled in a bite of food as an excuse to quit talking.

"Where'd you bunk down?"

Trace mumbled around his breakfast and ignored the look Emma shot him for his rude table manners. "Seth, did you learn to walk while I was gone?"

"He's running a five K next week. Where'd you stay?"

"Why does it matter? I'm sorry I didn't make it home last night."

"I don't care about that. He's sleeping through the night, and it's no big deal. I'm just curious—"

"In town." There. "I stayed in town. Okay? Is that a problem?"

Peyton eyed him for a minute, then shrugged like she hadn't just brought the Spanish Inquisition down on his head and went back to her own breakfast.

Women. Trace rolled his eyes and finished his own food. "I'm gonna run up and change Seth and myself before the day gets started." He picked up his son, who wailed at leaving two stray Cheerios behind on his tray.

"Welcome to the world, son. Disappointments abound."

Bea floated in, looking . . . different. "Hey, Bea."

"Hello, brother." She reached around Seth and gave him a kiss, then a quick pat on the kid's back before walking into the kitchen.

Trace looked over his shoulder at Peyton. "Was there something different about her?"

Peyton nodded slowly. "She was wearing jeans."

"Like, denim ones?"

"Yeah. And blue, too. Not that stupid pair of white jeans she wore last month and insisted they were practical." Peyton's look of astonishment grew. "Oh, my God, you don't think she's got plans to go into the stables, do you? Because that's all I need, is her going in there and trying to distract the hands."

"Like I would be caught dead in that pigpen." Bea sniffed as she settled down with her half a grapefruit. Emma, it seems, had caved and was keeping the kitchen stocked with Bea Food. "It smells like animals."

Peyton rolled her eyes.

"Besides, these are Dior. They are not for tromping in mud."

"They're denim! If you can't go out to the barn in them, they're not real jeans!" Peyton yelled to the ceiling. "What's the point of jeans if you can't get them dirty with work?"

"If you have to ask, you're clearly not going to understand," Bea shot at her. "They are for looking exquisitely casual."

"An oxymoron if ever I heard one," Peyton shot back.

A knock sounded at the door and then it opened. Morgan Browning, the ranch's vet, popped in. "Hey all."

Emma waved him in. "Have you eaten yet, Morgan?"

Toeing his boots off, Morgan nodded. "Yes, ma'am, I have. My mama does a mean breakfast."

"That's right, she does. You sit down and eat something anyway. Always too much food around, since that one doesn't eat anything." She pointed a spatula at Bea, then huffed back to the kitchen.

"I told you months ago to stop making me a share of grease and you'd be fine!"

A clatter of pans was the only answer Bea got.

Morgan gave Trace a handshake. "I still can't get used to seeing you back here all the time."

"Just like high school," Trace said.

"Yeah. High school." Morgan grinned foolishly, then gave Seth a tweak under the chin. "Except I don't think this guy would have quite fit in with our crew."

"Little too young to go keggin' and silo climbing."

Peyton waved from the table. "Morgan, if you're done playing Remember When with Trace, I have a few—"

"Morgan!" Bea called from across Peyton. "You can solve a little argument we're having here."

"Sure thing." His attention was immediately riveted to Bea.

Bea leaned to the side and held up one leg straight in the air, looking like a ballerina stretching before a routine. The skinny jean tapered at the ankle, showcasing a pair of killer high heel sandal things with so many straps Trace wondered how long it took to actually put the shoe on. "Are these jeans?"

Morgan looked like he wanted to pass out. He nodded dumbly.

Peyton rolled her eyes and gagged a little to the side.

Bea shot him a dazzling toothpaste-ad smile. "Thank you, sweetie. I appreciate a man who understands these things. Really, I just appreciate anyone who agrees with me."

Morgan nodded again, then sat down with a thump when Peyton grabbed his wrist and tugged.

Trace could see "lovelorn" written all over his old friend's face. He debated for a moment taking Morgan aside and warning him off—not for Bea's sake, but for his friend's. Bea would chew him up and spit him out like he was a piece of fat on one of Emma's chicken thighs.

But some things a man just had to figure out for himself. And hell, who was he to lecture anyone about getting in over your head with a woman? Wasn't he the one planning on using his next night off to go catch Jo in bed again?

The woman who would rather call him cowboy than by his name.

He shook his head in self-disgust and headed for the stairs.

"Little man, when you're old enough, I'm gonna write you a manual about women. We'll just call it a survival guide."

"You look like shit."

Jo flipped Stu the bird and poured herself a Coke. Three cups of coffee hadn't done a damn thing for her, so maybe a different form of caffeine would do her some good. The first sip had her gagging. Too sweet for the morning.

She would commit several different kinds of felonies to get a good espresso in town. Despite her own efforts, she'd never fully mastered the art of making a good jolt herself. No point buying her own beans and grinder if she couldn't even produce results worthy of the time and effort.

But on days like today, the added punch would have been more than welcome. Hell, she would have just chewed straight espresso beans if they would have helped.

Her lips twitched as she remembered exactly why she was so exhausted. And his name was Trace.

Mentally, she wanted to cross his name out and insert "cowboy." Make it less personal. But something about the way he'd commanded her to use his name in bed had it sticking.

Damn it. Either that was the most interesting trick of the subconscious ever, or he was a sneaky bastard.

She wouldn't rule out either until she'd had more time to think about it.

"Wanna tell Stu all your troubles?" The cook sat down at the bar in front of her and motioned for her to serve up a Coke.

"Hardly. I think we'll just keep what goes on upstairs separate from what goes on down here."

Stu snorted before taking his first sip. "Sure. Right. Let me know how that goes. If whatever kept you up was actually a who, it'll get around. Sooner or later, it always does."

As he disappeared back into the kitchen, Jo drummed her fingers on the counter. It didn't have to get around. Not if they were careful. If Trace waited until after all the customers and servers were gone for the night, then slipped into her place and back out again . . .

Wait. Was she considering a full-on affair? Not just writing it off as a one-night thing. How very unlike her. . . .

But when the sex was as good as it had been . . . how could she blame herself for running in that direction full force?

Her servers trickled in one by one, smiling and waving. Of course, Amanda couldn't ignore the chance to shoot the breeze. She wandered over after clocking in, tying her server apron around her waist.

"You look like hell. What's up?"

Jo threw her hands in the air and let her forehead fall to the bar top. After a few quick raps on the wood, she sat up. "Why am I surrounded by people who care when I look like hell?"

"Because we love you, naturally." Amanda grabbed a dish tub of clean silverware and sat across from her to roll napkins. "Something wrong?"

"Not at all." Jo dismissed the conversation easily. She wasn't about to do the exact opposite of what she'd asked

Trace and start talking to Amanda about their night to-gether. She liked the girl, a lot. But she had a mouth on her and God knew what she might spill in a moment of weakness.

Amanda finished up her rolls and grabbed a piece of chalk to write the day's beer specials on a blackboard above the back of the bar. "You know, you might start opening up to people," she said casually while concentrat-ing on looping her B just right for Blue Moon.

"And do what with them?"

Amanda laughed. "Typical."

Opening up meant getting hurt. Being dragged around—physically or emotionally—with no say in your own future. Thanks, but no thanks.

"So how's your own cowboy?"

Amanda beamed, since someone else had brought up her favorite topic: herself. "He's awesome. I mean, there's no future there. But he's adorable anyway. He brings me flowers when we meet up." She scrunched her nose. "I told him he didn't have to, but he said he likes doing that sort of thing. So I guess that's just his way of handling a lover."

Jo debated sharing her opinion on the matter—that Amanda's mystery cowboy wanted to be more than lovers—but bit it back. Not her place.

Amanda finished underlining the advertised price on the last special and dusted her hands off. "Now, to the bathroom to wash up and then open the doors."

"I'll open the doors. You go wash up."

Chapter Nine

Jo was pouring her second cup of Coke, and making a face at it, when someone sat down at her bar. She turned and smiled genuinely. Not her *you're a paying customer and I'm in a bad mood, but I'll pretend I'm not* smile, but the real deal. "Hey, Jeff. Back for lunch today?"

He grinned and put his worn Marshall High ball cap on the bar in front of him. "Couldn't help it. You convinced me to come back. Service can't be beat. Plus, you're one of the only people in this town who remembers to call me Jeff."

"Benefits of being a newbie. I don't have to forget embarrassing childhood nicknames. Drink?"

"Just a Coke. I'm out running errands for my mom today." He made a face.

"Aw, that's cute," Jo teased and passed him the drink. When he scowled, she patted his shoulder. "It's nice. A man who is good to his mother makes the women look twice."

"Yeah?" He sipped his drink and looked over the top of her head, like he was considering the statement, weighing its truthfulness.

He was a cutie. With his dark brown hair a little shaggy, thoughtful brown eyes to match and quick smile, he was going to slay the co-eds in law school. She imagined he already knew that, though. He seemed to carry an innate boyish charm that told her he'd gotten his way more often than not by flashing that dimple. But in a good-natured sort of way, not a sleazy way.

He didn't dress like a lot of the other young men around town. Both times she'd seen him, he'd been in a collared shirt. Today a polo, last time an Oxford button down. His jeans today were fresh, and he had simple Adidas running shoes on rather than the crease-worn denim and scuffed work boots she was used to. But then again, not everyone who lived in the area was a rancher.

Jo sent his food order back to the kitchen and wiped down some more glasses to place on the top shelf, ready for the real rush.

"Quiet in here this time of day."

Jo nodded. "Not many people are hitting the bottle this early, and while I think we've got a kickass menu, the diner still wins the lunch race by a long shot. But since they don't serve alcohol . . ."

"You make up for it with the dinner crowd," Jeff finished. "I like your style, Jo."

She winked at him. "I like yours, too, Jeff."

The lunch hour passed rather quickly, thanks to Jeff and his company. When she mentioned once that he should get on with his errands, he waved it off and said his mother wasn't going to be home until later anyway. "Miranda Effingham is a busy lady. She's one of those committee people," he said in a deadpan whisper.

Knowing exactly the type, Jo laughed. "You lucked out, then, only running errands instead of being roped into going to a meeting or setting up a cakewalk or whatever."

"Can't argue there." He set some bills down on the

bar—way over-tipping, by Jo's quick estimation—and stood. "But you're right. Eventually the chairwoman will be home and I should have all the things put away like a dutiful son."

He was adorable. The girls at school were goners. "Off you go, then. Shoo. I can't be responsible for the chairwoman bringing down the law on you."

He stared at her a moment, and she almost wiped a hand over her face to see if she had something stuck there. "What?"

He replaced his hat and shook his head. "Nothing. Have a good day."

"See ya." She bussed his area and took the bills to the register. Yup. Over-tipped by a long shot. She shook her head and hoped he didn't see their conversations as a reason to have to go so far over the typical fifteen percent. Maybe she'd dial back the friendliness a little.

But something about him just struck her heart. He was almost like the little brother she'd wanted when she was younger.

"Cutie pie gone?" Amanda walked by with an armful of dishes and deposited them for the dishwasher to handle.

"Cutie pie?"

"J. J."

"Oh. Jeff," Jo corrected. "He's going by Jeff now, as he informed me."

Amanda rolled her eyes. "That'll stick, like, never. He's been J. J. since he was born, and J. J. he shall stay, if anyone in this town has something to say about it."

They shouldn't, but Jo didn't bother saying anything.

Amanda cocked a hip on the edge of the bar and surveyed the dwindling lunch crowd. "I know you have this thing about gossip, but if it's about another business, it's more like industry news, right?"

Jo raised a brow. "Sure, I guess."

"Gimmie's is closing."

Jo's hands nearly dropped the tall glass she was hand washing in the bar sink. "Run that by me again?"

"Gimmie's, down the street. It's closing."

"I know where Gimmie's is," Jo said softly, eyes staring straight ahead. Gimmie's was one of the other two bars located within town. Though neither of her competitors offered a selection of food like hers, they did have their own draw. Gimmie's was the nicer of the two, in her opinion, with decent flat screens and far more room for dancing and more pool tables than she carried. Her space was taken up with more tables.

"I think the glass is clean," Amanda said dryly.

"What? Oh, huh." Jo turned the water off and set the glass in the side rack to dry. "Any reason why they're closing down?"

Amanda pursed her lips. "Now would this be more of that industry news, or gossip?"

Jo swatted her with the bar towel.

She laughed and danced out of the way. "All right, all right! Don't bruise me. I've got another date with my cowboy!" She held up her hands in surrender. "From what I hear, Meldon—that's the owner—is getting too old to handle the place, and he doesn't have any kids to pass the business on to. He's willing to sell, but I guess he's been looking for a buyer for a few months now on the DL, and no nibbles. So he's packing up shop and heading to a retirement villa in Arizona. His brother's there."

"That's specific, all right." Jo mulled it over. One less bit of competition. One more step up in being recognized by this town as a staple. An institution. An insider. "Maybe I should send him a fruit basket or something. I'm sorry to see him go."

"Sure you are." Amanda's smug smile said it all.

"Hey, a little competition never hurt anyone. And besides, it's hard to close up a business you put your soul into, I'm sure."

Her friend watched her for a moment, and Jo realized she'd gotten too emotional. Time to get back to work. "Okay then. Thanks for the heads up." She shot Amanda a serious look. "But no more gossip."

"Industry news," Amanda sang as she headed back to bus her remaining tables.

"Industry news," Jo muttered again, but smiled. One more step. One more very important step.

Trace saddled one of the brood mares currently not pregnant and led her toward the main house. After loosely looping the reins around a column, he headed in the front door. "Emma?"

She poked her head out from the kitchen, with Seth in the Bjorn in front of her. "Your boots off?"

He took one giant step back onto the entry mat. "Just wanted to take Seth out for a bit." But he couldn't help smiling at the picture of the housekeeper and toddler. Two peas in a pod, that duo. Seth adored his Emma. "If you can spare him, that is."

Emma rubbed a hand over Seth's head and the boy giggled. "He's quite the help. He spent the morning tearing through a laundry basket of folded clothes."

Trace winced. "Sorry about that."

"Just as well you're taking him out. He needs the fresh air. Not to be cooped up in the house with an old lady." Emma slipped the carrier from her shoulders, expertly keeping one supportive arm under Seth.

As she handed him his son at the door, Trace bent down and kissed Emma's cheek. "Where's this old lady you speak of? I only see you, the awesome Emma."

"Go!" She swatted his arm and shooed him out the door. "Bring him back in one piece!"

Trace lifted a hand in acknowledgment and undid the reins of the mare. Then he stared for a moment. How the hell would he get up in the saddle without dropping the kid?

"Need a hand, big brother?" Bea walked out in a pair of bright pink pants and a cropped top.

"Hold him while I hop up."

She still grimaced, but willingly accepted her nephew without complaint. Improvement.

"He's drooling."

Okay, one minor complaint.

"They do that sometimes. He's getting another tooth." Trace swung up easily into the saddle and reached down for Seth.

Bea handed him up willingly. "Okay, you two up there are adorable. And you know I don't use that word lightly. I'm taking a picture. I'm sure Peyton would love it for the website."

"Hear that, son? We're adorable. Watch out, ladies under two. Seth Muldoon comin' at ya."

Bea reached around to her back pocket and pulled out her phone. A quick snap later, she waved as they walked sedately toward the hot walk area.

Trace settled one arm comfortably around Seth's middle as his son clapped with glee. The rocking of the horse was soothing, while the elevated height and forward motion provided entertainment. Plus, they were on a horse. It was a natural progression for a Muldoon.

As they entered through the open gate of the hot walk area, Steve tipped his hat back. "New hire?"

"You know it."

"Looks a little green. Maybe we should start him mucking some stalls."

Trace smiled. "Soon enough."

He realized after a moment, the entire picture was laid out perfectly. His son, a few years from now, helping him clean stalls. Learning how to take care of his tack. Groom a horse. Fix a thrown shoe.

All on Muldoon land.

For once in his adult life, he could look years down the road and mentally picture himself in the same place.

Was that supposed to be frightening, or exciting?

He let the horse do her thing in a slow, plodding circle. The horse knew what to do, and if Trace hadn't held his son, he could have put the whole thing on autopilot. While the pace would have bored Trace by age three, Seth's not-quite-one-year-old self was thrilled with the action. And Trace remembered all over again exactly why he'd fought to keep his son, rather than walking away when Rose came to him to tell him she was pregnant.

And no, her husband wasn't the father.

He'd been so close to losing Seth altogether. . . .

His hands tightened on the reins, and he loosened them again with effort. Going back there was not where he wanted to be. Seth was with him, where he belonged, and that was the end of it.

Seth was a Muldoon, and he belonged at M-Star.

Why was it so hard to remember he did, too?

Trace stretched his back, wincing at the twinge. But he manned up and grabbed his saddle, ready for a workout.

"Freeze."

Red walked up behind him and put a hand on his shoulder. "I think after the spill you had, you should take a day or two off."

"I've already been up once today."

Red snorted. "I'm sorry, but a breeding mare walking in a circle at point-two miles an hour while you've got your son does not exactly count. Rest up. The work will be there tomorrow. Stretch, heat, the whole deal. I'll ride Lad for a while."

Trace made a face. "You shouldn't be doing my work for me."

Red sighed. "I hate admitting this, but it's been too long since I've done the workouts on an experienced animal. I want some time. Give me the excuse, will ya?"

His lips quirked. "Is this another 'Please do me the favor of going out for a beer with Red' moment?"

"Not at all," Red lied easily. Trace wasn't fooled. He patted Trace's shoulder and grabbed his own saddle. "If you insist on working, I have a few errands you could run."

Errands. Trace rolled his eyes. "Pass."

"Ah, well. Thought you might like the chance to catch some lunch in town, but hey. No skin off mine."

The idea of grabbing a quickie with Jo during a lunch lull appealed too much to resist. "I—wait. Why do you think I want lunch in town?"

Red stared at him with disappointment. "How stupid do you think I am?"

"I'd say very, just to piss you off, but right now I'm in no shape to defend myself so I'll just let you go on."

"I see the way you watch that cute bartender. The owner. Jo? Every time you've gone in there and I've been with you, you track her like you're on a hunt and she's the game. So I'm guessing you wouldn't mind a chance to do a little more hunting."

No point in mentioning he'd already technically bagged the game. And wasn't that just a horrible metaphor? "Yeah, well . . . fine. Whatever." He jabbed one finger at Red. "But this isn't about lunch, or hunting. I need to pull my weight. And if you're not going to let me up on a real horse today, then I'll run your damn errands."

"Suits me. Peyton's got the list at the main house. She's in her office."

Trace heard Red chuckling as he left the stables, but he ignored it. He paused to remove his boots at the front door, freezing a moment to see if he could hear Seth. But then, noticing the time, he knew his son would be down for his morning nap.

A quick knock on the office door was all the warning he gave before walking in. "I'm informed by Lover Boy you have some errands for the gimp to run."

"Yup." Without looking up, Peyton held up a sheet of paper. "This stuff is piled in a corner of the storage barn. Grab one of those big boxes and fill it up, then run it to the animal shelter. If you make a quick pit stop to the feed store for the things at the bottom of that list, I'd appreciate it."

The animal shelter? "We've got an animal shelter?"

"Morgan started the ball rolling on that little venture about four years ago. Runs mostly on donations. Whenever we've got blankets too worn for the horses, we pass them on. They cut them down to puppy-appropriate sizes." She frowned and keyed a few more figures into her spreadsheet of doom. "And a few other things they ask for from time to time."

"Got it." Easy enough. And just like Morgan to see a need and go filling it. He'd guess the place never lacked for donations. People loved the Brownings, and they adored Morgan. Always had. Now that he was a respected vet, and likely worked for every family in the surrounding area, he must have a whole host of donors.

He was still reading the list as he slipped his boots back on. Otherwise, he would have seen the danger he stepped into.

"Trace!"

Bea hustled up the front steps, her heels clattering noisily over the old wood. "You heading into town? I'm dying to get out of here for a while."

Aw, shit. "I've just got two quick errands and that's it. It's not a shopping trip."

"Where are you going?"

"Animal shelter." That'd shut her up.

Instead, to his shock, her eyes lit with excitement. "Oh, puppies!" She grabbed a bag hanging from the nearby hook and shooed him. "Go. Let's go. The dogs await."

"I thought you hated animals."

"Puppies are not animals," she said, staring at him like he was an idiot. "Puppies are adorable little balls of fluff that melt into you. Plus, it can't hurt to play with them for a while, can it? They're all caged up in there like fuzzy puppy jail. And now I have that awful, sad Sarah McLachlan song stuck in my head."

His own head was starting to hurt. "I'm just dropping off a donation, Bea."

"I'm sure you wouldn't mind some help, would you?"

He watched as she struggled over the dirt path in her heels. The white of her capri pants was already turning dusty. "It's old blankets and junk. You wanna carry an old blanket?"

"The puppies need blankets? I'll carry a blanket."

He shoved open the large sliding metal door leading to the storage. "You asked for it."

Jo's heart added an extra beat into its rhythm when the door opened and Trace walked in. She wasn't used to seeing him in the daylight, but the sight added another memory to her store. His jaw was freshly shaven, and his dangerously good looks were . . . not downgraded exactly. He was still sinfully handsome. But the edge of illicitness was gone. More boy next door, less dangerous to make out in a dark corner.

She smiled, doing her best to mask the jolt she felt at the sight of him. "Hey, stranger."

"Hey back." He settled down at the bar and looked her over. "You look good."

"Ditto." She tossed a coaster in front of him. "Drink, lunch or both?"

"Water, and I'll be ordering lunch in a second. I'm just waiting for . . ." He trailed off and glanced at the door as it opened again. "That."

Jo remembered Bea Muldoon—Trace and Peyton's youngest sister—as she glided through the door. There was no other word for it. Some women wore heels like they were born to wear them, and Bea was one of them. Jo watched, amused, as several male heads turned and followed her every move, the gentle sway of Bea's hips as she walked up to join her brother at the bar. Normally, Jo would call it practiced, and respect the dedication to the art. But Bea made it look as natural as breathing.

Bea patted her brother's shoulder, then looked horrified at herself. "I need to go wash my hands, repeatedly. Jo, sweetie, do you have any lye soap, or maybe a sand blaster back there?"

That's one of the things Jo loved about Bea. She immediately treated you like her best friend. As someone who moved around often, she'd been grateful to meet people like Bea. "Sorry, just regular soap and paper towels, though they might be rough enough to qualify as low-grade sandpaper."

Bea sighed and headed in that direction. "It'll have to do." She didn't look around to notice if others were staring as she walked to the bathroom. But they were.

Trace laughed. "She's just pissy because she had to get a little dirty. All for a good cause, though. And I did warn her. Not my fault she didn't take me seriously."

Jo set the glass of water down on the coaster. "What in the world did you drag her into?"

"Drag? Hell, she jumped at the chance. I think she's bored at home." He looked thoughtful for a moment. "She probably needs to get out more, see a few friends. But she claims nobody around here gets her."

Jo sympathized. "Years away from home will do that to you sometimes."

"Didn't happen to me," Trace rationalized. Then his face brightened. "Hey. Two city girls, you might get along. You should hang out."

"Thanks, but I can get my own date." She winked at him and started pouring Bea a Diet Coke when she saw the woman walk their way. "I assumed . . ."

"Thank you, God." Bea gulped down half of it in one very un–Bea-like slurp. "I think I had five pounds of dust coating my tongue."

"Jesus, Bea, we were in there for less than an hour. And frankly, I had to drag you out."

"Where'd you go?" Jo couldn't handle the curiosity any longer.

"The animal shelter," Trace said. "Went to drop off some donations from the ranch, and Miss Priss here"—he cocked his head toward Bea— "begged to come along."

"It turned out for the best, didn't it?" she shot back.

"Not if you keep complaining and whining like a girl."

"Hey," both Jo and Bea said simultaneously. Then they laughed.

It felt good, laughing with another woman. She appreciated Amanda's friendship, but the employer-employee relationship added a complicated line she didn't want to cross. It held them back from being closer, forming a more permanent bond.

Okay, so maybe Trace was on to something.

"Ready to order, or should I lock the cage door and toss in a rare steak to see who wins?"

"Salad." Bea scanned the menu quickly. "You can do that, right? Something that doesn't come with a side of buffalo or cow?"

"Yes, smartass." Jo grabbed the menu and tossed it on a pile behind her. "You want yours with bacon and three cups of cheese, right?"

Bea stuck her tongue out, but smiled. "If you have a raspberry vinaigrette . . ."

"You get Italian dressing."

Bea turned to Trace. "The service here is lovely. I can see why you suggested it."

So it had been Trace who'd brought the siblings to the bar. Jo bit back a smile at that. "You want haute cuisine? Meet up with the other foodies in New York."

Bea's eyes fluttered closed and one hand paused dramatically over her heart. "If only."

Trace handed Jo the menu. "Burger, rare as you can make it. Fries."

"I like the easy ones." She punched in the order on the screen and then did her best to keep her distance. Not just out of principle, but because she didn't want to intrude on the sibling bonding.

Yeah, they bickered like kids squabbling over a toy, but she could tell they loved each other. And they still had some work to do in order to catch up. So she'd give them their space. Besides, she had other customers at the bar, and more than one of them wanted to chat about Gimmie's closing.

Her standard "It's too bad, a strong local economy is good for everyone" line was received well enough, with nods and smiles. But inside, every time, she couldn't help but do a little mental shimmy in response. It wasn't her fault the bar was closing; it wasn't as if she'd run the owner out of town. He'd been looking to sell, he didn't have a buyer, and he wanted to move closer to his brother. No guilt involved.

She glanced up as Bea answered her cell phone. Her rushed tones told her something was up.

Trace gave her a smile and shook his head. "Probably her agent." Jo took that to mean nothing was really wrong, just Bea being Bea.

A few minutes later, Trace waved her over. "We need to cash out. We've got to head back to the animal shelter."

Moving on autopilot, she printed their ticket. "Don't tip," she said as she handed it to him. When he raised a brow, she shrugged. "I'm the owner. Technically, you aren't supposed to tip the owner."

"Learn something new." He handed the trifold back with cash. "Just the same, you did the work so you'll have to accept the gratuity. Do whatever you want with it." Before she could argue, he winked and followed Bea out the door.

Just as the door closed behind them, Bea popped her head back in. "Hey, Jo!"

"Yes?"

"We're going to hang out sometime, okay?"

Jo couldn't answer before the door closed again.

Pushy bunch, those Muldoons.

Jo found herself looking forward to the next time she ran into either of them.

Chapter Ten

Peyton was on the front porch with Red when Trace and Bea pulled up. She hopped off the rail and onto the first step, then froze in shock as the dog Trace had stashed in the bed of the pickup hopped down and raced at her.

Her freeze was melted when the dog leapt up on her legs and started licking her hand. "Hey, buddy, where'd you come from?"

Trace jumped down from the cab and shut the door. "Oh, wow, a stowaway."

Peyton's hands sank into the fur around the dog's pudgy body. "I assume we have a new work dog?"

"More a pet than a work dog." Feeling stupid now, he called the dog to him. The dog ignored the summons. "I was thinking Seth might like a pet."

"Seth has a barn full of horses, a loft full of cats, and two ranch dogs." Red squatted down next to Peyton and gave the dog some attention.

"Those are working animals though." Yeah, he was an idiot. "This is more like . . . a pet. He'll stay out in the barn with the rest of the dogs. Emma would skin me for bringing a dog in the house. But I just thought he might be some fun for Seth. Watch them grow up together."

"By the looks of these paws, this one's got some growing to do." Peyton spread out one paw. "Boy, you'll have to grow into these saucers."

"Breed?" Red asked.

"Mix. Collie, shepherd, Lab . . . they did their best to identify him, but he's just an all-around mutt."

"Luckily we love mutts." Peyton gave him one last belly rub and stood. "Name?"

"Still working on that. Frank!" The dog ignored him. "Rover! Jim Bob? Lucky!"

Nothing.

Well, they'd work on it.

The passenger door finally opened behind him, and he sighed. "Just for the record? I had nothing to do with this."

"Do with what?" Peyton asked slowly; then her eyes widened as she saw what Trace knew she was going to freak out about. "What the hell is that?"

Red's lips twitched and he settled back down to watch the fun.

Bea came up beside Trace. "He's a dog."

"That is not a dog." Peyton pointed down to the mutt squirming between their legs, begging for more attention. "This is a dog."

"It's a Boston terrier. He's a purebred," Bea argued. The black-and-white creature—which Trace was still not convinced wasn't a large rat—shook slightly in her arms. "And you're scaring him."

"Too bad. Take it back."

"He needs a home just as badly as that puppy did. Maybe more so, since he's older." Bea snuggled the rat-dog-thing to her, cradling him on his back like an infant. "Older dogs have a harder time being adopted, they said. And he was just so sad in there, Peyton. Those big eyes and his little ribs sticking out, and he was shaking because all the big dogs scared him. And they can't keep all the dogs forever, and what if they had to put this sweet boy down? Could you handle that on your conscience, Peyton?"

The dog's bug-eyes stared straight at their sister in a silent, upside-down plea, his scrawny chest heaving in the canine version of a sigh, as if gearing up for a large disappointment. Bea's own baby blues welled convincingly.

"Look, even his ears are sad. They're all floppy because he was anemic from starvation." Bea used the tip of one finger to gently flick the dog's ear, which folded back over.

Peyton stared for a minute at their baby sister and her new acquisition. "You have to tell Emma. That thing isn't a farm dog. And she's going to skin you alive when she hears you're bringing a dog into the house."

"Done," Bea said quickly. "Besides, he'll be at my place mostly."

"You're over here more than you're over there," Red pointed out logically.

"Don't worry, he won't be a problem at all."

"That's what Daddy said when he and Mama brought you home from the hospital," Peyton said dryly, then spun on her heel and headed into the house.

"Good one," Trace muttered under his breath. How long had she been saving that up?

Bea held out the dog, nose to nose, and spoke directly to him. "You're going to live in my apartment. And I'm going to get you sweaters, because it gets cold here. And maybe some booties, because your little feet will be so chilly in the winter. . . ." Walking up the stairs, she tucked the animal under her arm. "And in the summer . . ." She disappeared into the house, voice trailing behind her.

"Are we sure that really was a dog?" Red asked.

"I asked at the shelter. They confirmed." Trace ran a hand over his head, then bent down to scratch the pup currently gnawing at the hem of his jeans. "I warned her this would happen. But she just wanted to get him out to play with him. And that led to taking him on a quick walk around the building. And that led to signing adoption papers and asking where the nearest pet store was so she could buy him a cute collar."

"There's no pet store around here." Red tipped his hat back. "And who cares if the collar is cute? It's a dog."

Trace shrugged. "That's Bea." He slapped his thigh once and No Name followed easily. "Let's go meet your new friends, boy."

She should call him.

No, that was stupid. She wouldn't call. This wasn't a relationship. And who cared if she hadn't heard from him in three days? He had a life, and so did she.

But Jo found her hand reaching for her back pocket where she kept her cell phone anyway, before she forced herself to pull back.

"Something wrong?"

She looked up and smiled at Jeff, who had become something of a regular at her bar. "No, just having a mental debate with myself."

"Who's winning?"

"Not me. Which is a problem, isn't it?" Jo poured him some water after he finished his beer; it had become habit now. "You're in here often enough. Shouldn't you be out running around, enjoying the last moments of freedom before you go back to school?"

"I get enough running around as it is. I like the relaxation. Plus, if I'm not there, my mom can't send me on more errands." He grinned, a cute boyish gesture.

"Well, we're closing up in ten, so drink your water." He was one of only two people left, and her closing server's last table was cashing out.

"I could hang around a bit." He didn't look at her as he suggested it. "If you're the last one to close up, just to make sure you get back to your place okay."

Warning bells rang in the distance, but she ignored them. This wasn't some slick guy trying to make a pass. She was in cowboy country now. Chivalry came free with every pair of boots. Plus, he was like a little brother. "Thanks, but I make it home okay every other night on my own." She waved a hand. "I'm just around the corner, anyway. No trouble at all to walk the twenty steps. That's the benefit of living where you work." She checked her watch. "Besides, after you're gone, I've only got about ten minutes of cleanup time. Then I'll be in my apartment stretching out."

He hesitated, then nodded, a smile spreading. "I got ya." He finished his water and set some cash down, heading out behind the last tabletop as they walked toward the door. "See you later."

She waved and started to clear his area. "See ya!"

Once the table was cleared, Jo cut her server loose. No point in making her stay when she could easily clean the last of the place herself. A quick mop job around the few tables they'd missed as things started dwindling and a last-minute double-check with the registers, and she was ready to roll. She patted her back pocket to make sure her phone was there, grabbed her keys, and then headed out the front door, locking up behind her.

She'd taken two steps when a movement to her left had her swallowing a shriek. She turned and flattened against the wall, then nearly sank to the ground as Jeff stepped back out into the light from the shadows.

"Jesus, Jeff." With one hand over her racing heart, Jo concentrated on steadying her breathing. "You almost made me scream like a girl."

He stuffed his hands in his pockets and smiled sheepishly. "Sorry. I didn't think that one through, did I?"

She bent over and took a few quick huffs of breath, then straightened again. Jeff was there, hand on her back.

"Geez, sorry. I didn't mean to catch you so off guard."

"I'm fine. Just recovering." Another moment and she almost felt back to normal. "Did you forget something at the bar? I can go unlock and—"

He was on her before she could finish the sentence. Flattened against the wall, his body laid out over hers, he kissed her with more enthusiasm than skill.

Aw, shit. This was so not how she wanted things to go with him. Now she'd have to let him down and he'd be embarrassed—because guys always were when they got shot down—and it'd end the nice friendship they'd been starting. Damn. *Damn, damn, damn.*

She waited, unresponsive, for him to pick up the cue there was only one participant in the kiss. When he didn't seem to notice, she tried pushing gently on his shoulders. He merely rolled a little, squishing her harder into the brick of the wall behind her. Her elbow scraped on a particularly rough brick, stinging a little.

Okay. Fuck being gentle.

"Sto—"

But Jeff's tongue swept in before she could finish the word. It was like being French kissed by a puppy. Good Christ, the kid was bad. She made one final attempt to shove at his shoulders, but when he didn't budge, she started to raise a knee to hit his groin.

But the weight, the oppressive strain against her, was gone before she had the chance to nail the death blow. She took one deep, fresh gulp of air before opening her eyes a crack.

Jeff stood a few feet away, hands balled into fists at his sides, weight on his toes, looking like he was ready to go a few rounds. And Trace Muldoon stood, hip-shot, relaxed, with what Jo determined was a deceptively easygoing smile on his face.

"Hey, Jo."

"Hey, Trace." She refrained from wiping her mouth with the back of her wrist. She still liked Jeff, even if the kid couldn't take a hint or kiss for shit. This wasn't going to end well regardless—no need to embarrass him more. "Wasn't expecting you."

"Do you mind?" Jeff shot at him.

"I think the point is Jo minds." Trace looked to her for confirmation, though it was unnecessary. She nodded slightly but held up a hand when he would have said more.

"Jeff . . ."*Don't be cliché, don't say you're flattered.*"It's just not like that for me. Sorry."

He stared at her a moment, then at Trace. "It's like that for him. Right?"

Trace watched him carefully, not moving an inch as he spoke. "That would fall under the category of none of your damn business."

It was the stillness that alerted her to an impending problem. "Trace," Jo warned. More softly, she added, "I'm sorry, Jeff."

He recovered quickly, and she was relieved. With more bravado than truth, he held up his hands and said, "Whatever." But if he felt like he saved face, that's what mattered.

She waited until Jeff headed toward his car. But neither of them spoke until the car was nothing but dual pinpricks of light in the distance.

"Dick," Trace muttered.

Jo frowned. "No, that's not right. He was just confused. And by the way, how did you know I wasn't totally into that?"

"Because you're the one who said no others. You're not the type to go back on your word."

She liked that. That he took her word at face value and didn't assume she was playing games. "That wasn't fun."

"Never is, breaking a man's heart. Right?" He smiled

and held out a hand. "Or were you a big man-killer back in all those cities you lived in before?"

She laughed and took it. "Oh, yeah. Can't you just picture it? Me wearing an all-leather dominatrix getup, waiting for men to walk into my black widow's web of seduction." She chuckled again, and almost stumbled on the third step after looking at his face. "I was kidding."

"So, you don't own a leather dominatrix outfit?" His tone was morose.

Time for some fun. "No. I gave it away before I moved." She waited until they stepped up to the landing in front of her front door, then trailed a hand over his chest on the way into the apartment. "I kept the whip though. Just a memento . . ."

She wasn't even completely through the door before he swept her up from behind and slammed it shut. Jo clung to his neck and waited for the dizziness to pass when he put her down somewhere unexpected . . . the kitchen table.

With a quick spin, she was bent over the cool laminated top. His long fingers found the button of her jeans and flicked it open with no help, zipper sliding down easily. She wasn't shocked, but she appreciated the originality.

The lack of foreplay definitely was a surprise. He searched her out with two fingers, testing quickly. Yeah, she was already wet. Just walking up the stairs with Trace, knowing what they would get into, was enough to get her going. But rather than taking his time, he unzipped behind her, reached in his own wallet for a condom—clearly a replacement from the other night—and was in her before she could say the magic words.

Please, God, please . . .

Her hips pushed against the edge of the table, which bit into her skin. Her cheeks flushed, a contrast to the smooth cool tabletop. And her hands clawed at the edges, trying to find a grip as he took her from behind. Her arms were too short to reach the other end and she scrambled until she realized there was no hold. Instead, she flattened her palms and pushed back against him the best she could, given her position.

His hands were rough, not the gentle, playful lover from the last time they'd joined. Insistent, dominant, demanding. He made her body follow, didn't allow her to give in when her muscles screamed, wouldn't let her give up or beg for another spot.

It was amazing. He knew just when to flip her over, onto her back, and ram back into her. Knew she wouldn't have lasted another second in the first position.

He ripped her shirt up, pushing her bra with it and latched onto her breast with his mouth, pulling on her nipple as hard as he thrust into her wet center. Her hands came around his head, clutching, gripping, doing whatever she could to gain traction on the feelings rushing through her. Physical, emotional, whatever the hell was happening to her body that made her want to scream and cry out and beat at his shoulders and pull him closer to her.

Her legs curled around his waist, her heels digging into his ass, pulling him into her, deeper and harder with each thrust. Her head fell back and *thunked* against the table, but she didn't care. And when she came, she screamed and arched until her body couldn't give another inch.

Trace followed her swiftly, his own climax seeming to take as much out of him as hers did from her. But through the sexual haze, the sweetness of her name on his lips cut through and made her want more.

More what—that was the question.

Chapter Eleven

Trace stared up at the underside of the table. "This might be the weirdest place I've ever recovered, sexually."

After they'd been able to move again, Trace had helped Jo up from the table. But rather than lead them to bed, as he'd assumed, she'd stripped what was left of her clothing and headed into the small kitchen.

When in Rome . . . he'd followed suit. And found her digging through the freezer. Her nipples tightened into sweet pink buds while she practically crawled into the appliance to find what she wanted.

She'd produced a half-eaten carton of Moose Tracks ice cream, found two spoons—one of which was a cooking spoon, that she'd claimed for her own—and ended up lying on her back under the table, eating spoonfuls straight from the carton.

He really needed to stop assuming about Jo. The minute he had her figured out, she changed things up again.

"I could think of weirder spots for things." Jo licked her spoon, giving extra attention to the spot where the bowl met the stem. Damn it all if his cock didn't start getting jealous of that piece of cool metal. "Behind a Dumpster, for example."

"You had sex behind a Dumpster?"

"No, that would have been gross." She smiled. "I just

got dumped by the Dumpster. Which, I realize, is more than a little ironic. But hey, the guy clearly wasn't a prince."

"Asshole." He dug another bite out. "This is chick ice cream, you know that, right?"

"Chick . . . ice cream."

"Yeah, all these chunks of stuff in here. Ice cream has like, four flavors: chocolate, vanilla, strawberry, and maybe swirl, if you're feeling crazy."

Jo rolled her eyes and beat his spoon away with her larger one to get another bite. "For a guy who insults the ice cream, you're digging in without much problem."

"I need my strength. You wear a guy out," he said innocently. Partially true. But really, he was more interested in watching her face while she ate.

Every moment of pleasure, each drop of ice cream was reflected in her expression. The half-closed eyes, the little moans, the way her tongue darted out to lick a stray drop. He could watch her for hours.

"Have dinner with me tomorrow night."

She froze, spoon halfway to her mouth. "No."

His brows lowered. That was fast. "Maybe lunch next week. There's a nice spot in—"

"Negative." She said it so calmly, digging in for another bite.

"Okay, why don't you pick the day?"

"Because I'm not interested."

Ouch. Damn, direct hit. "Interested in having a meal with me, specifically? Or anyone?" He wasn't sure which was worse.

"In general. The whole dating thing, I'm not up for it." She shrugged and rolled to face him, her hand resting on the floor beside her breast for support. "I'm not looking for a relationship. I said that outright in the beginning."

She had.

"And I didn't think you were, either."

He hadn't been. "Well, a meal's just a meal. It doesn't have to mean anything." He trailed a finger from the corner of her lips down her jaw, circling over her shoulder. "I like looking at you. Maybe I wanna do it more often."

"So eat lunch at the bar." She swatted at his hand when he headed for her breast. "I don't date. Period, end of story."

"Is it the timing? Or is it the concept of dating altogether?"

She rolled onto her back, and he lost contact with the breast he'd been playing with. "You're chatty tonight."

"Sorry." He scooted out like he was getting out from under a car and searched for his pants. "I wasn't aware our arrangement had so many damn rules. From my memory, I thought we covered not banging other people, and me wearing a rubber. Now I can't even ask to see you outside of your apartment?"

She didn't say anything.

"Right. Here's the thing, Jo. I like sex as much as the next guy. Hell, I love it. I think it's one of the best ways to pass some time. But I also like you. I think you're someone worth knowing. And if you're telling me my time in your bed means we can't even have a decent conversation while grabbing a freaking hamburger, then this probably isn't for me. I thought I was signing up for a lover, not a fuck buddy."

Jo bit her lip, her eyes closing a moment. "I'm sorry, okay? I'm sorry. Don't . . . don't do that. Don't just get dressed and leave." She held out a hand. "Stay. Please?"

He paused, shirt in hand. She looked so confused. Like she wasn't sure whether she was sticking to her guns, or about to back down. Did he want to find out which?

Hell, yeah.

He dropped the shirt but left the jeans on. Scooting back under the table, he waited for her to talk.

"I've never been interested in domestic bliss. My mom's found it too many times to count. But for the sake of keeping track, she ended up married seven times. Oh, sorry." She snorted. "Five times."

"Which one of you can't count?"

"Regina math," she muttered. "Every time my mom found a new guy, we moved. Sometimes they married her, sometimes they didn't. But it was the same shit, different school year. Over and over again, I was the new kid in a city I'd never been to before. I saw what love does to a woman. I'm not interested. I like what I have here."

His heart hurt for the little girl, the new kid, year after year. "I'm not exactly looking to yank you out of here. I live here, too."

"Which almost makes it worse." She ran a hand over her forehead, as if trying to clear her thoughts. "I can't just ignore you when we're done, or move away. I have a business here. You have family. So eventually, when this thing is done, we'll still run into each other. Repeatedly."

The "when" in her statement rankled him. Sure, not all relationships lasted, but why did she assume from the get-go theirs wouldn't?

Probably because to her, it's not a relationship, dipshit.

The rough, simple reminder that she was in it for the sex alone hit him hard. Sex was fantastic. But he liked a little companionship when he could get it. He'd had enough of meaningless one-night stands and women whose names he couldn't remember a few months later.

"I haven't worked out in my mind yet how dating is supposed to work when you know you aren't leaving soon. All my relationships before this have had built-in expiration dates. Even if things were going well, I ended up moving. So I stopped having them. And now that I'm not moving, I'm not sure what a relationship looks like, or if I even honestly want one."

"I've done the anonymous lay before, Jo. I'm not a twenty-one-year-old guy looking to get some in the back of my horse trailer between competitions. I'm not trying to sneak in a blow job before I hit the road and never see What's Her Face again."

"What's Her Face?" Jo laughed. "Must have been memorable."

"Clearly." He closed his eyes and waited for inspiration. None came. So, he tried the truth. Looking straight into her eyes, he said, "I want you. More than that, I like you. And so when I say I want you, I mean all of you. Not just what I can get in the dark."

She sighed. "This isn't a ploy to get me to put on an apron and stand barefoot in the kitchen, is it?"

"That depends."

She eyed him warily. "On?"

He grinned. "What's under the apron?"

She snorted, then rolled into him and fit herself against his side. "I like you, too."

"Then have dinner with me. It's just a meal, served sometime after lunch but before you go to sleep. You ate ice cream with me. Just bump it up a little to something more substantial and we've got ourselves a compromise."

"Dinner," she muttered, lips brushing against his neck. "The man wants dinner. I can bring up leftovers from—"

"Nope. That's cheating."

She groaned, a low sound deep in her throat, and bit him on the shoulder hard enough to sting. "You win."

"I pick the restaurant," he said quickly. Knowing her, she'd choose something with a drive-thru and insist on eating in the freaking car. "I won't take you too far, but I think we can do better than the diner down the street."

She shrugged. "Fine. Let me know when you want to go."

"Don't have to wait for a night off?"

She smiled and dragged herself over him, her warm body pressing into his in all the right areas. "Sweetie, that's the beauty of owning your own business. It can always be my night off."

Trace left an hour later, his body loose and relaxed as he climbed into the cab of his truck. Anticipation already filled him for the next time he'd see her. But he'd have to wait on that. They both would. He'd already been gone enough nights lately.

It irked him again, remembering how hard he'd had to argue to get her to agree to one single date. Jesus, the woman was stubborn. But that was probably part of her charm.

Maybe forever wasn't in the cards for them. But hell, who could say until they both laid their hands down on the table?

Dinner. A real restaurant. Something nice, but nothing to sweat over. Trace used the powers of Google to search out restaurants in the nearby area—which were slim to none—and extended the search a little farther out.

Something tugged on his pant leg. He smiled. Seth's crawling had taken on a new ninja status if he'd managed to get into the office without being heard. "Just a minute, buddy. I'm trying to find a nice spot for some dinner."

Tug. Tug.

"I know, I know. Hold on." He clicked one more link, jotted down the possibility. "Gimme a second."

Tug. Rip.

"Seth. What the . . ." He looked down and stared into the biggest bug eyes he'd ever seen. "Aw, hell. Seriously?"

The dog picked up a stuffed frog and stared at him with four long, neon green legs dangling from his mouth. Then, with a mouth full of frog, he whimper-whined.

"Don't do that."

More whining, louder now. The tip of one ear flipped up a little, as if in silent plea, before folding back over.

Trace sighed and scratched the top of the pathetic dog's head. "You're a sad case, you know that? Have some pride."

Pride was a nonissue for the dog, apparently, as he tried to jump into Trace's lap for more attention. His too-short legs wouldn't allow it, though, and so the whining started all over again. Muffled through the stuffing, of course.

"You're a little shit." He reached down for the frog, thinking if he played fetch, he could toss the toy out of the room and shut the door behind him. But the dog evaded him, not letting go of the toy.

Next plan. Trace scraped the chair back from Peyton's desk and yelled, "Bea!"

Bea's head popped in. "Have you seen Milton? Emma's going to slaughter me if I lose sight of him again."

"Who the hell is Milton?"

She stared at him as if he'd just asked who the president was. "My dog."

"You named your dog Milton?"

She sniffed. "It's distinguished. He's a gentleman."

Trace looked down and grimaced. "Your distinguished gentleman just pissed on Peyton's office rug."

"Oh, my God." Bea ran around the corner of the desk and stared at him. The dog, not Trace. "Milton! Why? We were outside five seconds ago! Why!"

The dog bounced happily, frog legs flopping around his jowls, pleased to show off his puddle.

Bea picked him up and thrust him at Trace. "Hold that. I have to clean this up before Peyton or Emma sees it."

Trace held the dog at arm's length. Those bug eyes really did freak him out a little. "You know, you keep that up and Emma's going to feed you to the barn cats."

The dog stared back, unimpressed.

"They're bigger than you are, and mean as spit."

He cocked his head to one side, considering the insult.

"Or she might just make you sleep in the barn."

At that, the dog seemed to realize perhaps piddling on the floor wasn't the best choice. He began his whine again, that nails-on-a-chalkboard noise making Trace want to rip his eardrums out. "Stop."

The sound grew louder.

"Hell." Trace brought the dog to his chest, holding him the way he used to hold Seth when he burped him. The dog quieted down immediately and snuffled into his neck. His wet nose made Trace tilt his head away. "Jesus, don't do that."

"Oh, look, he likes you. He's bonding with his uncle Trace." Bea hustled back in with a wad of paper towels and some carpet cleaner.

Amazed, Trace watched Bea clean the spot. "I didn't realize you even knew what carpet cleaner looked like."

"I spend most of my day in the house with Emma. Trust me, I've seen carpet cleaner." She scrubbed furiously, a woman possessed.

"Why are you even over here? You have your own apartment now. You could leave him there."

"No, I can't. He has separation anxiety."

"He has what?" Trace looked at the dog again. For something that weighed fifteen pounds, max, he came with a lot of problems.

"Abandonment issues. I mean, he hasn't had a great life, Trace." She looked up and cooed at Milton. "No, you haven't. But now you have a nice life, don't you?"

"So you're over here because . . ."

"My place doesn't have Internet yet. I had a Skype date with a friend back home." She sat back on her heels and evaluated the spot. "If either of those two see this, he's doomed. He already christened one of Peyton's boots the other day."

Trace looked at the dog. "And you're still alive?"

The dog licked his neck in response.

"Yes, because Peyton isn't heartless . . . completely. But I'm not willing to push it." She stood and threw the paper towels in the trash can. "There. Hardly noticeable."

Except for the fact the carpet was wet.

Bea seemed to sense this. "Okay, so . . . maybe she won't come in her office for a few hours."

As if realizing that was a vain hope, Bea reached out for the dog. "Come here, baby. We'll go for a nice, long walk."

"Why is it," Trace mused, "when I hand you Seth, you act like he's a ticking time bomb? But you hold that animal in your arms like he's the most precious thing you've ever seen?"

"Because he is. Isn't he sweet?" She held the dog up for inspection.

What Trace saw was an underbite, those creepy bug eyes, and ribs sticking out.

"Whacha doing?" she asked, craning her neck around to see the computer.

"Nothing." He quickly hit the power button to the monitor. "Go feed him something. He's too damn skinny."

She shrugged, as if already forgetting she'd asked him anything. "He's on a specific weight-gaining diet. He'll fill out, won't you, sweetie?"

It amused Trace no end that his sister, who refused responsibility as easily as most people refused brussels sprouts at the dinner table, had willingly taken on another living thing as her own. And was willing to clean up the mess afterward in order to save the responsibility's worthless hide.

Maybe she was changing.

Bea headed out of the office, dog slung over her shoulder. The frog's legs flopped against her back. "Come on upstairs, Milton. I ordered you a cardigan online and it came in this morning. Let's go have a fashion show!"

Or not.

Trace pulled out his cell phone and quickly texted the name of the restaurant to Jo. She wouldn't answer right away, he assumed, since she was likely working. So he pocketed the phone, headed to the kitchen, and made himself a sandwich. Carrying the sandwich, wrapped in a paper towel, to the front porch, he found Emma and Seth playing with the still unnamed dog he'd brought home from the shelter.

"Hey, little man." He sat down and watched in amazement as his son crawled to him. That he could get around on his own now was such an awesome thing. "Soon enough, you'll be too big to crawl. You'll be walking all over this place."

Emma shook her head. "Don't remind me. I've gotta keep an eye on that one already, and he's just crawling. Once he gets his feet under him, I'm done for."

Trace watched Emma over his son's head while Seth used his father as a prop to practice standing. She was unmatchable for strength, in his mind. Emma had been his mother-figure growing up. His soft place to land, his hard line for consequences, and everything in between. In the years between leaving home and coming back, he'd painted her as a conquering hero.

But she was a woman, same as any other. And she was getting older. Keeping up with both the housekeeping duties and chasing after a soon-to-be toddler couldn't be easy for her.

"Maybe it's time to look into an assistant for you," Trace said, testing the waters. "Someone to run errands, to look after Seth while you cook dinner or whatever."

Of course, by "assistant" he meant babysitter. And the

job would come out of his own paycheck, just as Emma's raise had when she'd taken on the added task of nanny.

Emma's steely gray stare pinned him like a nail in a still-fluttering moth. "I'm not dead yet. I can handle him."

"I didn't mean you couldn't."*Retreat, retreat. Sound the alarm.*"Just that, as more people come into this house, it might be more work than any one person could handle. Even a superhero like you."

Emma looked disappointed in him and his lack of faith. She bent down and scooped up a wobbly Seth. "Come on, boy. We have some vacuuming to do. Yes, you like the sound. I know you do."

That went well. Trace let his head fall back to the porch rail with a *crack*. He deserved it, probably.

Why were none of the women in his life cooperating?

Chapter Twelve

Jo watched the bar, surveying for signs of struggle, signs of impending trouble. Anything she could use to delay going out. Something to keep her tied to the bar.

An excuse. Yeah, it was an excuse. But damn, she wasn't ready for this. They could play with semantics, just calling it a nice dinner between lovers or whatever. But she knew what it was to Trace.

A date.

The words sent a chill down into her belly the way the words "serial killer" might another human. She didn't date. She'd tried that, and didn't care for it. She didn't do permanency. Her bar was the most permanent thing in her life. Even her friends—Stu and Amanda and the others—would eventually leave. Restaurant staffers were a fluid group. And so, she was resigned to the fact that she would be mostly alone, unless she invited someone into her life for a period of time.

But the way she'd arranged her life, she reminded herself, nobody would leave her. Nobody would kick her out with a teenage daughter and force her to find yet another sugar daddy to pick up the slack. Move her ass across the country to find the next meal ticket.

She would do this on her own, all the way. She was now

a big fish in a small pond, not the other way around. And she liked it. So she would maintain the status quo.

"Hey."

Jo jumped a mile in the air. "Jesus." Turning, she looked up—and up—into the eyes of Bea Muldoon. "Are you on a stepladder or something?"

"Just tall. And you're short." Her answer was given so easily, it didn't carry the sting of insult.

"Why are you behind the bar? Go. Go over there and sit down. Or go find a table. Is Peyton with you?"

"Nope." Bea took her sweet time walking back around the counter to lean on the edge. The pose would have looked practiced, if it weren't so easy and fluid. She looked like a Vargas girl from the forties. At least a dozen male eyes took advantage of her position, ass out, to visually devour her.

"Do you do that on purpose?" Jo asked before she could think better of it.

Bea didn't bother pretending ignorance. "I used to. Now it's just habit." She winked. "Casting directors love a femme fatale, don't you know?"

"No, I don't know, said the short girl," Jo responded.

"Oh, men love a tiny woman, too." Bea waved that off.

"Tiny, I am not." Jo put a hand on her hips. "These are not tiny."

"You've got curves in your small package. It's the best of all worlds. Stop comparing yourself to me. The female race is like a buffet."

"Come again?"

Bea nodded. "To a man, females are a buffet. See, you have all sorts of different women. But there are men with different tastes. The broccoli should never feel bad sitting next to the French fries on the table, because there's always going to be a man who wants broccoli. Man after man might come for French fries. But eventually, a guy who has been dying for the perfect plate of broccoli is going to come by."

"Am I the broccoli, or the French fries?" Jo was pretty sure she knew the answer.

Bea ignored that. "You shouldn't compare yourself to me. I'm offering something entirely different."

Jo couldn't help but smile. "What's that?"

"Fantasy B. You, my dear, are Fantasy A."

Jo laughed, despite herself. "You're something else."

"In this town, I would have to agree." Bea reached out and touched one fingertip to Jo's right ear with its four piercings. "But so are you. Are we going to do the bonding thing now?"

Jo shrugged. "I'm working."

"No, you're not. You've got a date with my brother."

Jo shushed her and looked around the bar, waiting for people to start throwing questions—or rotten fruit—in their direction. "Shut up, loudmouth."

Bea looked insulted for a moment. "I didn't realize it was a big secret. Are you embarrassed?"

Jo's eyes closed a moment as she gathered patience. Then she reached in her pocket and handed Bea her set of keys. "This one opens my apartment. Go up there and wait for me."

Bea raised one brow. "Full disclosure—I have to tell you I'm going to snoop."

"Just stay out of the nightstand drawer."

"Done." Bea trotted easily on high heels out the door. Jo waited to see if any slobbering males would follow like little lambs following Mary, but they managed to resist the urge.

After checking with her night bartender, Jo concluded there was nothing holding her back. Damn it. She headed up the stairs to her own apartment.

Instead of rifling through drawers, Bea was sitting on the couch, legs crossed, waiting.

"Thought you were going to search my things." Jo headed to her kitchen for a bottle of water. She held it up and shook. "Want?"

"Yes, please." Bea squealed when Jo tossed it her way. "Watch it!"

"Such a girl."

Bea picked up the water and rolled her eyes. "If I wanted to be insulted, I would have stayed home and hung out with my sister." She glanced at her watch, a cute silver sparkly thing that caught the light with every twist of her wrist. "If I'm not mistaken, you don't have much time to get ready."

"First off, how do you know I'm going out with your brother?" Trace wouldn't have said anything. Jo knew that much for certain. She took a sip of water and wondered if Bea had as big a mouth as Jo thought she might have.

Bea shook that off with a smirk. "He was being secretive with his computer time. I went back through the computer history, found the name of the restaurant he looked up, and snooped in his phone to see who he was going out with and when."

"Could have been a friend," Jo reasoned.

"Hardly. Not a place like that. He'd go to the diner with Red, or here. Not out of town to a nice place like that." Bea scowled. "Give me a little credit."

"Which brings me to my second question, why were you so interested in what your brother was up to?"

"Boredom, mostly." Bea let one foot swing, lightly kicking the coffee table with her toe.

"You could get a job." Jo smiled slowly, an idea forming in her mind. "You could serve. I'm sure I can find a few shifts a week for you."

Bea's face had Jo doubled over in laughter. "God, the

look on your face . . ." she managed to gasp between hiccups.

"Hilarious, I'm sure." Bea picked at the edge of her top, smoothing it down, then flipping it over again. "I could be useful."

It was on the tip of her tongue to ask *so why aren't you?,* but she pulled back. Something in Bea's eyes told her now wasn't the time for sarcastic truths.

"I just don't know where I fit in here," her friend went on, looking around the apartment rather than at Jo. "I don't belong here, that's for sure."

Jo played silent supporter and sat in her armchair.

"But apparently I don't belong in Hollywood either. So . . ." Bea let her shirt drop from her hands. "Where?"

Jo shrugged. "I could tell you where I don't belong. New York, San Fran, Dallas, Salt Lake—"

Bea laughed. "Right, right. I know. My problem, nobody else's." She rubbed her hands together, then threw them apart, like she was clearing the space of negative energy. "Time for something more fun. What are you wearing tonight?"

Jo grimaced. "I haven't gone out in months. Probably a year. Everything I have is totally out of date."

Bea smirked. "Honey, if it's from this decade, Trace won't notice. They're not much up on haute fashion here. I'm guessing your years of city living have at least given you some sense of style."

"My sense," Jo agreed. "Not quite Paris runway but . . ." She shrugged and angled her head to the bedroom. "Any idea what your brother is wearing? That might help me narrow down choices."

"Hopefully not something with throw up on it."

"What?" Jo froze and looked over her shoulder. "Is Trace sick?"

Bea's eyes widened. "No, why?"

"What's with the throw up talk?"

"Because of . . ." Bea froze, as if someone had pushed the pause button on the remote. "Because of the dog," she finished slowly. "He got a dog the other day."

"Oh." Odd. Why would a dog throw up on his things? Wouldn't it be outside? "I'm assuming you're inviting yourself in for a fashion consultation."

"That I am." Bea stood and followed her into the bed-room. "This might be almost as much fun as dressing *my* dog."

Jo stopped short. "You got a dog? You mean the same dog as Trace, right?"

"No. A cute little Boston terrier." Bea looked proud and flipped through her cell phone a moment before holding out the screen. "See? His name is Milton, and he's adorable."

Jo stared at the face only a mother—or someone squinting—could love and her heart melted a little. "Aw, he's cute."

"See!" Bea pumped a fist. "I told them he was cute, but nobody believed me. He's going to be even cuter in the new sweater vest I'm giving him."

"Too far." Jo took another step, then paused. "Uh, is Peyton or Trace helping you take care of him?"

Bea looked offended. "Why does nobody think I can take care of another living thing?"

It was too easy. She let the softball pass her by.

Bea scowled. "I can hear what you're thinking. I'm not a screwup."

Jo dug through her closet, searching for outfits she would have worn to meet a man a year or so ago. They were deep in the recesses of her closet, she realized. Wow, she'd really packed that side of herself away, literally.

"I'm not a screwup."

"Okay." Her voice was muffled by a sweater.

"Everyone just thinks I am because I let them." The superior tone in Bea's voice made her smile. "It's easier to get out of things if people assume you don't know what you're doing."

"I think I just heard every feminist in the Western hemisphere gasp and cough."

"I'm not a feminist. I'm a Bea-ist."

Jo had to sit down before she laughed so hard she fell into a pile of last season's boots.

"What?" Bea crossed her arms and stared at her. "It's a real thing. My yoga instructor told me it was. Something about being your own advocate and finding your inner goddess and blah-blah-blah."

"Your yoga instructor was high on granola and downward dogs." Jo brushed at her eyes. "Okay. Let's do this."

Trace waited not so patiently on the small front step of Jo's apartment. He'd dusted off his only pair of dress slacks and a nice button-down shirt. No tie, too formal. No snaps, too informal. Just the right balance, he thought, pleased with himself.

He wondered how Jo would dress. He imagined she'd try to keep it as casual as possible, with her allergy to relationships. Somehow he could easily see her showing up in jeans and a T-shirt that said "FU" or something equally vulgar. Probably she'd assume he would rather stay home and slip into bed than take her out.

He grinned. He'd take her out, vulgar shirt and all. There was no way he would let her escape this important step.

After another few moments, he knocked again. The light was on, that much he could see. But the shades were closed, so he didn't know where she was in the apartment.

Finally, he heard footsteps approach the door, and the

locks disengage. All—he counted with each sound—five of them.

Five? Huh. Then again, she did live above a bar.

When she opened the door, he prepared himself to compliment her regardless of what outfit she'd decided to go with. But the predetermined words stuck in his throat at the sight that greeted him.

Her hair was down, waved and lightly curled in some just-out-of-bed look. Her makeup was more pronounced than he'd seen on her before, with smoky eyes and deep lips. The number she wore left her shoulders mostly bare but for thin straps that were sheer black, almost invisible when paired with her dark hair. The neckline was low, though not plunging. And the skirt hit right above her knee. The outfit complimented her body, showing off the curves he knew she disliked to their full potential.

But the heels. Oh, he would dream about those later. Slender straps, impossibly high heels, delicate little things that made him imagine all sorts of macho, politically incorrect things like sweeping her into his arms to carry her over puddles.

And he was losing his damn mind.

She chewed on her lip a little. "Too much?"

"No. Right. Very much right." He pulled one hand from behind his back and presented her with the flowers he'd picked out earlier. Yeah, they were from the grocery store. But it wasn't like Marshall had a first-rate florist. "These are for you."

He'd decided against roses —too cliché. Jo lived to sneer at clichés. Anything pale was out, not her style. So he'd settled for a cheerful flower—damned if he knew what it was called—in a deep purple. As she held the arrangement to her, the flowers skimmed her cheek and he knew they were the right choice.

He watched her eyes, the momentary panic followed quickly by reserved pleasure. "Thanks. I'll, uh, go put these . . . somewhere." She darted back in and closed the door on him. Then she opened it again with a sheepish smile. "Sorry. Come in."

He stepped through the door and pressed a light kiss to her lips. She was nervous. It pleased him as much as it made him want to calm her. They'd spent plenty of time together. Alone, not alone. There was no reason to be so worried.

But that she was worried meant she cared. That the results of the night were important to her. That was a good step.

Water ran in the kitchen, something scraped, and then she darted out to the dining table before grabbing a chair and dragging it back in.

"Want me to get something?" he called.

"No!" Her voice was strained. "I've got . . . it. Yes!"

Well, he'd offered. A moment later she appeared, a pretty blue pitcher filled with the flowers. She settled it on the table, stepped back, then rotated it a quarter turn and placed her hands on her hips, analyzing. Finally, she shrugged and held her hands up.

"I know nothing about flower arrangements. Looks good to me though."

He grinned. "Yeah, looks real good. Come on, honey, we've got reservations."

She took his hand after a moment of hesitation. Still not sure what to make of tonight, he realized. Uncertain, but maybe a little excited.

He'd play on both. They were both important emotions in the grand scheme of things. So he'd use them ruthlessly, until he got them both where he wanted them to be.

★   ★   ★

She relaxed slowly, almost by inches. Trace enjoyed watching Jo more than anything else that night. He barely tasted dinner. It could have been a five-star steak or baby food for all he paid attention to it. But he would never forget the pleasure in Jo's eyes when she ate something delicious, the flush in her face from her third—and final, she swore—glass of wine, her enjoyment of the quiet atmosphere with interesting art.

She was at home here. Comfortable. Her bar was home, too, but this was another sort of home. A coming back. It wasn't anything fancy, likely not for her anyway. But it wasn't peanuts and draft beer, cowboys in dirty boots, and women vying to be the next rodeo queen. It was . . . sophisticated. City.

Or as city as they could get within a reasonable drive of Marshall.

And she fit like a glove. But she fit in Jo's Place, too, with her hair back in a ponytail, her simple black polo and jeans, and her brash, easy way of handling customers.

Jo Tallen. Multifaceted woman.

He waited until the waiter presented the check, then sat back. "Enjoy yourself?"

"Mmm." She took the last sip of wine, dabbing a finger at the stray drop that clung to her bottom lip.

He resisted the urge—just barely—to reach across and lick her lips himself. God, she drew him like nothing else.

"Trace?"

"Yeah?" His eyes never left her lips. Couldn't. He was mesmerized by watching the way they moved while she spoke.

"This was nice."

"Very."

"But you know it's not going to change anything, right?"

The pleasure bubble burst and he looked up into her eyes. "What was that?"

She chewed a little on that bottom lip he'd been so intent on a minute ago. Then, as if she was mentally strapping on a suit of armor, she leaned back and slipped into Jo, the untouchable lover. "We've got a great thing between us in bed. And I like you out of bed, too, which is something remarkable for me. I like spending time with you. But I don't want you to get any ideas about where this is going."

Annoyance flickered, but he pushed it away. "Why don't you tell me where you think I'm trying to steer you?"

"Toward a relationship. A real one, where you spend every night with me, or me with you, and we date in public. You bring me flowers, we have an anniversary, and then people around town start speculating about when we're going to tie the knot." She looked like she wanted to throw up, either from nerves or pure distaste at the thought.

"And that would be plain awful, right?"

Her brows drew together. "It's not my style. I didn't think it was yours, but you're starting to worry me a little. Maybe you're more 'hearth and home' than I originally thought."

"Kiss of death, apparently," he muttered into his napkin.

"What?"

"Nothing." He tossed the linen on the table and held out a hand, standing with her. "What is it about relationships that kills it for you?"

"They tie you down," she answered quickly. This wasn't something she'd just thought of. It was a very real deal to her. "They weigh on you. They make you change, take you places you didn't want to go."

"Physically?"

"That, too, but mentally, emotionally as well." She

shrugged into the jacket he held out for her. "It's not my thing." She moved her hair so it slid out from under the collar, the strands moving together like inky silk. He wanted to bite the back of her neck, hold her in place like a stallion pinning down its mare.

"It's too limiting," he summarized.

"Can be." She took his arm and followed him out to the parking lot. Thanks to the long drive, they'd made it to dinner on the late side, and were one of the last to leave. His truck sat in the back of the lot. "I'm not a fan of that whole settle down, build a picket fence, have two-point-two kids and the dopey lab thing. I mean, I live above a bar, for Christ's sake. And I like it there."

Minus the last one-point-two kids, she'd all but described his current life. Problems abounded if he was going to get her to come around to his side of the fence, picket or otherwise.

So he'd ease her in. Get her hooked on him, on them as a unit. And once that happened, maybe he could get her used to the idea of more than just a commitment that ran from one evening to the next.

"Relationships are boring, huh."

She headed around to her side of the truck and waited while he reached for the door. "I'm just not convinced being in a full-blown relationship could keep me excited."

That was it. He whirled her around until her back hit the door of the truck and pressed against her. "I think that was a personal challenge."

Her eyes widened in the weak light of the parking lot. "It wasn't meant to be."

"Sweetheart, I'm taking it as one." He didn't give her a chance to argue, but kissed her with all the passion, confusion, annoyance, and desperation he felt. He let it all pour out of him, into their kiss, communicating the feelings behind it.

Yes, feelings. He had feelings for her, ones he couldn't quite describe yet. But they were intense and he wasn't about to walk away from them—from her—because of a simple challenge.

Jo lifted one leg and wrapped her ankle around his knee, drawing him in closer. Trace pulled her more firmly against his chest with one hand at the small of her back and groped for the door handle. He managed to pry it open before lifting her up by the ass and setting her down on the bench seat.

She stared down at him a moment, panting. "Well. That was something. I should unintentionally challenge you more often."

He stared at her, shaking his head. "You think I'm done?"

One brow rose, a silent question.

"Jo, that was just an appetizer."

Chapter Thirteen

Jo shivered and wondered just how fast he could drive them back without breaking too many laws or getting pulled over. The ridge of his cock had been so hard, so full against her stomach as he'd pressed into her, she knew he was hurting as much, maybe more than she was. Ready, primed to go.

Apparently, Trace wasn't concerned with the drive back. He vaulted into the truck like a cat, crouching over her, blocking out any of the miniscule light from the lone lamp in the parking lot. His figure was only a shadow over her, poised and ready.

But she knew him. She knew the shape of his face, the angles and planes of his body, the gentleness he used when he wanted to. The tenderness she sometimes caught him watching her with. That same tenderness that made her want to jump at him and wrap her limbs around his torso and never let go. The tenderness that made her want to sprint for the hills and never look back.

"I'm at the point of no return here, Jo. So if you want me to stop, say it." He pressed the hard length of his erection against her crotch, the panties and denim a pathetic barrier between the heat they both burned with.

"Don't stop," she managed to gasp. It seemed like hours—but was really less than a few seconds—before he lifted himself off her to reach in the glove compartment and fish out a condom.

"The glove compartment? Really? Aren't you worried your parents might find that when you return the truck at the end of the night?" she teased.

"The way you make me feel, stashing these babies all over the damn state wouldn't be enough." He slapped her thigh playfully. "Take those panties down. Now."

She'd barely managed to get them off one leg when he was back on her, thrusting her knees wide and pushing inside her. Her whole body tightened, contracting under him, around him, and they both groaned.

In their frenzied pulsing together, she knew it wouldn't last. Couldn't last. Nothing this intense, this primal could go on forever. Could even go on for more than a few minutes. They'd combust otherwise.

And her body responded to the urgency, the danger of being caught and the unholy pace Trace was setting. After only a few more thrusts, she tightened and her body vibrated with an impending climax.

"Baby, I hope to God you're close because—"

"Yes." She placed a palm on either side of his face. "Yes, yes, oh, my God . . ."

The rest of her prayer was lost as his mouth took hers and he joined her in climax.

"Well." Jo sat up beneath him and wiped a hand across her face. A piece of hair stuck to the corner of her mouth and she couldn't seem to get it. He reached down and fixed it.

"Thanks." She settled herself a little more. "Wonder if any of the staff came out here and saw us."

Trace snorted and hopped down to the pavement, the open door sheltering him from anyone inside the restaurant. "If they saw the truck rocking like I think it was, they'd have been idiots to come investigate."

He wasn't sure how he expected her to react to that. Blush? Moan? Hang her head in her hands?

Nah. Not Jo. A small, secret smile crept across her lips, like she was the cat who found the stash of cream and was quite pleased with herself at the discovery. "You're right. Besides, no need to make anyone jealous."

Damn, he wanted her again already. Wanted to taste that satisfied smile, spend hours rediscovering all the secret places on her small, curvy body. Only this time, he'd rather do it in a bed.

He bent one knee, shook it a little, trying to work out the stiffness. After his fall from Lad, the leg was still giving him some trouble when he didn't move it around enough. That would ease over time, though. He'd had enough experience with being thrown to know that.

"Ready to drive this thing home, cowboy?" Jo patted the dashboard, and he realized he was still half-frozen, hand on his belt, pants not quite fastened yet.

"Yeah, sorry." He finished dressing and closed her door, walking around the front to get in and start the truck. As the engine came to life, he knew what he wanted to say next. Needed to say next.

"I like you."

Jo's hands paused in the middle of pulling her hair into a tail. "I like you, too. That's why we went out to dinner, isn't it?"

"Of course it is." He rubbed a hand down his face. Why wasn't he good with words? "I mean, I really like you."

Jo just shook her head. "I got it. We did our date thing."

"I want another."

She opened her mouth—likely to argue—then shut it again. "Why? What's wrong with what we had? Sex when

we want it, no commitment when we don't. No obligation."

"Because there's more here." He watched her, focusing
hard on her face in the dim light. Damned if he was going to turn on the cab light just to have this stupid conversation. One he should have waited until they were at
home to have. "I want to try having more with you.
You're not an obligation to me."

Her shoulders slumped forward, as if defeated. That was
not the reaction he was trying for, and he felt guilty for a
moment. But only a moment.

"What if I say no? Are we done? Done with everything?"

"No," he said slowly. "That's shooting myself in the foot
for spite." He grinned sheepishly. "Much as I like you, I
like being with you in bed, too." She snorted, and he
shrugged with a sheepish smile. "Why deny it?"

She laughed hard, shoulders shaking, her hair falling
from the messy tail and framing her face. She laughed so
hard she had to reach up and wipe tears away.

"You know, just when I think I have you pegged, cowboy, you surprise me. I like that. It keeps me on my toes."

He leaned over to haul her against him. "Say yes." He
nibbled at her lips, along her jawline. "Say yes, Jo."

"So . . ." Her voice was breathy, as if she couldn't get
enough air in to make the words solid. "So we'd, what? Be
going steady?"

He didn't respond to that. He was too busy with a delicious spot just below the ear where several earrings decorated her lobe. The delicate skin seemed especially tender
at the moment.

"Would you let me wear your varsity jacket?"

"They don't give letter jackets to rodeo kids." He licked
a patch of skin, blew gently against it until she shivered.

One hand rose up to cup her breast, the nipple peaking into his hand.

"I'm at a loss as to how to define us."

"Us." His other hand came up to massage the other breast. "Isn't that worth leaving labels behind?"

She was silent, long enough that he wondered if his attention to her body had been a mistake. But then she whispered, "Yes."

Triumph surged, and he knew if he didn't get the truck on the road in the next ten seconds, they'd be in for a repeat performance. Only his body just wasn't up for another round of truck sex, much as his hormones begged to differ. He slid back, pushing gently on her shoulders until she was a good foot away.

Her eyes, dreamy and half-closed, snapped open. "What?"

Trace buckled his belt and nodded at her. "Seat belt."

She just stared at him, mouth open.

"I can't drive without you buckled in."

Jo's mouth set in a serious line and she faced forward with a cute little huff. But she latched her seat belt and he started the drive home.

"If I hadn't pulled back, I wouldn't have stopped," he said quietly. The only noise competing for sound was the tires rumbling over pavement. The night was clean, clear, and quiet.

"Who asked you to stop?" Jo's arms crossed over her chest.

"I did." He smiled a little and angled the truck toward the highway. "Next time I get inside you, I want a mattress. I'm not as young as I used to be."

She smiled a little at that, and he let her ride in silence.

She was so worried about being pegged into the domestic role, so worried about being tied down. He had to approach things more cautiously from here on out. He'd managed to corner her into agreeing to the relationship . . . sort of. Into an "us," which he wasn't sure was quite the same thing. But he'd take it.

His gaze slid over the dashboard and across the clock. He calculated how much longer he wanted to spend away from Seth before heading home.

Seth.

Damn. In all their time together, he'd never mentioned his son. That hadn't entered into the arrangement. He'd even liked that she hadn't known, hadn't heard gossip and been one of the women wondering what had happened to Seth's mother. Now that he'd brought Jo into the "us" category, dragging her heels, it would be awkward to spring news of a son on her. Damn it.

His hands gripped the wheel. They'd play it by ear, that was all. Dating was all about getting to know each other. He'd ease that one in. Get her comfortable with the relationship and then casually mention it. That was reasonable, wasn't it?

He'd walked himself into this mess—albeit unintentionally—now he had to walk himself back out of it.

Trace raised his legs toward the ceiling, keeping his feet flat. "Here goes the airplane!" To his son's delight, he made the engine sound and jiggled him. Seth laughed and drooled a little, but it landed on Trace's shirt rather than his face, so he let it pass.

"Looks like fun. Can I have a turn?"

Peyton lay down next to him, her feet going the opposite direction so her head was right next to his.

"Sorry, riders must be two feet or shorter and weigh less than twenty pounds." Seth wriggled his body a little in a c'mon gesture and Trace obliged, swirling his legs in a circular motion while still keeping a firm grasp on his hands.

"So, gonna tell me who his mother is?"

"Nope."

She shrugged, as much as his sister could while flat on her back. "Well, whoever it was, she must have been beautiful. Because this little cutie looks nothing like you."

In fact, he looked quite a bit like his father, but Trace could take the jab. Peyton's routine of asking once a week—give or take—hadn't slowed down one bit. He figured she would give up asking after awhile. Emma had, and Emma was a pit bull with a bone when it came to that sort of thing. But if Emma was a pit bull, Peyton was a liger.

Yeah. A liger.

Emma walked by and stared down at them, hands on her hips. "Is this how you two spend a Sunday morning?"

"We would have gone to church, but we didn't want to get fried by lightning," Trace said innocently.

"If you—"

"Neeeerrrrroooom!" Seth squealed in rapture.

"It wouldn't be—"

"Bbbbbbbrrrrrrwwwww."

His son nearly fell from his perch, saved by some quick maneuvering from Trace.

Emma eyed him narrowly. "That's not—"

"Pfffffttttt."

"Amusing!" she yelled before he could make another plane noise. She dropped the wet dish towel on Peyton's face, stifling his sister's laughter. "Just for that, Trace Muldoon, you get to go on the grocery run."

He froze, Seth still stuck in a half nosedive. "Aw, Emma. C'mon."

"Someone's gotta go, and you just got yourself nominated." The housekeeper shot him a grin a shark would turn tail and hide from. "I'll have the list ready in ten minutes."

Peyton turned and watched him for a moment. "Don't even think about hiding. She'll just find you and add more to the list. I know. I tried it once."

"Damn," he muttered and lowered Seth to his chest. "Well, little man, looks like we're going shopping." He shot his sister a look. "Unless Auntie Peyton wants to bond with you a little. . . ."

"We bonded last night. I'm off poop duty today." She rolled to her stomach and pushed up to her feet. "Besides, you had your hot date last night. I've got one for myself today."

"Where's Red taking you?"

"Red?" She huffed a laugh. "I've got a buyer coming in. One with quite a bit of disposable income, if word is correct."

Since Red was likely where she got the word, and Red knew everything, Trace figured correct was an understatement. "Good luck with that."

"You should hustle back and talk to the guy. He saw you and Red about two months ago."

"Name?"

She described the man and he shook his head. "Don't remember."

"Well, either way, he was impressed with both of you. Try to get back so you can pander and strut a little." She reached over and pinched his cheek before he could evade. "The customers really like it when you boys strut."

"Trace!" Bea's voice carried down the stairs like a whip. "Are you going to the grocery store?"

"Yeah," he called back up. "If your list isn't ready in five minutes, it's not coming with me."

"I'm coming with you. I need things and I can't trust you to get them."

"What the hell, am I incompetent?"

Her head popped around the railing, as if leaning over without taking the next few steps down. She smirked at him. "Fine, if you want to pick up my tampons for me . . ."

"You have ten minutes to be in the car." He rolled his eyes and hitched Seth up on his hip. "Time to get changed. They don't let men shop in their footie PJs at the store."

Jo opened her small pantry and scoffed. Right. Should she have the stale bread or the handful of goldfish crackers for breakfast? She let the doors close with a snap and tried the fridge. Unfortunately, it seemed her grocery shopping genie hadn't shown up for work. After a quick debate, she decided she needed to suck it up and get some food. Real food. Not just whatever she could make herself from the stash downstairs. Adult food.

She dressed quickly, not bothering with makeup. An old sweatshirt, a pair of jeans from the floor, and her long hair in its customary ponytail and she was ready to rock. She grabbed her keys from the table and locked the door behind her. She'd only get a few bags and walk rather than drive the three blocks. It was the beauty of living above the bar. Everything was handy.

She was nearly down the stairs when she spotted the truck sitting at the curb. Her heart did a traitorous little dive into her gut before she realized it wasn't Trace's.

Jeff stepped out and she groaned. Her first thought was *why me?* The second was . . . how long had he sat in the truck waiting for her? How long had he already been there?

Jeff stood by the side of the truck and waited for her to hit the bottom step. She debated walking on and making him chase her if he wanted something, but that seemed petty. He wasn't worth even a petty gesture.

"I came over to apologize. I'm sorry."

The words softened her. A little. But not much. The kid

looked like hell, though, and that softened her more. "You should be."

He raised his hands, as if not sure what to do with them, then stuck them in the pockets of his jeans. One sneaker kicked at the dirt, and the entire performance reminded her of a sullen little boy. "I misunderstood the situation."

Misunderstood, her ass. Maybe he'd misunderstood if she was interested, at first, but there was no mistake after she'd started pushing him.

When she didn't reply, he went on. "I got lonely and freaked out about school and I just sort of lost my head a little. I'm sorry. I'm really sorry."

It wasn't an excuse, but she understood. A young kid made mistakes. She'd made more than a few, and was lucky enough none of them had been permanent. She made a split-second decision—some of her best decisions were in the heat of the moment, after all—and ran with it. "Just remember that for the next time. Otherwise, you might get your ass handed to you."

He grinned, quick as lightning. "You woulda laid me out, wouldn't you?"

She shrugged, then smiled a little. "If I felt it necessary."

He stepped forward, then back again, hands still in his pockets. "Can I still come by before I head out?" When she watched him, he clarified, "The bar, I mean. Like for lunch."

"Sure. I know you're good for the tab." The joke made him smile again, and she waved and walked off to the grocery store, feeling a little lighter.

He wasn't a bad kid. Just a moment of stupidity. Hell, they all had them. Like her, the night before.

What had honestly possessed her to think a relationship with anyone—least of all someone rooted in this community—was a good idea? She was a business owner

in a tenuous position. The outsider still trying to prove
herself. A woman in a man's business, trying not to get
kicked in the teeth with ass–backward cowboys. And she
had to go and add *feelings* to the mix.

Brilliant. How the hell had Trace talked her into that?

Her body tightened at the reminder of exactly how he'd
primed her for that one. In a parking lot, no less, like a
couple of teenagers. Christ.

She paused and made a big show of window shopping
in the closest store. Somehow, she didn't think anyone
would believe she was deeply considering buying a
muumuu in size triple XL with puppies frolicking on the
front. But she needed a minute to calm the flush or she'd
really embarrass herself.

Nothing like the word *muumuu* to stifle a sexual heat
wave.

As she reached the grocery store, she grabbed a basket,
then debated and put it back in favor of a cart. She needed
to stock up. If she was going to have Trace over more of–
ten, she'd have to feed him meals. A man like him ate, and
ate well. She smiled at that, and considered the various
ways of serving meat and potatoes without being tedious.

"Jo."

She turned at that, recognizing Bea's voice. "Hey.
What's up?"

Bea practically sprinted at her and hooked one arm
around Jo's elbow. "You're just the person I needed. I'm
looking at this pitiful selection of dog toys they carry and
I'm not sure which one to choose."

"Shouldn't you go to the feed store for that?" Jo looked
back toward the produce she was being dragged away
from. "I need food, Bea."

"You're in a grocery store. You'll get it. But this is im–
portant. Look." She halted at an end cap and held up two
toys. "The blue one? Or the pink one?"

"He's a boy, right?" When Bea raised a brow, Jo shrugged. "Just checking. The blue."

"But this is the twenty-first century. Why can't men have pink?"

"The pink, then." A headache loomed like a black cloud over a picnic. "I need to go get something other than instant soup for my kitchen."

"Oh, great. I love veggies." Bea swung her arm around Jo's shoulders and tossed the pink toy in Jo's cart. "Let's talk cucumber."

"Do we have to?" Jo eyed her warily. "What's going on with you?"

"Me?" Bea's eyes widened. "Why?"

Jo picked up a head of lettuce and ignored Bea's feigned innocence.

"Not that one." Bea handed her another head and grabbed the first to put back.

Jo rolled her eyes and stuck the bundle of leaves in her cart, moving on to the tomatoes. When she picked up a four-pack of prepackaged ones, Bea moaned quietly.

"Oh, my God. What is wrong with you?"

"Those are so bad for you. The prepackaged ones are always hot house tomatoes, which are tasteless and devoid of any real nutrients."

"Not what I meant," Jo muttered, but put down the plastic with caution and picked out a few from the bin individually.

Bea hovered, but kept her mouth closed, which suited Jo just fine. And when Bea nudged one tomato over toward the sack with her index finger, Jo figured the silent gesture was better than listening to a lecture, so she gracefully accepted the tomato and moved on.

"Where are we going next?" Bea bounced next to her.

"Frozen foods."

"No!" Bea grabbed the cart and swung it around, nearly knocking Jo into a display of Oreos.

"What the he—Bea!" Jo regained control and avoided a collision with a mom and two toddlers by inches. "Jesus, what's your problem?"

Bea ran a hand through her hair until little blond tufts stuck out awkwardly. "Frozen food is awful for you. All those preservatives and nitrates and . . . stuff. You know. Let's revisit the fresh vegetables. So much better."

"I happen to like preservatives and nitrates." Jo yanked the cart back in the direction she'd originally intended. "And it's easy to pop in the oven when I've had a long day. Which I almost always do."

"Okay, but first . . ." Bea glanced around and pointed. "I need your opinion."

Jo sighed. "My opinion is you're being a pain in the ass."

"I'm not—hold on." Bea held up a finger and reached in her bag for her phone, currently belting out the theme song to *Legally Blonde*. Oh, for the love of God. "Let me just . . . oh, damn."

"What?"

"My agent. We've been playing phone tag for a while. Stay right there." Bea shot her a dirty look. "Don't you dare move."

"Okay." Jo shrugged and watched Bea answer the call and wander off, one hand over her free ear to block out noise. After she'd taken a few steps and looked suitably busy, Jo swung the cart and headed for the frozen food section.

Yeah. She'd lied. Oh, well. All's fair in love and frozen pizza snack bites.

She turned a corner and smiled when she recognized Trace. Or rather, his back. She should have known Bea wouldn't come to the grocery store alone. Or at all.

God, he looked good. Even just from the back. The way he stood there, weight on one leg so his hip cocked out, one hand in his back pocket, stretching the aging denim quite nicely over his adorable ass. She could barely see a piece of paper over his shoulder, and she could imagine, thanks to the way he stood frozen, he was reading an entire list of things he had no clue about. Men sent grocery shopping . . . not always a good idea. Well, she would just have to save him.

Slowly, Jo crept up behind him, then reached around and covered his eyes with her hands.

"Cut it out, Bea."

Jo pressed her breasts into his back and whispered, "Not Bea."

"Jo?" She thought she heard him mutter, "Jesus," but she couldn't be sure, and then he turned around. "Hey. What are you doing here?"

Why was everyone asking her that? "A girl's gotta eat. Listen, I was thinking about picking up some steaks for tonight. Do you want to . . ." She trailed off, her eyes catching something to the left of Trace's sleeve. "What's that?"

"What?" He looked behind him, and froze again. But not in that cute *I'm so confused, what's the difference between virgin and extra virgin olive oil?* sort of way. More like in the *oh, shit, I'm caught* sort of way. Which really had her heart racing. "It's a baby."

"Yeah. I can see that." The fact of its existence made her want to take two steps back for sheer preservation. "Why is it in your cart? Are you cart sitting?"

"Cart sitting?"

"Yeah, you know . . ." Her mind raced as she stretched for a plausible reason why a baby would be in Trace's cart. One that wouldn't ruin the very thin, tenuous thread of happiness they'd started to build on. "Someone needed to pop into the other aisle so you, you know, offered to watch the cart in case some weird baby snatcher came by. Cart sitting."

"Are there a lot of baby snatchers running around the Piggly Wiggly?" He looked a little horrified and started surveying the aisle, as if some masked robber was going to pop out from behind a freezer and yell "Gotcha!"

"Not the point." Okay. Starting to sound a little hysterical. Breathe. Breathe. "Whose kid is this?"

Trace reached back and rubbed one hand gently over the kid's head. "He's mine."

Chapter Fourteen

For a moment, Trace wondered if he'd have to catch Jo. She paled, faster than he'd ever seen anyone go pale, and he really thought he had a fainter on his hands. But she recovered and took another step back. Why did she keep doing that?

"You have a kid."

It was a question, though she'd stated it as fact. He nodded. Seth grabbed his hand and squeezed, working his fingers around and playing.

"You've, uh, always had a kid?"

"Long as he's been alive."

She stared at Seth, like he might be a cross between a rabid dog and a charging bull. "And he lives with you."

Another question in a statement. "Yeah. He stays out at the ranch."

"Oh, my God." She breathed it, and he almost didn't catch the words. "How stupid am I?"

"You're not stupid. Jo, I—"

"No. No, it's okay." She held up a hand to halt his progress. "It's totally okay. It's just a reminder, that's all."

A reminder of what? By the way she took another step back, he was pretty sure her "okay" wasn't code for "I love babies and this is the best surprise ever!" Damn it, he was going to lose her. "Jo, we need to talk about this."

"Yes." Her eyes went a little glassy and she nodded. "Yes, we do." But she said nothing else, just watched as Seth tugged on the rolled-up sleeve of Trace's shirt, silently begging for attention.

Someone rolled by them, slowing down enough to grab a frozen pizza from the freezer across from them. The older woman shot them both a confused, slightly annoyed look that said *stop loitering, hooligans* and went on. But it was enough to break whatever trance Jo had slipped into. She turned around and started back down the way she'd come, squeaky cart bumping over cracked tile like she was running from the devil.

That wasn't talking. That was the opposite of talking. But he couldn't very well give chase with Seth in the cart.

She couldn't hide from him. He knew where she lived and worked. They'd talk. And though he'd meant to get to this a little sooner, he'd say everything he needed to. It'd be fine. There was no way he was letting this ruin what they'd started.

Bea skidded around the corner in her heels, looking frazzled and a little lost. "Where's Jo? Did you see her? Did she see you?" Her eyes went round. "Did she see Seth?"

"Yes, times three. And I don't know where she is. Checking out, I assume." Or fleeing the country. "Where'd you go?"

She held a hand to her chest and bent over like she'd run a marathon. "Trying to find her before she caught sight of you two. I was distracting her in the produce section and then I got a call from my agent and . . . it doesn't matter. I was trying to be helpful."

"Why would you distract her?"

"Because she doesn't know about Seth. Right?" She winced. "Or at least, she didn't. I was hoping to prod you enough to get you to tell her soon, before she found out some other way."

"Too late for that," he murmured, reaching in the diaper bag and finding a toy to distract Seth from gnawing on his own fingers. He located Sophie the giraffe and handed the toy over. "Here, buddy. Try this on for size." With Seth content, he focused back on his sister. "And why would you think it mattered if Jo knew? We weren't exactly public with our . . . thing."

"Your sister isn't public." She smiled smugly. "I have my ways. But that's not the point. The point is, you need to go after her and explain."

"No, I need to finish shopping and take the groceries, and you two, home. Then I can give her time to cool off and get over the shock, and try to explain."

Bea rolled her eyes. "Sure, if you want to be logical about it. I swear, sometimes you're too much like Peyton for your own good."

He bent and kissed her forehead. "I'll take that as a compliment. But thanks, for trying to help." In her own messed up sort of way. It was a good thing, Bea trying to be helpful. It meant she was investing in the family again.

They eased the cart around and headed for the checkout. "I thought you were getting something for your dog."

"Casualty of the moment. It was in Jo's cart. She probably put it back." Bea shrugged. "Another time." As they stood in line, Bea perused a magazine with the latest *American Idol* winner on the front cover, then added another magazine with what appeared to be TV soap stars.

"That's not food."

"It's food for my soul. Calm down." She flipped through a few more pages, then without looking, asked, "Are you going to fix things with her?"

"If it kills me," he answered immediately. When he wanted something, he got it. Period. He wanted Seth, he got Seth. He wanted to make things work at home, they were working. And now, he wanted Jo. The trouble was making her want him—all of him, now, which included his son—back. The whole "ease her in" thing was not going to happen. So back to square one.

"Flowers are nice," she said absently.

"Flowers?" He debated running to the floral department, then shook his head. "Not going to work." At least, not for a big apology.

"Hmm. Giving her clothing is too weird. Lingerie is always nice, but sends the wrong sort of message for the situation. More of a let's have wild rutting animal sex vibe."

"Bea," he muttered, holding his hands over Seth's ears. That's just what he needed, for his son's first sentence to be about wild animal sex. The matron who had given him and Jo a dirty look turned around and shot Bea a nasty glare.

Bea ignored it. "The whole rutting, primal animal sex thing is nice," she added, almost wistfully. "If you can get it, I mean."

"God. Why don't I have two sets of hands so I can cover my own ears?" he moaned. When the scandalized woman in front of them paid for her purchases and hauled ass to the parking lot—likely cursing the Piggly Wiggly for allowing such people to shop there—he gratefully started loading the conveyor belt with their items and ignoring Bea.

"But you need something that says, *I get you. I get you, and you're important.* And you can't do that with lingerie or flowers. So think harder."

He paused in the act of setting a bag of beans on the belt. "Is that it? That's your big help? *Think harder.*"

Bea patted his arm. "You're on your own from here." She weaved around him and cooed at Seth, pushing the cart out of the lane. "Let's go to the car and get you all hooked up in your car seat. Does that sound like fun? Yes, it does!"

Trace shook his head and reached into the cart for the last item before they pulled away. He came back with the soap magazine. Naturally, Bea would expect him to pay for it and not put it back. He sighed, debated, and then tossed it on the belt.

Why not? He might have a hell of a lot more free time on his hands now. Maybe he could watch reruns.

"He's got a kid." Jo slammed her palms down on the bar, making Amanda jump. "Why didn't anyone tell me?"

Amanda looked up from the server notepad she was doodling in. "Probably because most people assumed you knew?"

"Why would I know that? I'm still 'new' here." New in the Bumfuck Nowhere sense, which meant you were the new person until you'd lived there at least a decade.

"People talk." Amanda shrugged. "But regardless, you hate gossip. You shut it out the moment you catch a whiff of it."

"You could have made me listen," she muttered.

"You weren't exactly public with your relationship."

Relationship. There was that dirty word again. "Apparently you knew." Jo walked around the bar and sank into a chair next to Amanda. "What, did everyone know?"

"Nope," her star server chirped. "But I was here late more than once, and I saw his truck hovering by your side of the building. Plus, you've been in a way better mood lately. I put two and two together and figured you two were playing Ride 'Em, Cowgirl at night."

"Awful. That was awful."

"Thanks. I liked it." She ripped out the sheet of doodles and wadded it up, closing the pad and stuffing it in her server apron with the other hand. "It's not the end of the world, right? You're just doing the nasty nasty. He's not exactly bringing his kid with him on adults-only dates. So what's the big deal?"

The big deal was they'd recently made the joint decision to start something more than just the nasty nasty. And she, despite her bitching, had been looking forward to it with nervous anticipation. Now it was shot to hell.

She let her head fall to the table with a dull thud. "Why is being an adult so hard?"

"Because we had it too easy as kids? Something about our grandparents walking uphill both ways in the snow . . . I don't know. I usually blank out after Gramps gets going." Amanda rubbed her back soothingly.

"It's going to be okay. You're you, and you'll get through it. You'll get what you want out of the bargain, because that's what you do. You wanted the bar, you got it. You wanted to be top dog, it's coming to you. You wanted a hot man in your bed, and he was. Now you can keep him there, and pretend he's not a daddy on the side, or you can find another strapping cowboy to fill in. There's no shortage of them in this area, if you didn't notice."

She opened her mouth to argue, but closed it again. Might as well let Amanda think that. But the fact was, she didn't *want* another cowboy in her bed. She wanted her cowboy. The one she already had.

But a kid? What did she look like, June Cleaver? She didn't do kids. She really didn't even do relationships, but she got talked into that one. Hearth and home, for her, weren't on the table. She wasn't stepmother material. She wasn't even sure she was good girlfriend material, but at least if she fucked that up, Trace was adult enough to get out of the way before the shit hit the fan.

God. What the hell was she supposed to do?

★   ★   ★

Trace ran Lad through another obstacle course, cutting corners a little closer than he normally would. When a client was in the building, it wasn't a bad idea to show off just a little. But rather than riding herd on the horse, he was more concerned about keeping check on his own emotions.

Ruthlessly, coldly, he blocked Jo from his mind. Blocked it all out until it was him and the horse. Lad and Trace moving together. Anticipating the horse's movement, ticks, every breath so they were one fluid creature rather than rider and mount.

He'd already run through the same course with two younger horses, still in training. So seeing it done with his own horse, seeing what the Muldoon training could accomplish with raw talent, was usually an eye-opener for the customer.

And when he finally rode Lad over to Steve, waiting to take the horse to cool off, he saw the look of appreciation in the client's eyes.

"Fine mount, gentlemen." Flint rubbed his jaw and watched as Lad walked away, his eyes tracking the horse's legs. "Nice show."

Trace watched as Red all but stepped into his new persona, in full showmanship mode now. This was never Red's favorite part. But it was part of the package.

Red slapped a hand on Flint's shoulder. "Not just a show. Our horses know what they're doing, because we know what they need. It's an equal partnership. . . ." Red winked and Trace almost choked on his laughter. "As long as the horses remember who holds the sugar cubes."

Flint laughed in big guffaws. "Isn't that the truth?" He rubbed at his jaw again. "I'm not entirely sure. I was over at Three Trees the other day. Tanner said he let you go a year ago."

Red's eyes twitched, just a little, but his smile was easy

and smooth. "Well, that's a matter of opinion, I suppose. My work there was done, and I moved on. But here at the Muldoon spread, we—"

"He warned me about this place. Said y'all were going bankrupt. That it would be foolish to even step foot over here."

Trace's hands balled into fists. That's how the competition was going at it? Throwing mud?

"Something about unethical practices," he went on. "I didn't stick around for the details, of course. Not one for gossip myself." Flint's eyes told a different story.

"Flint, you know me, don't you?" Red began easily.

He nodded. Everyone did. Red's name was synonymous with superior horse training.

"I think I'd like to let my reputation speak for itself. I've always held myself to the highest standards, and I expect the same of those I work with. I've stayed here for as long as I have because I believe this place to be the pinnacle of ethics. And between you and me, it's an up-and-comer for stock. You start business with M-Star now? Men will be calling you brilliant in a year. You'll be ahead of the game."

Flint nodded again, but took a small step back. It was a gesture most might overlook, but Trace saw it for what it was. Separation, a step in the direction he intended to continue. Despite their quality stock and unmatchable trainer, rumors and hearsay would take them down.

"Gentlemen, you've given me some things to think about. I—"

"Yoohoo!"

Three heads swiveled in unison, and all took in the sight walking toward them.

Trace groaned.

Red closed his eyes in a *this is not happening* sort of gesture.

But Flint? His tongue all but rolled out of his mouth and dragged on the floor like a cartoon hound at the sight of Bea toddling toward them. One arm was out for balance, the other holding that stupid dog against her shoulder like a baby. And damn if she wasn't wearing an imitation Daisy Duke outfit, right down to the skimpy, ripped up cut-off denim shorts and cowboy boots, with a shirt—was that his shirt?—tied up around her navel.

The dog, poor thing, was sporting a red bandana and looking miserable about it.

Damn it. Just what they needed. Red had spent the past five minutes assuring Flint they were a serious business, one to contend with. And now Bea was going to undo it with one shake of her on-display ass.

Bea finally made her way down the dirt path and held out a hand to Flint, who grasped it without hesitation. "I heard in the big house there was a new cowboy to come and see. I couldn't resist."

Flint—the fifty-year-old man who looked like he could chew up railroad spikes for breakfast—blushed. He actually blushed under that salt-and-pepper beard. "Ma'am."

"Oh, Bea, please. Everyone calls me Bea." She rubbed her dog lightly over the back and angled herself slightly so they could see his face. "And this is Mr. Milton."

The dog shot them a mutinous look that said, *Get me out of here. I'll share my kibble with you.*

Flint chuckled and rubbed the dog on the top of the head with two knuckles. "Not quite a farm dog, is he?"

"Oh, no. He's my baby." Bea snuggled the dog a little and smiled. "But you must understand about that. The horses are like your babies, right?"

The man stared, glassy-eyed, then shook his head. "I wouldn't say—"

"I could tell you were a nurturing man," she cooed, interrupting him. Flint didn't seem to mind anyway. Hooking one arm through his, Bea pulled him toward the house. "A man that cares about his animals is a man you can trust, don't you agree?"

"I do," he said, getting into the swing of things. The man could have been her father, but that didn't stop him from clearly fantasizing about Bea. He followed along with her like a dog on a leash. Except Bea never used a leash for her damn dog.

"That's why you're just the perfect fit for me!" Bea laughed and bumped his shoulder with hers, much to Milton's disgruntlement. "I mean the ranch. Red's just the best there is, isn't he? And did you see my brother up there on that horse? It's magical."

Trace turned around and doubled over, hands on his knees, trying his hardest to not bark out a laugh. Red kneed him in the thigh and motioned to follow behind the pair heading toward the house.

"Well, I agree Callahan's got a good rep," Flint said as the magic of Bea's spell started to wear off and common-sense took over. "But I'm still not sure yet."

"Oh." Bea stepped back a little and bit her lip. "I'm sorry, I didn't mean to push. It's just, there was this other man here a few days ago and I thought you two were friends. I thought he sent you. Oh, darn it, what was his name?"

Trace looked to his left and watched as Red's face went blank. What the hell was she pulling?

"It reminded me of a bird. Ostrich? No, that's silly. Oh, well. No matter." Bea swatted the thought aside. "I just thought you two were friends for some—"

"Partridge?" Flint said, stopping dead in his tracks.

"Oh, that's a bird, isn't it? Maybe that's it!" Bea lit up and patted Milton's butt. "You're so good at this. Yes, a man—maybe it was this Mr. Partridge, though I'm not exactly positive—was around the other week and I'm not sure how I got it in my mind you two were friends."

"More like enemies," Red muttered to Trace. "Confirmed enemies."

Ah. The dawn broke. Trace debated ending the little act now, sending Bea off to the house and wrapping up the meeting. It's what Peyton would have done. But something, call it instinct, held him back. Since Red wasn't jumping in to stop the show, Trace could only assume his infamous gut was talking and saying to let it play out.

Bea squeezed Flint's arm, and her eyes widened. "I think your arms are bigger than Trace's!"

And that was his punishment for following instinct. He stepped forward, intent on breaking it up, but Red put out a hand. "Let her finish," he said from the corner of his mouth.

"Did Partridge buy anything?"

Bea's nose scrunched as she thought. "Um, I'm not sure. I'm not really a businesswoman, you know. I don't handle that sort of thing. But he looked so happy when he left, and he said he'd be back soon. . . ." Bea chewed on her bottom lip and hugged Milton tighter. If it was possible, the dog's eyes bugged out even more. "Oh, no. Did I get this wrong? Maybe it wasn't Partridge after all. There are so many bird names. I can't be sure now. Don't hold me to it."

Flint shook his head. "I'm not worried about that."

"Oh, please don't tell anyone I mentioned it!" She grasped his wrist in a desperate move, her eyes going wide and a little watery. She blinked rapidly, as if trying to hold back the tears. "I don't want to make a mess of things and I hope I didn't ruin any secrets or surprises. Please don't tell."

Flint patted her hand, looking more fatherly now than

lecherous. "I wouldn't dare. You did the right thing." He angled his head back a little. "Callahan, should we head back to the office and talk numbers?"

Red tipped his head in agreement. "Sure thing. You head on up there—Emma'll let you in. Tell her to grab a plate of cookies. They're an experience not to be missed."

"I'll take him!" Bea called and once more hooked her arm through his. "I always love a handsome cowboy escort. I can never bring myself to say no."

The two men watched in silence as Bea Muldoon, self-proclaimed shallow actress and airhead, led Flint, a hardened horseman with a keen business sense. It was much like watching a skipping child with a balloon and a lollipop lead a docile bull by the ring in his nose.

Once they were out of earshot, Red turned to him, grinning madly. "Brilliant. She was brilliant."

"Yeah, she pulled that one off, that's for sure. You know, I don't think I gave her enough credit for her talent." Trace dragged one heel through the dirt. "So who's gonna be the one to tell Peyton how this all went down?"

The men stared at each other for a moment, then in unison muttered, "Bea."

Chapter Fifteen

"You what?" Peyton's yell thundered inside the small office. Trace wondered that he didn't see some of the picture frames rattle. "You let our sister do the talking? On one of the most important business deals we've seen yet? *Her?*"

"Jesus, Peyton," he muttered, rubbing the back of his neck. "She's right here."

Bea sat in the club chair opposite the desk, ignoring them both and filing her nails. One leg was crossed over the other, bare foot lazily dangling. She'd changed the moment Flint drove off into a regular tank and khaki shorts that were—to his eternal gratitude—about three inches longer than her ripped cut-offs, but remained barefoot.

"She knows nothing about horses. She can't even name all the freaking tack. She won't step foot in the barn. And she thinks dogs are accessories. But you let her have the reins with Flint. What the hell were you thinking?"

"I was thinking—"

"He was thinking," Bea interrupted, not looking up from her fingers, "that you were about to lose the deal. No amount of fancy horsemanship by Trace was going to save the day. No superior knowledge or reputation from Red was going to push him over the edge of signing on the dotted line. I'd been listening in before I ran out there." She glanced up momentarily to look at him. "Am I wrong?"

"She's not wrong," he told Peyton, and Bea resumed filing. "The guy heard some heavy shit from Three Trees. He was ready to walk. Bea added a nice little imaginary incentive for him."

Peyton dug her thumbs into her eyes and pushed hard. "Do I even want to know what it was?"

"I merely mentioned that a gentleman with a name that reminded me of birds stopped by last week to look and chat, and he might be back soon."

Peyton stared at Bea for a moment, then looked to Trace for help.

"Partridge."

Peyton's mouth dropped. "But he wasn't here. Last week we had Bullock and Robins stop by, but—"

"Robins!" Bea said, holding a hand in the air. "That's it. That's the bird-sounding name." She grinned maliciously. "Whoops. My bad."

Ignoring their sister, Peyton asked him, "Did she ever come right out and say Partridge was here?"

Trace ran back through the conversation, then shook his head. "No. She mentioned the bird thing, and Flint came up with it on his own. She even told him she wasn't sure and not to hold her to it."

"Just said the man I was thinking of said he'd come back next week."

"Robins is scheduled in on Thursday," Peyton murmured, watching Bea closely. "How did you know that?"

Bea sighed, then stretched her long legs and stood. "I hear more around this place than anyone else thinks. And I pay attention more than anyone else thinks. You don't give me enough credit."

The words were said simply, but their implication bit hard. Both Trace and Peyton glanced away, chastened.

"Anyway, I need to take off. Any other questions?" When neither spoke, she shrugged and headed for the door. "I'm taking Milton over to see the vet."

"Morgan?" Peyton asked, arching a brow. "What's wrong with him?"

"I think he has allergies, poor thing." Bea glanced out the window. "Is it supposed to get windy? Do you think he needs a sweater?"

Peyton, who'd just started to look at Bea in a new light, deflated. "No. Your dog doesn't need a sweater. Go."

"Toodles!" Bea waved and sauntered out the door, closing it behind her.

Peyton's eyes bored holes through the door. "I'm not even sure what to make of her anymore."

"Why make anything?" Trace sat in the chair Bea had evacuated and crossed one boot over his knee. "Bea is who Bea is. She's not an idiot, much as she would like some people to believe. She likes being underestimated."

Peyton pondered that for a moment, then shrugged. "Whatever. It worked. But don't do it again. We can't let the Bimbo Sister act define us."

"Point made." He waited a beat, and then grinned. "It was pretty ingenious though."

Peyton's lips curved in a reluctant smile. "It wasn't bad."

"She's trying."

"Yeah." Peyton's eyes turned to the door again. "For how long? It's been months. I thought she'd be ready to escape by now. She knows she can. Why is she still here?"

Trace laced his fingers over his stomach. "Have you asked her that?"

Peyton scowled and turned to her computer. "You've got your own problems. Go figure out how to fix things."

"Does everyone know about me and Jo?" he asked, throwing his hands in the air in exasperation.

"I do now," she said, a smug smile creeping over her face.

"Damn it." This stupid town.

Peyton's smile slipped a little. "You used to tell me everything."

"We were kids back then. The stakes were lower."

"And then," she went on as if he hadn't said anything, "you disappeared. You were my best friend, and then you were gone."

"Jesus, P." He rubbed a hand over his face. "I was nineteen. I needed to get out and do my own thing."

"But you barely even said good-bye. Just packed up and left." She rolled her lips in a little, then went on. "I was left running this place. Me, by myself, battling that woman every step of the way. Knowing for everything I did right, she'd blow in and do three things wrong just to spite me. I think she enjoyed watching Dad's work crumble."

He shut his eyes.

"I felt like you abandoned me. Left me alone to deal with her."

"Peyton."

"Had you planned to go? I need to know that. Had you been planning to leave, and you just didn't share it?"

"Does it matter?"

"It does to me. It won't change things, but I need to know."

Trace settled back and stared at the ceiling. How much to tell her? What to leave out? "Mom made my life hell."

"Mom was hell, period." Peyton snorted. "Sylvia was a piece of work."

"The last weekend before I left, you were away with the 4-H group. The weekend trip. Bea was sleeping at some friend's house. And I was alone with her. She had one of her wino friends over for a weekend bender. I think she forgot I even lived here half the time, since I was gone so often."

"Working at the feed store," his sister murmured.

"The money was nice. Being away from her was better." He smiled ruefully. "I don't think Monroe's ever had someone who liked coming in to work overtime as much as I did.

"But I was off for the weekend and he didn't need me to come in. So I holed up in my room and prayed she'd forget I was there. She might have, but her friend didn't." He closed his eyes, then opened them again, praying the images didn't come back while he talked. "That woman— I couldn't tell you her name even if I gave a damn—crept into my room and fell on me. I thought she'd gotten the wrong room at first. God knew she smelled like she was half-drowned in a vat of wine. So I meant to push her off and lead her to the guest bed. But then she started groping."

Peyton winced but didn't look away.

"I rolled out from under her, heard her calling me to come back. When I hit the hallway, I heard Sylvia snickering in the family room. She knew what was going on and just sat back to watch."

"Jesus," Peyton moaned and let her head fall into her arms on the desk.

"Yeah, He wasn't gonna help me, either," Trace said dryly. "When I asked what the hell her problem was, she just kept laughing and saying she thought I'd like it. A nice eighteenth birthday present, a little early."

"And you were already nineteen." Peyton's voice was muffled through her arms. "She never was good about keeping up with birthdays."

"I'm fine with that. I'd have rather she forgot my existence. After that, I knew I couldn't stay. Any woman who would sit back and watch her own son get molested in his sleep was evil. But what could I tell you to explain why I was going?"

"The truth?" Peyton raised her head and looked at him with such hurt in her eyes, it killed him. "I thought you were just done with me, with the family. Her, I get. But me? Even Bea? The ranch? I thought you were just . . . too old to deal with a kid sister anymore. And Bea was still practically a baby. I thought you were sick of playing man of the house and wanted a fresh start, damn whoever it hurt."

It needled him that she wasn't entirely wrong, when he stepped back to look at his feelings. While staying with Sylvia had no longer been even remotely possible, he also hadn't been ready to carry the burden of the ranch, of his sisters, of the family's well-being.

And that shamed him. "I left you with her. The whole time, it never occurred to me that while I was saving my own hide, I left you behind."

Peyton huffed out an unsteady breath. "Yeah, well . . . at least I didn't have anyone groping me."

There were other violations, like trust and safety, she'd endured instead.

"I'm sorry. I was an adult, and I should have put my feelings aside and stuck it out."

Peyton stretched her neck, then her arms. "Hardly. You couldn't have made her change, couldn't have kicked her off the property, and couldn't have taken us with you. So in the end, not much would have been different. We would have been stuck and you would have, too. Your getting out was probably what saved us all."

"How do you figure?" Relieved she didn't seem to harbor intense anger about it, he settled a little.

"I stopped hoping you would step up and did it myself." She shot him a quick grin. "Lazy ass."

"Management was your style, not mine. Daddy's desk

looks good with you behind it." And it was true. Trace loved to ride, loved to work with the horses, but in the end he wasn't a businessman. Haggling the price of a horse wasn't the same as running a ranch, and Peyton was ready to do both.

"So." Peyton blew a piece of hair out of her eyes, tucked it behind her ear. "Now that we've had our little heart to heart, I have one more question."

"Anything."

"Who's Seth's mom?"

"Anything but that." He stood quickly, afraid the openness he felt would reveal his one other shame and he'd let it all flood out. A man could only take so much kumbayah for one day. "Speaking of, he'll be getting up from his nap soon."

"Off you go, Daddy Dearest." Peyton waved at him, already engrossed with her computer. Probably adding up the astronomical figures of Flint's offer, and how far out of Sylvia's hole it would dig them.

He accepted the dismissal and bounded up the stairs, hearing Seth the closer he got to the top. Turning to the left, he entered the nursery and just stood, watching his son babble to himself and play with his toes in his crib. Safe and sound, perfect and pure.

"Well, little man, looks like we've got some work ahead of ourselves." He walked over and picked Seth up, taking him to the changing table. "Our little run-in with Ms. Jo earlier didn't go so well."

Seth batted at his father's sleeves as he changed the diaper.

"Somehow, we'll figure this out. I mean, how can she resist a pair of handsome Muldoon men? It would be downright criminal, wouldn't it?"

Seth whimpered a little, a sure sign he was hungry for a snack.

"You can think of your stomach at a time like this? Well, I suppose that's natural." With a final snap of the onesie, Trace picked Seth up and headed back down the stairs for some puffs and Cheerios. "First, food. Then, women."

It was the natural course of things.

Jo wiped the bar again, for the twentieth time, before she caught herself at the mindless task and put the rag away. At this rate, she would have to refinish the bar top from all the abuse. But her mind wasn't in the game. She wasn't sure if she should be happy with the slow night, so her stupidity wouldn't be on display for that many people, or wishing for a busy night so her mind wouldn't have a chance to wander.

Two days. Two days with nada from Trace. Was this his version of the brush-off? His way of saying, "Now you know, so we're done." Or was he biding his time, figuring out his own move, and would slink back in to apologize somehow?

And more to the point . . . did she want the apology? Or the space?

A smooth breeze washed over her and she watched Jeff walk through the door.

Great. Just what her confused mind needed . . . a night when she had to watch every word she said. Pray God the kid didn't start getting ideas again.

"Hey, Jo." He hopped up on the seat, grinning easily. Apparently for him, the entire incident with Trace was behind him. "How's it going tonight?"

"Good. Great." She forced a tight smile and got down a glass for water. "In for dinner?"

"Dinner and a drink. I'll have a Bud to go with that water you're pouring." He smiled. "I'm in no hurry tonight."

She pulled the beer and handed him the glass, waiting while he looked over the menu.

"What's good tonight?"

"Salad." She laughed a little at his grimace. "Try the bacon cheddar burger, if the thought of rabbit food hurts your manly sensibilities."

"Sold." He handed the menu back and waited while she entered the order in the computer system. "So how are things with you?"

"Good. Great." She held back the wince when she realized that was the same answer she'd given already. And that raised brow of his told her he heard the falseness. "Just really busy right now, with the bar and all. Debating adding on another bartender."

"You could use the break." He paused, then asked, "Are people hassling you?"

"Hassling me?" She looked around the slow-but-steady dining room, full of calm patrons and low music. "No, why?"

"I mean about Trace."

Oh, shit. Here it comes. "Why would they do that?" She grabbed a bar rag and started wiping down the bar again. *I'll refinish the damn thing if I have to.*

"It's just that Judy Plumber saw you two arguing at the Piggly Wiggly the other day, and she said—repeatedly, mind you—that it didn't look like you were having a tussle about frozen entrée selection, if you know what I mean."

He blushed at that. "The last part was her phrase. The 'if you know what I mean' bit. I wouldn't say that."

"I'm sure you wouldn't," she murmured, staring for a moment across the bar until her vision blurred and all she saw were vague blotches of color moving around the room.

A touch on her hand brought her back. Jeff covered her hand with his.

"If there's anything I can do, let me know. If you need

me to talk to him, I can. If you two have broken up or anything, and he's still bothering you, I—"

"Thanks." She said it briskly, not wanting to discuss the situation. Why confirm to him she had zero idea whether they were broken up or not. A week ago, there was nothing to "break up." Suddenly they were in a relationship, and now there was a kid. Poof. Insta-family.

The thought had her going clammy. She squeezed the back of her neck at a pressure point the chiropractor— Regina's husband number four—had showed her until her vision stopped swimming. God, she had to stop thinking like that or she'd pass out.

"Jo?" Jeff stood up, started walking around the bar before she held up a hand.

"I'm fine. Just . . . got a little dizzy. That's all." A weak excuse, at best, but he seemed to buy it and sat down again. Concern didn't leave his face though.

"So you two are . . . done. Right? I just assumed that was what the fight was over."

God, not again. "It's no big deal. Your burger will be out in a minute or so." She turned toward the kitchen, but he caught her wrist as she walked by.

"Jo, come on. If he's out of the picture, then why can't we—"

"Because I don't think about you like that." Rip the bandage off, nice and clean. He wouldn't take the gentle route, so time to cut cleanly. "Look, it's not going to happen with us. Whether I'm with someone else or not has nothing to do with it. I'm begging you, stop thinking about it. It's not a possibility, not even close. So don't ask again, okay?"

She shook her head, so tired now of men and bullshit in general, and walked into the kitchen for a minute. "Stu, can you watch the bar for five? I need a break."

"Yeah, sure. I'll deliver this burger while I'm there." He

headed out with Jeff's plate and left her to a nearly-empty kitchen, her only company the busboy washing dishes in the corner. He didn't even look up as she grabbed a bottle of water from the small fridge for the workers and headed out into the back alley for some air.

The male species were brain dead. It was the only explanation. They were all born idiots, and it was a female's lot in life to knock sense into them, one brick at a time. God, what a tiring thought.

She gave herself four and a half minutes, then headed back inside. She plastered a fake smile on her lips, but when she pushed back into the bar from the kitchen, Jeff was gone. Next to his untouched plate was a twenty and the empty glass that had held his Bud. She prayed he hadn't chugged it, but who knew. Then again, only one beer shouldn't hit him that hard. With a sigh, she walked the plate into the kitchen and scraped the food into the trash.

Waste. All of it.

She hated waste.

Trace sat in the truck, engine still on, arguing with himself.

Go in, face the wrath, face the accusations and the anger. He deserved them all. And if she was done with him, he'd have to walk back out into the night and accept it.

Or turn around and not know for one more day. Have one more night to pretend Jo was his, and he had something to build on.

Trace had never considered himself a coward before. Never bolted at the thought of breaking a horse, of possibly taking hard kicks or being stepped on, knocked around a stall. He'd never shied from a fight. But the thought of knowing, without a doubt, Jo was done with him had him seriously debating turning tail to deal with it another night.

Fuckwit. He growled at himself and jerked the key out of the ignition. Then he took five deep breaths. Just what he would need . . . to fuck up his car so he couldn't actually leave after she kicked him out.

Climbing out of the truck, he paused, hand wrapped around the top of the door as that kid from a few nights ago walked out of Jo's bar and down the street. His hands were stuffed in his pockets, his head hung down low, and his feet stomped like a little boy's going to time out with a pissy attitude.

Trace smirked. *Kicked you out again, huh? Serves you right.*

Then his good humor died. Odds were, he'd be walking in the same footsteps in a few minutes. Cautiously, he opened the door and waited for a moment for some bad omen to slap him in the chest. But when he walked in, the bar was oddly quiet. A few tables had patrons, a server worked here or there, cleaning or talking to customers, but otherwise, slow night.

Jo was behind the bar. She caught sight of him and smiled a little before the expression slid from her face. She grabbed a rag, started to wipe down the bar, then scowled and tossed it away.

"Mind if I sit?"

She motioned to a chair. "Free country."

He eyed her as she started filling a water glass. "Is that to toss in my face?"

"If it is?" she asked, not looking up.

"Can you at least skip the ice?"

She snorted, then sighed. "No, it's not to toss at you. Here." She slid it at him, then poured herself another glass. "I figured water would suit better than a beer for this conversation."

Likely right. He glanced up at the clock over the bar, next to the flat screen. "What time are you closing up?"

"Whatever time I want." When he shook his head, she shrugged. "No sense in paying servers tonight. It's a Tuesday, no sporting events going on tonight, and clearly nobody's killing time out and about. I'll have them lock up at nine."

Have who?

She motioned to someone behind him, and Amanda slid up next to him. "Yeah, boss?"

"What's this *boss* crap?"

Amanda smiled prettily. "Just being dutiful in front of the customers."

Jo rolled her eyes. "You're on bar duty for the rest of the night. Reposition the stations so the other three can cover the floor."

The woman huffed and walked around the bar. "Yeah, so we can all manage the big rush?"

Jo sighed, grabbed her cell phone from under the bar and stuffed it in her back pocket. A back pocket hugging a very fine ass he was hoping he'd get to see again sometime soon.

Wishful thinking, cowboy.

"Just have Stu lock up at the end of the shift, and call me if there's trouble."

"Like there's ever trouble." Amanda shooed them away. "Off you go. Both of you."

He watched her for a minute, then shrugged. If Jo had told her about them, or she'd figured it out, it was fine with him. He never really cared for playing the invisible man anyway.

Chapter Sixteen

Trace followed her up the stairs and into her apartment, keeping a close-but-respectful distance away. Hands off, unlike any other time they'd climbed those stairs. No gentle guidance at the small of her back, no playful pats on her ass or carrying her up on his back. Nothing that said *we're still lovers.*

Not good.

Jo dumped her keys in the dish by the door and set her cell phone on the table, then pointed to a chair. "Sit."

He did so, not wanting to anger the bear by getting out of line. She sat across from him, hands close enough to her body to discourage reaching out for her.

"I feel lied to." And the well-deserved punches started coming.

He winced. "I'm sorry."

"Not done." She held up a hand, then let it fall to the table lightly. "I feel like you held back this whole time. You had something in your life that affected our relationship, and you never let me in on it. I won't say I'm hurt, because that's going too far."

He could see the lie in that written all over her face. But if she needed the small half-truth to soothe the wound, he'd let it go, gladly.

"But honesty is big with me. And I can't tell you how

shitty I feel being lied to. Not just that you did it, but that I didn't expect it, see it coming. Whatever. I pride myself on reading people, and I hate feeling like I got it wrong."

She paused for a long moment, and he hoped that meant it was his turn. "I don't want you to be wrong. I want to be that guy you thought I was. And I'm sorry I didn't mention Seth."

"Seth." She said it slowly, like she was committing the name to memory. "That's his name?"

"Yeah. Seth Muldoon."

She nodded, but said nothing.

"I didn't mention him at first because, well, we didn't really start out with anything that needed full disclosure. I wasn't in a relationship, and you weren't either. Two adults, unattached, attracted to each other . . ." Okay, he needed to skip that part before he got off track. "It just didn't factor in. You didn't seem like you wanted to know more. And I was out to get away from being a dad for a bit. I wasn't about to break out the baby pictures and play Proud Papa while we were recovering in the sack."

She nodded again. "Okay. I see what you mean. Sharing intimate details during something like that isn't really a requirement."

He started to breathe a little easier.

Then her eyes narrowed, and his throat constricted again. "But you wanted more. You were the one pursuing a relationship. A real one, not just fuck buddies."

"Guilty." He stared into her eyes, unblinking. "And I don't regret it for a second."

"But now there's a tiny little elephant in the room. One you failed to mention."

"I'll admit, I screwed this one up." He sighed and ran a hand through his hair. "I just got in the habit of not talking about that side of my life, and by the time I realized I'd left it out . . ."

"You didn't want to scare me off," she said quietly. Her gaze was firmly on the table.

"No, I didn't. After I realized the clusterfuck I'd backed myself into, I had this whole plan to sort of . . . ease you into the idea." As he said it, he realized it was a shit plan. But at the time, he hadn't known what else to do.

Jo said nothing.

"That's wrong. I get it. Full disclosure and confidence that you know what you're walking into is important." He reached across the table, and this time she let him take her hand. He chose to view that as a good sign. "I screwed up. And, spoiler alert, if we stay together for longer than five minutes, I'll screw up again at some point. I'm sorry for it. And I'm hoping you'll give me another shot."

Her eyes drifted down to their joined hands.

"Here's the thing . . ."

His heart, which had only just begun its slow crawl from his gut back into his chest, slid again. He pulled his hand from hers and crossed his arms over his chest, needing the extra layer of armor to absorb the coming blow.

"I'm not into the whole family thing. I don't really have a family, and God knows my example of a mother was . . . well." She smiled a little. "Less than perfect, we'll say."

"You know those spiders that sometimes eat their babies?"

Jo looked mildly grossed out. "Yeah."

"My mom made them look like mother of the year."

"Okay then." The corners of Jo's lips twitched, and he knew she was fighting back a real smile. "So neither of us came from super awesome parenting stock. Still, I'm not really set up, emotionally or physically, to be in a family. A couple?" She lifted her hands, let them fall back again. "I was gearing up to try, but even with that, I had reservations."

"I know," he murmured. He'd driven right through the wall she'd set up against him. He'd do it again, if he had to.

He'd rather she opened the door, though. Much less messy.

"But this?" She laughed, but it wasn't a pleasant sound. "I'm nobody's mother."

"I'm not asking you to be." What the hell did she think he was doing, trolling for nannies? "My son is a major part of my life. He's the biggest part. But he doesn't dictate who I date."

"Doesn't he?" She closed her eyes and sighed. "Would you get into a relationship with someone you didn't trust him with? Someone you really thought would be bad for him?"

"No, of course not."

"So that right there proves the point. I'm no good for a kid. I run a bar, for God's sake. I live above it. I'm not someone you should trust with your child. I don't even think I've ever held a kid before."

She was starting to edge on hysterical again. "Look, when it's us, it's just us. You and me. Nobody else. I had plans on easing you into the whole 'hey, I'm a dad' thing. So let's go back to that plan. We do what we're doing. And eventually, maybe one day you come over and we just hang out, the three of us." He looked a moment at her face, frozen in, well, he hoped not in horror. "I'm not asking you to change diapers or anything."

"Better not." She mimicked his pose, arms across her chest. "Fastest way to end this thing is to hand me a diaper."

"Duly noted." He couldn't help but gain a little hope again at her wording. "So is there still a thing?"

She breathed in deeply and scrunched her eyes shut, the heels of her hands digging into her temples. It almost looked like she was fighting off brain freeze.

"Yes."

The word came out as a squeak and he wasn't entirely sure he'd heard her correctly. "Did you say yes?"

"Don't make me repeat it before I take it back."

"Done," he said quickly and before she could even open her eyes, he was around the table and kneeling next to her chair. "You're not going to regret this. Whatever happens with us, we'll take it one step at a time."

"I'm not Mary freaking Poppins," she warned.

"Well, thank God. She sings way too much for me to handle."

She laughed and grabbed his ears, yanking him up for a blistering kiss. "Any more family members I need to know about? Any wives or foster monkeys lurking in closets?"

"Foster monkey? We don't even think about him like that. Bobo's one of us now."

She squeezed his ears and he yelped. "Nice one, Muldoon."

He kissed her again, and was reaching one hand under her bar uniform shirt when her cell phone rang.

"Leave it." He worked his mouth over to her neck. "Leave it and make me a happy man."

"I will, after I check the . . . shit." She pushed at his shoulders a little. "It's the bar. They wouldn't call if it wasn't something they could handle. Hello?" She stood as she answered the phone, leaving him leaning over her vacant chair, all but heaving in deep breaths.

Cold shower, stat.

"Shit. Is he . . . okay, that's good. How about everyone else? Yeah. Thank God. But why . . . no. No, I absolutely did not. Yeah, two minutes." She shut her phone and set it on the table with deliberate care. Then she turned to him and smoothed down her polo. "Do I look like I've been making out with a horny cowboy?"

"No . . . but I just got started. Gimme a minute or two

and you'll be nice and mussed up." He reached for her, but she stepped back.

"That was the police."

Nothing doused lust quite like the mention of local authority. "What's wrong?"

"Apparently a patron who came in earlier this evening was drunk driving and plowed into the side of someone's house."

"Jesus." He stood and ran a hand down his face to help him refocus. "Whose house?"

"I don't know. Didn't get that far. They're downstairs and want to talk to me." She shrugged and grabbed her keys with one hand, stuffing her cell phone in her back pocket with the other. "Sorry to cut our little make-up session short, cutie."

"Good luck with that whole mess."

"I'm not worried. He only had one beer at my place. They're likely just tracing back to double-check. Everyone's okay, though. Nobody was home, and he was already at the hospital getting the okay from doctors when he was questioned."

"Lucky break." He opened her door and followed her down the stairs. "Want me to wait for you?"

"Nah." She patted his chest. "Go home to—"

"Don't." He flattened her hand against him. "Don't let this start changing things. I offered because I have the time available."

She paused a moment, then nodded. "Okay. You can go home, but we'll continue this another time."

"Okay then. Call me later." He bent to kiss her once more in the dark shadows of the corner before heading for his car.

Damn drunk driver cutting things off short. But he couldn't stop the curving of his lips as he started the engine. It might have delayed things, but their relationship had survived its first scuffle . . . a doozy of one. In his mind, this only meant more promising things in the future.

Despite the abrupt end, it had been a very good night.

Jo forced herself to walk calmly into the bar rather than running full speed the way her pounding heart dictated. Between hearing the words "police" and "in the bar" together in the same sentence, and recovering from that kiss upstairs, she was on the ragged edge of control in so many ways.

She opened the side door and walked in through the kitchen. Stu gave her a long look and a shake of his head.

"Never good for business when the cops show up and don't order something."

"You're right there." She patted his shoulder as she eased by him and walked into the dining area. The place was deserted, though that wasn't totally surprising as it was near closing time. But two officers in khaki uniforms sat at the bar, listening to Amanda as she told some amusing story that had them both laughing.

Good girl. Keep them amused and entertained. Always good to have the law smiling when in your home. And the bar was her home, come hell or high water. "Officers, welcome to Jo's Place."

"You're a Ms. Josephine Tallen, correct?" One of them glanced at the pad of paper in front of him.

"That's me. You can call me Jo." She held out a hand and shook with both as they introduced themselves as officers White and Nelson. "Can I get you something to drink? Water? Soda?" Both politely declined. "Well then, what can I do for you this evening?" She knew why they were there, but she wanted to hear it directly from them.

The one on the left, Officer White, scratched his chin. "We had a bit of an accident earlier tonight. Car drove into the Peckinpaugh place a few miles down the road. Quiet subdivision, not much traffic through there. Guy was heading home."

"I hope nobody was hurt." She also hoped she sounded sincere, since she knew the answer already.

"Minor injuries to the driver, nothing a night spent in observation won't fix. Nobody was home, so only property damage on their side of things."

She nodded, then waited. People who asked a lot of questions tended to look guilty. She had nothing to hide, but she wasn't going to start volunteering information either.

"The driver, a Mr. Jeffrey Effingham, Junior, informed us he'd spent the time before going home here, at the bar."

"He was here earlier, yes." She patted the bar.

They played the same game as she had, waiting to see if there would be any more information. She stuck to her guns.

The man on the right, Officer Nelson, glanced at his partner's pad. "He informs us he ordered dinner and drinks."

"Dinner and a drink. I served him one beer, which he drank. He didn't touch the dinner."

He nodded, then asked, "Was he intoxicated when he arrived?"

"Not at all. He seemed in a pleasant mood, but there was no indication he was under the influence." She gave them both intent stares. "I've been doing this long enough to pinpoint someone under the influence pretty quickly. I don't over-serve my guests, and I don't give someone who's already buzzed fuel for a fire already started."

"Good policy. We've just got one problem here."

Oh, goodie. A problem. "Yes?"

"Mr. Effingham blew a point-one-five at the hospital."

Good Lord. Talk about overkill. "I see."

"He says he didn't stop anywhere else to drink."

"Okay." She leaned against the cooler.

"He tells us you were his only stop before going home."

She shrugged. "I don't know. I didn't follow him."

"He also says, you plied him with beer, encouraging him to drink. Made him believe he was less intoxicated than he was."

"Say what?" She shot off the cooler, causing the beer bottles to rattle. "What, like I funneled his beer while he was fighting me off?"

"Nothing so dramatic, ma'am." The officers glanced at each other, as if silently asking each other how to approach the bear, and how long a stick they should use when poking.

"Just tell me how nondramatic it was, please."

Officer Nelson tried again. "It simply appears as though his story and yours don't quite . . . match."

Officer White added, "He says you served him several beers—he doesn't remember how many. Then he got in his car and drove off."

The little piece of shit. "Do you want his receipt? He paid cash but—"

"That'd help, yes. But he also mentioned the beer was on the house, as you two were close friends. And when he asked if you would call a cab, you encouraged him to drive home, as he was"—the officer glanced at the pad—"just fine to drive."

The *big* piece of shit. Drinks on the house wouldn't show up anywhere. "All I can say is, that's not true. He had one beer, a Bud, which I served him and he paid for, and that was it. I stepped into the kitchen as his meal was being served, and when I came back out, he was gone, his pint glass was empty and his meal was untouched. What he did after leaving here, I don't know. But I do not over-serve my customers. I never have, and I never will."

When Officer Nelson pulled back a little, she realized she'd advanced until her palms were slapped down on the bar. Great way to uphold the image of respectable business owner. Charge cops just doing their job like a bull seeing red.

Relaxing her stance, she gave them an easy smile. "Is there anything else I can help you gentlemen with?"

White looked up and around a little. "Any cameras inside?"

"I've got two inside, but they're focused on the front and back door. Nothing trained on the dining area or bar."

"Hmm." He drummed his fingers on the bar, then scooted the stool back and stood. His partner did the same. "Thank you for your time, Ms. Tallen."

"Jo, please." The formality worried her. People around here didn't *do* formal.

She showed the officers out the door, then locked it. There was nobody else in the bar, and it was only a little before nine.

"Bad news bears?" Amanda poked her head around the corner of the kitchen door.

"I wouldn't say that. Not great news, either." Her hand curled into a fist against her heart. "That little rat bastard tried to blame me for his drunk-driving problem. I can't believe it."

"I can." Amanda shrugged. "Sorry, I didn't think you wanted to hear anything negative about the guy. You seemed like you were getting along with him. And not in the sexy, giddy up cowboy way you are with Trace."

Jo rolled her eyes and headed toward the bar, then froze. "Why is it so quiet in here?"

"Because we're closed?" Amanda said slowly.

Stu peeked around. "Because Amanda sent the other servers home an hour ago."

"Oh. Okay then." She would have given Amanda a small lecture on taking such action when she wasn't technically a manager . . . but tonight her decision was fortunate. Fewer people to see her talking to the cops. Even though she was innocent, it never did any good for business to be associated with the po-po.

"So now what?" Amanda grabbed a take home cup and filled it with ice and diet soda. "Are we going to court?"

"What? No. Calm down, Judge Judy. We gave our side of the story. And our side includes a receipt that shows he ordered exactly one beer."

"Or, shows we only charged him for one beer." Stu followed in Amanda's footsteps, getting a diet soda for himself as well. Apparently, he was watching his liquid calories. "Which could look just as bad, if not worse."

"Mary Sunshine, not helping." She reached for a take home cup herself, filled it with ice, a little soda, then stepped on a stool to find the good stuff on the top shelf, Jack Daniels. "Hello, Jack. I've missed you."

"Ditto." Amanda held up a cup, but Jo shook her head.

"Hell, no. You're getting in your car soon and there is no way I'm giving you a drop."

"One shot won't . . . ah. Right. Well, sucks to be me." She tipped her cup in acknowledgment. "But you can't keep everyone who comes in here from drinking. How are you going to play this?"

"Play what?"

"The nasty ju-ju. Negative press. The bad rap. The—"

Stu nudged her with an elbow. "She gets it."

"Yes, she does," Jo said sullenly. "I thought being an outsider was bad enough. People still aren't sure what to make of me. Now I have to add in *I don't over-serve immature twenty-two-year-old man-children* to the list of things to make clear?"

"Afraid so." Amanda sipped. "I'll vouch for you, but that might not be enough. I've got a financial stake in seeing you pull through this. You're my meal ticket."

"Same here," Stu put in. "You could look back at the receipts of anyone who was here eating dinner when he was. See if the cops would talk to them and get their take. It's usually memorable when idiots drink too much. If other customers can at least acknowledge he looked no worse for the wear, it couldn't hurt your side."

"No, it couldn't. Good call." Though she remembered just how empty the bar had been at that point in the day. Witnesses would be few and far between. But few was a better number than zero. "I'll look into it."

"Now on to the good stuff." Amanda leaned in, elbows on the bar, chin in her hands. "Has Trace talked to you yet?"

"You're relentless." Might as well get it over with. "Okay, fine. Yes, he talked to me. Yes, we worked it out, sort of. And yes, we're still an item. But I don't want to share more. We are what we are, and I'm comfortable with that. We're not pushing to be more, and we're not going to make a big deal about it. Right?" She shot Amanda a hard look.

Unfazed, the other woman smiled, catlike. "Did he convince you in bed? Was it a wrestle to the death?"

"Let's pretend you didn't ask that, and we can move on."

"Thank you," Stu grumbled.

"How are you going to handle the baby?"

Jo's eyes closed at the reminder. Ugh. "Yeah, I'm not sure yet. We're sort of . . . ignoring that elephant in the room. At least for now. That won't last forever, but I'm hoping things will be clearer when we reach that stage."

"Good idea." Stu nodded. "Single parent dating can't be easy. Don't wanna introduce the kid to every woman who comes by. If you're taking time to get to that point, it can't be anything but good."

"Yeah." She didn't know how to explain the whole *wait and see* thing wasn't just for the kid's benefit, but hers as well. But hey, if this approach made her look mature and capable, then she'd grab it.

"Oh!" Amanda's eyes lit up. "Oh, my God, I totally just remembered! This is perfect. Now you can find out who the mystery mama is."

"The . . . no. I'm not even going to ask." Jo sipped her doctored soda and sighed. Jack Daniels, the best man of all.

"I'll tell you anyway. Trace went off to do the rodeo thing, and we all watched from a distance. Marshall is very proud of our local cowboys when they go off and do their own thing, you know." She puffed up a little with town pride. "But he didn't come back all that often, so any news we got about Trace was either through the circuit, or from Peyton. And then one day, poof. He's just back, seemingly for good. Only now, he's got a kid. Which is so weird, because he did not at all seem like the type to play doting daddy." Her eyes went a little soft. "But from the few reports I've heard, they say he's actually really good at it."

"None of that sounds mysterious," Stu pointed out.

"Shush, I'm building. So anyway, we expected to see some buxom blonde trailing behind him any day. But a week went by, then two, and no sign of the kid's mom. So delicate inquiries were made, and it appears nobody knows who the kid's mother is. Not even his family. Or if they do, they're completely quiet about it."

"Does it matter who the mother is?" All this intrigue over one man and his son. It boggled her big city mind.

"Well, no," Amanda conceded. "But I'd just like to be the first—or second, or even third—to know. Spill."

Jo smiled a little wicked smile. "My lips are sealed."

"So unfair!" Amanda posed with a pout, then shrugged one shoulder. "Oh, well. If you need someone to unload your burdens to, my phone is always with me."

"Uh-huh," Jo said dryly. "I'll remember that. Now scoot. I'm closing up." Amanda stood, and Jo gave Stu a pointed look. "You, too, big guy. I appreciate the support, but as Semisonic said, it's closing time."

Amanda started humming the tune as she grabbed her purse and walked out the door. "See ya later!"

Stu waited a moment more, then bent down to buss her cheek. "Call me if you need some muscle. Or call Trace. He's a cocky son of a bitch, but he'll watch out for you."

"Thanks." She patted his arm and followed him to the door. "But I'm a big girl. I can watch out for myself."

"I know you can, but nobody's got panoramic vision. Having someone there to watch your back isn't a weakness, it's a strength." With a wink, he left her alone in the bar.

A strength . . . to depend on someone? She just couldn't wrap her mind around that one. If you needed anyone but yourself, you were that much weaker, weren't you?

Jo scrunched her eyes shut and massaged her temples. The end of a long day was definitely not the time to get philosophical. It was the time to get drunk.

She reached for the best man in her life, Jack Daniels. Jack could watch her back any day.

Chapter Seventeen

Trace popped into the kitchen to check on Emma. "Everything going okay in here?"

She shooed him back until his toes were at the edge of the tile. "Out of my kitchen or there'll be hell to pay."

He obediently watched as she fluttered around the kitchen, pausing every so often at an appliance or by a cutting board, never in one place for long. Like a bee moving from flower to flower, constantly in motion.

"Is everything going to be ready?"

Emma shook her head. "The boy brings a girl home and acts like suddenly I don't know what I'm doing."

"I'm sorry, Emma." He chanced losing a limb and stepped behind her to kiss her cheek. She scowled, but leaned into the gesture. "I'm nervous, okay?"

"I know. Which is why you're still breathing while you stand in my kitchen. Out."

He gave her a grateful smile and headed out, pausing at the doorway to ask, "You sure you won't eat dinner with us?"

"Buncha young people talking too loud and constantly using those i-whatevers you have attached to your hand all through dinner? I think not." She wiped a strand of hair back with her wrist, never losing her grip on the butcher's knife she wielded with expert care. "Besides, who would keep Seth occupied upstairs?"

Good point. "Seth will probably sleep through dinner anyway." It was one of the main reasons he'd asked Jo to dinner so late in the evening. He wanted a chance to spend time with her on his turf, but knew having a typical family dinner would scare her off. There was nothing like a teething ten-month-old who currently hated his high chair and drooled like he was paid by the ounce to dampen the mood. So it would just be the five of them: Peyton and Red, him and Jo, and Bea.

Bea, of course, had no problem being a fifth wheel. As far as she was concerned, it meant she got more attention. Always a win with little sis.

"If he gets to be too much, just let me know."

Emma rolled her eyes. "I had you three how many years ago? I know what I'm doing. Now if you want dinner to actually start on time—which is hours too late, if you ask me—you need to go and leave me in peace."

"Thanks, Emma," he said and left her to finish up.

He found Red at the dining room table, setting placemats down.

"How'd you end up setting the table?" Trace inched a candlestick to the left, then stepped back. Too far. He inched it the other way.

Red watched him, one brow cocked. "You need a ruler?"

"Do you have—bite me." He flipped Red off and stepped away from the table before he started rotating all the placemats a quarter turn or some equally ridiculous shit. "Sorry for wanting things to be nice. Not all of us can woo our women in the barn."

"Takes real skill," Red agreed. "Maybe someday you'll be man enough."

Trace kicked at him, but Red was already out the door and heading toward the living room, laughing.

"What could he possibly have to laugh at?" Peyton strolled in, looking like a hot mess.

"Why haven't you showered? Jesus, Peyton." He checked his watch. "She's going to be here in like ten minutes."

"Jo's not stuck up. She won't care what I look like. It's just us at home. We're not carpooling to the Ritz or anything." She sat down in her usual chair and reached for a carrot from the plate Emma had set out.

He debated slapping her hand away and knew that was too much. "I give up. I'm going to go watch for her. . . ." He listened a moment. "That's her. Do not embarrass me, or I'll be forced to break out The Pictures." The ones from her Rodeo Princess days. Oh, yeah. That was a real threat.

Peyton smiled smugly. "I burned them."

"Not the copies I hid in my room before I ever left home." He had the pleasure of watching her face drain of color before he headed to the front door.

He stepped out on the porch and waited for Jo to climb out of her car. She did, a simple skirt flowing around her knees. She adjusted one strap of her tank as she straightened and ran a hand over her hair. Down again, the way he liked it. A river of black silk just begging for his fingers to play with. When she looked up and saw him, she smiled. But the gesture held a hint of wariness that he wanted to erase.

"Hey." Trace held out a hand and led her up the last two steps. "Welcome to the ranch."

She glanced around, taking in what little she could see in the last light of day. "I've never been here before. Looks huge."

"It's a good size, though not the largest in the state by

far. Definitely not what we might call huge." He led her through the front door and waited while she took in the house. He tried to see it through her eyes.

The natural wood and warm tones of the floor clashed with the industrial sculptures and sleek artwork his mother had picked out for the space before her death. Sylvia had insisted that spending money so the place looked as if they were already loaded made them more attractive to prospective clients. Since their father had been little more than a doormat where Sylvia was concerned, she'd let loose a decorator and—in Trace's mind—ruined the natural appeal of the house.

But it hadn't been his house to say otherwise. Still wasn't, no matter what anyone said. Peyton didn't have an eye for stuff like that, or else she likely would have changed it months ago. Not that they really had the money, anyway.

Maybe if they sold some of that artwork . . .

"The house is awesome. And, just for frame of reference, my first apartment in San Francisco could have fit on your front porch." She held out a bottle he hadn't noticed. "This is for you guys. A little nicer vintage than what we normally stock at the bar. Not many wine drinkers in the area, but I thought . . ."

"I love a good white." Bea sailed—not walked, sailed—down the stairs and enveloped a confused Jo in a hug. Her runt of a dog followed in her wake and sat a short distance off, looking forlorn. Though Trace thought that might just be depression due to the fact that he was wearing a collar designed to resemble a man's shirt collar and tie. The dog had no dignity left. And why was he even over here? Bea had her own place now. Why didn't she use it?

"Thank God you're here. Save me from the testosterone and horse talk. Remind me of my days in civilization. Bring me some city charm."

"City charm. An oxymoron if ever I heard one." Peyton lounged in the doorway, one shoulder propped against the frame. She nodded to their guest. "Hey, Jo."

"Hey, Peyton." She smiled and waved, not seeming at all put out by the casual welcome. "Hey, Red."

"Jo," Red said, walking up behind Peyton and sliding one arm around her waist. Trace watched as his sister's face softened just a little, and she leaned back into him. Despite all his initial concerns, he knew they were all but perfect together.

Bea took the wine from her hand. "I'll just go put this on the table so we can have it with dinner."

Jo nodded, then looked around a little more. Her eyes caught on something, and he turned to see what had snagged her attention.

Seth's play gym. He'd done his best to remove reminders of the child from the first floor, to give her some time to breathe and relax. But he'd missed that one. Damn it. He took her arm and steered her toward the dining room.

"Emma's so glad to have company, she's probably outdone herself. But she always says that and manages to top herself the next time. She made chicken—you like chicken, right?" He was babbling. Damn it, why did he have to let this build in his mind so much until he all but ruined it with nerves?

Either she sensed his unease or she just naturally knew what he needed. Jo placed a hand on his cheek and leaned in for a slow, sensual kiss. There was heat, but it was a slow burn, not a flash of fire. And it ended too soon as she pulled back and smiled up at him.

"Thanks for inviting me to dinner."

"Yeah. No problem." Yeah? No problem? Jesus, he was a regular Casanova. "I'm glad you were able to come out. I worried about you the other night, leaving you to deal with that mess."

"What mess?" Peyton walked in, passing them on the way to the kitchen.

"Just a customer giving us a little trouble." Jo waved it off and sat in the chair he held out for her.

Red waited for Peyton to return and held out her chair as well. Peyton paused, an amused smile on her lips. "We should have company over more often. I could get used to this kinda treatment."

He bent down and bussed her lips, using the opportunity to slap her playfully on the ass. "Get in the chair, woman."

Peyton slid easily into her seat and leaned over to stage-whisper at Jo, "He knows I love it when he plays caveman. If you stick around long enough after dinner, you might get to watch the clubbing before he drags me—"

"Dinner!" Emma called out cheerfully, backing into the dining room carrying a platter.

"Thank you, God," Trace muttered, and shot his sister a look. One that his sister knew meant *Don't ruin this for me.*

She smiled brightly and winked. "Sure you don't wanna stay, Emma?"

"I've got a date tonight with *Matlock* reruns and that handsome fella upstairs." She patted the table next to the platter. "Enjoy!"

"What was the trouble?" Bea took her seat and accepted the bowl of peas Red passed her. She spooned some on her plate, still watching Jo. "Nothing serious, I hope?"

"I don't think so." Jo took a slice of bread. "A patron left our place, somehow managed to drink until he was intoxicated somewhere else, then drove into the side of a building."

"The Peckinpaugh house." Red nodded. "Heard about that this morning when I went into the feed store. J. J. Effingham was drunk as a lord when they got on scene. Though that might have been what saved him, since he was so relaxed when he crashed. His body didn't have a chance to tense up. A relaxed body doesn't get hurt as badly as a tense one."

"But nobody was seriously injured?" Peyton asked.

"No. Only now . . ." Jo glanced down at her plate as if trying to debate how far to go. Then she shrugged and reached for her glass to hold out to Trace. "Now he's claiming I'm the one who gave him the alcohol. The implication is that I plied him with drinks until he didn't realize how drunk he was, and then I made him feel like he had to drive home by not getting him a cab."

"What a jerk!" Bea held her own glass out for wine. "Thanks, bro. That sneaky bastard. What's the kid's name again? We should send Trace and Red out there to beat him up."

"What is this, *West Side Story*?" Red laughed. "You can't just send us out like thugs whenever you're mad at someone, Bea."

She huffed. "What's the point of brothers—pseudo-brothers included—if they won't play muscle for you?"

"Poor thing," Peyton whined sarcastically. "The world is against you."

Bea turned her shoulder to Peyton and stared directly at Jo. "The police understand your side of things, right?"

"Well . . ."

Trace felt the stirrings of something cold in his blood. "This isn't causing trouble, is it?"

Jo sighed. "No. I'm handling it. Nothing a few receipts and some witnesses can't fix."

"I know the Effinghams a little," Peyton said, staring at her glass for a moment. "Not well, of course. God knows I wouldn't be running in the same circle as the parents, and J. J. was too young for me to be in school with. But they're all over the town. On every committee or board that pops up."

"Sounds like they could cause some trouble," Trace said easily, though he wanted to wring the kid's neck.

"They're the kind of parents who think their kid can do no wrong. Or, if they see the wrong, they'll step in to minimize the damage to save face." Peyton shrugged. "Appearances, you know. She might have gotten along with mama, if Sylvia wasn't a drunk. Same theory on the appearance bit."

There was silence around the table. Mentioning their mother in such a casual way was a new thing for them all. Then Red spoke. "If you need something, Jo, let us know."

"Thanks." She smiled widely. "So, Bea, what's going on this week in the land of the soaps?"

Bea launched into her favorite topic—other than herself—and kept the conversation moving at an easy pace with funny quips about evil twins, faked suicides, and hidden jewels. But it was minutes before Jo relaxed. Trace reached under the table and found her knee, squeezing lightly in a reassuring gesture. Her leg inched toward his, brushing lightly against him.

He resisted the urge to pull that caveman stunt Peyton had accused Red of not ten minutes earlier.

But it was a near thing.

Jo resisted the urge to lick the dessert plate. Instead, she scooted the plate toward the center of the table. "That was amazing. Emma is a genius."

"Which she never lets us forget." Peyton winked. "Ask anyone. Emma runs this place, hands down. We couldn't function without her."

"Wouldn't want to," Trace put in. "She practically raised us. And we weren't an easy trio."

"Speak for yourself. I, for one, was an angel." Bea batted her lashes.

Peyton coughed into her napkin, "Bullshit."

The angelic moment was shattered when Bea shot her sister two middle fingers.

"Ah, sibling love." Jo sighed and rested her elbows on the table. "I never got to experience this. How about you, Red?"

"Nope. Only child here, too. Gotta say, walking into this family was an eye-opener."

Peyton elbowed him. "A good one, right?"

Red exaggerated a wince that made Jo smile. "Of course, sweetheart. A great one. A brilliant eye-opener."

Trace gagged a little.

"Oh, please. Like you two aren't adorbs over there," Bea accused. "Just bring Seth down and you'd be the cutest little fam . . . ily. . . ." she ended lamely, realizing her mistake a beat too late.

There was a moment when the only sound was the huffing of Bea's little dog-child panting under the table.

"Well, this was great," Peyton said, pushing back from the table. "We should do it again. Jo, you need to come during the day so you can get the full tour. Do you ride?"

"Ride? A horse? I'm more of a subway kinda gal, myself."

"We'll get you up on one. Everyone learns to love it. Except that one," she added with distain, pointing at Bea.

Red gave Bea a look Jo couldn't quite interpret, then reached over and started gathering plates. "It's our KP night. So you guys are free to escape."

"We're free! We're free! Come on, Milton. Let's go watch whatever's on the DVR." Bea sauntered out toward the living room without a backward glance. The dog trotted behind her, tiny legs working furiously to keep up with Bea's mile-long stride. The tinkle of his tags, like a bell, made Jo smile.

"That dog is something else."

"I'm still not sure it is a dog, frankly." Trace looked disgusted at the whole thing, which made Jo swallow a laugh. "But she loves that damn animal. I don't have the heart to tell her no dog likes getting dressed in the morning and . . . *accessorizing.*" He broke out the air quotes for that last one and shuddered.

She started to crack a joke, but broke off when he glanced around her.

"Sorry, hold on a sec." He rubbed her arm and walked around her and up to the stairs. "Yeah?"

"Sorry." Emma's voice, unnaturally soft, came back. "But he's having a hard time going back down and I thought maybe you could just give him five minutes. But if not, I—"

"I'll be right there." He gave her an apologetic smile. "Sorry. I didn't wanna play Daddy tonight but needs must."

"Go, it's fine." It made her smile a little that he didn't hesitate to drop her like a hot potato because his son needed some cuddle time. She might not get it from a maternal standpoint, but she did know it made him a good man.

A good man deserved a chance, didn't he? Was she tossing the, well, the man out with the baby and the bathwater?

She took a breath and held it, listening. Footsteps above, and they sounded like they were moving in a circle. Curiosity tugged at her, and she tried hard to battle it back.

But then, damn it, she heard what she thought was the start of a lullaby, and she couldn't resist. Taking the stairs slowly, trying not to creak, she snuck up the steps. She wasn't sure what to expect, but it felt as if she'd left one house and entered another. The sleek, modern artwork and showroom quality furniture had given way to a simple, comfortable, lived-in family room. The carpet was a beige shag, the couches were a dark brown, and there was a flat screen hung on one wall. From the top of the stairs, she could count several doors. Some to bathrooms, she assumed, others to bedrooms. Pausing, she waited to hear more of the song Trace crooned to his son.

Emma's silver-tipped head popped over the top of the couch, nearly startling Jo into falling back and tumbling down the stairs. The woman's grin was infectious, and she tilted her head toward the door with a sliver of light peeking through the opening.

Jo took this for an invitation and crept over to the door, pushing it open just a little. And what she saw made the breath catch in her throat.

Trace walked the floor with his son over one shoulder. The little boy looked sad, almost angry, but he was quiet. One fist was up by his mouth, the fingers red and a little wet as if he'd been sucking or biting on them. His cheeks were flushed, his eyes watchful. They caught sight of her before Trace did. The boy struggled against Trace's hold, twisting to watch her.

Trace glanced over and saw her.

"Sorry," she mouthed and started to step back. But he shook his head and motioned her in.

Frozen, Jo tried to move—*pick a direction and just go!*—but she couldn't. Couldn't step back, couldn't move in. She was completely tied to the doorway, as if unable to make a choice one way or the other.

Sensing her problem, Trace walked over and held out the hand not cradling the boy to his shoulder. "He's fine, just a little cranky. Another tooth coming in."

"Ah," she said, as if that made any sense to her at all. But when he took her hand, she let him lead her into the room.

"Seth," he said quietly, turning so the boy faced her over his shoulder, "this is Jo. Remember her? You scared her at the grocery store last week."

"He did not," she whispered back. Seth watched her with big eyes, exactly like Trace's deep blue ones. He was a miniature of his daddy. In twenty years, he'd be beating women off with a stick.

Or not. She smiled at that and tentatively reached up. His little fuzzy head, with wisps of dark hair curling around his ears, begged to be smoothed over. Then she snatched her hand back. Not her kid. Not hers to touch.

"It's okay," Trace murmured. "He likes the attention."

Once more, she lifted her hand and let it smooth from the boy's forehead down to his back. She was going on instinct, mostly. Seth moved into the caress, like a faithful dog wanting another scratch behind the ears. Okay, maybe she shouldn't be comparing someone's baby to a dog, but she was adrift on the whole kid thing.

"Hey, Seth," she said softly. "I hear you're not having fun with a tooth. I'm sorry to hear that."

Between Trace's gentle sway and the soft words, it seemed Seth struggled to keep his eyes open.

"You look a lot like your daddy, you know." She glanced up to see Trace watching her. "Lucky for you, he's a handsome guy. So it seems like you scored the genetic lottery on that one." Taking a chance, she let one fingertip trail down his forehead, between his eyes to land on the tip of his nose with a near-imperceptible touch.

The touch seemed to soothe him, and he closed his eyes, nestling one ear against his father's shoulder, and smiled a little. Or maybe it was gas. Jo couldn't help but smile back. He was so darn cute, all snuggly and bundled up in his cowboy pajamas with feet meant to look like boots. What kind of woman could resist the picture these two men made?

"He's pretty calm now. You want to hold him?"

And then the spell was broken. She stepped back, knocking into a table holding a lamp. She managed to reach back and grab the lamp before it crashed to the floor, but the damage was already done. Seth's head jerked up, and his lower lip quivered.

Shit.

"I'm gonna get going." She backed up, rapped her elbow on the open door and cursed under her breath. Then louder, "Sorry, I didn't mean to say that. I'm gonna . . . thanks for dinner."

The sound of Seth's wail and Trace calling her name chased her down the stairs. Bea poked her head up from the living room couch and called to her as well, but Jo didn't even bother waving.

Escape. It was the only thing she could think of. Escape the domestic bliss she'd nearly slid into like a comfortable pair of sweatpants. No. No, no, no. Not her thing. And she'd almost forgotten. She didn't do the kid thing. She was nobody's stepmother.

Damn it. How had she let herself be lured into that?

She settled her bag on the passenger seat and started the car. She waited for one moment, then two, but realized what she was doing and forced herself to back up and turn around in the dirt road. She didn't need Trace chasing after her. And waiting for him to come down behind her smacked of manipulation.

So back to the drawing board. It annoyed her she hadn't seen this coming. Hadn't realized the two males together—one big, one little—would hit her so hard. Make it so easy to forget what she needed in life, what she wanted.

Back to just using each other for sex, she supposed. It wasn't a bad idea, over all. But now it felt a little hollow. A little shallow compared to what she'd just left.

What she'd just left wasn't for her. She was a bar owner who lived alone and liked it. The end.

She just had to keep repeating that to herself.

Chapter Eighteen

Jo opened the bar the next morning and greeted her first two patrons of the day with something close to dread.

"Officers," she said, holding the door she'd just unlocked open for them. "Here for lunch?"

They both shook their heads, though Nelson gave her an apologetic look. "Sorry, ma'am."

"Jo. And it's all right." She walked back behind the bar and set two coasters down in front of them. "Something to drink while we chat?"

Nelson ordered a water, White a soda. She poured both, got herself another water, and leaned in. None of her servers would barge in on the obviously private conversation. But still, she'd rather keep things as quiet as possible. "Do you have more questions for me?"

"First off, do you have the receipt from the other night?" White took a sip of his soda. "And any names you could think of that would serve as witnesses in the restaurant that night?"

"I do. Just a second." She headed to her tiny office and came back with a folder containing the few scraps. "It's a copy of the receipt. Is that a problem? I have the original but I'd like to keep it for my normal records."

"No, though I wouldn't toss out the original just yet." White took the folder and opened it, glancing down the list. "Thanks for this. Saves us a little legwork and helps to close things faster."

"Best all around," Jo said, agreeing with that. "Can I do anything else for you?"

"Well . . ." White looked around, then leaned in a little farther. "Just so you know, there's been a petition to the city council to shut you down."

"What?" she shrieked, then clamped a hand over her mouth. She saw her servers staring at her from the back wall, but she waved off their curious glances. "Sorry," she tried again, quietly. "Why in the world would—"

"Jeffrey Junior's mom." White shrugged, as if it wasn't any big deal. "She's sticking by his story that you're an alcohol pusher. Took advantage of the kid, led him astray, it's not his fault, yadda-yadda."

"I'm assuming she thinks if she gets you shut down, or even just tosses suspicion at you, it makes her son's story look more legit." Nelson gave her a sad smile. "She's got some pull, I hate to say. Unfortunately, that's not police business. What we do doesn't have too much to do with licenses and the like. I don't know how easily she could have you actually shut down for any period of time, but the odds are good she will at least give you a headache."

"I've got aspirin," she murmured, and they both chuckled. She stared off into the distance for a moment. "So what, I have to just go plead my case to the city council? Tell them my side of the story and let them know I'm not an irresponsible businessowner?"

"Well . . ." White said.

Jo's stomach plummeted.

"She's also mentioning something about you running a bordello in the bar, or just above the bar, or something like that. That men are seen coming and going often."

Jesus. A bordello. What was this, 1880? "I don't even know how to respond to that."

Nelson looked completely uncomfortable with the whole thing. "We are supposed to give a quick glance around today, with your permission. We don't have a warrant, but it was asked that we try."

Jo shrugged. "You can look wherever you want." She dug in her pockets and held out her key ring by one key. "My apartment is upstairs. Lock up behind you when you're done."

The officers looked at each other, as if debating the wisdom of taking her at face value. Then Nelson took the keys with an outstretched palm. "We won't be long."

"I'm sure you won't." The implication of *because I have nothing to hide* wasn't lost on either of them, she noted, as they nodded.

The moment the door closed behind them, she turned on her heel and walked through the kitchen, ignoring Stu's questioning look, and straight into the back alley. She doubted anyone would follow her.

And there, in the quiet morning, she bit her lip to fight back the tears

She'd been praying this was her fresh start. She'd been here a year, damn it. And suddenly, because one stupid kid had done something dumb, and one community leader decided she didn't want her precious boy to face the consequences, the city was ready to toss her out on her ass.

She pinched her arm to focus on something other than the tears. Focus on the anger. Focus on her resentment at being treated like a second-class citizen because she was new. Not being considered trustworthy, despite her spotless records and fair business management.

She'd show them. Maybe someone else would take this as a sign to skip town and start over somewhere else. She wasn't going to. Hell, no. She'd been drawn to this place, this bar, before she even knew what the town's name was.

And she wasn't going to give up on it without a fight. This was her chance to grow some roots, and she was doing it.

Jeff—J. J.—freaking Effingham be damned.

Trace walked into the bar, hands in his pockets. He had a real purpose for being there, other than seeing Jo. He was grabbing lunch to take back to the ranch, giving Emma a break and thanking her for babysitting the night before. But still, he could have chosen the diner, or one of the few fast food joints in town. Jo was the main draw, and he had no shame in admitting it.

"Hey, cutie." Amanda walked up and grabbed his arm, pulling him around the bar and behind it.

"Should I be back here?" he said, looking around.

"You should because I say you should." She pushed open the swinging doors to the kitchen, firm grip still on his arm. "Hey, Stu. Bye, Stu."

The massive man at the cooktop didn't even turn to look at them as they passed behind. Either the man was really intense about his work, or he just wasn't easily fazed.

"She's out there, and she's had a really shitty morning. So go do something to change it." Amanda halted at a door that clearly led outside.

"What happened?"

"Cops were back. They dropped off her keys with me and took off, so I have no clue what's going on now. But you need to go out there and fix it. Whatever it is, fix it." With that, she planted both hands on his back and shoved until he was out the door and into the alley.

Jo's head snapped up from her position leaning against the opposite brick wall. "What are you doing out here?"

He looked behind him, but Amanda's face was already gone from the small window on the door. "Your head server is really pushy."

Jo smiled a little. "Yeah, she is." She pushed off the wall and walked toward him. "Sorry I ran out last night."

"Too much, right?" He rubbed her upper arms with his hands, pulling her into his chest for a hug. "I hadn't intended . . . but then he needed me and I couldn't—"

"It wasn't that. I mean, I get why you went up to him. I'm not upset by that. It was the right thing to do. I just shouldn't have gone in there. I wasn't . . . ready for it."

"Ready for it. You need to psych yourself up for meeting a kid?" He dropped his head until his cheek rested on the top of her hair.

"Yes, actually. I told you, kids and I don't get along. I made Seth cry."

"Honey," he said with a chuckle, "he was already in a horrible mood. I made him cry ten minutes later by stepping on his stuffed dragon. He's teething. Anything and everything ticks him off right now. It's nothing personal. Five seconds before he adored you."

"But I scared him. I don't know what to do with kids. I've never really wanted them. You know?" She pulled away so their chests were apart but their legs were still tangled together. "I feel like girls hit this wall in their twenties where they suddenly know they want kids, and it's time to find the right guy to make them with. They pass by the baby section of Target and they get all gooey over the shoes or they see a commercial for formula and they tear up and whine about how they want one. And I never did that."

"That's a good thing. Seth doesn't need any more shoes." Her lips twitched, and he knew he had her. "I don't need someone to play mommy. I'm his father, and although I have help, I think I've been doing an okay job by myself. I'm not in this for a stepmom. I'm in it for you. How we fit together, both you and me, and then the three of us, that'll come later. Or it won't. But don't let this one experience stop you trying, please?"

She took a deep breath and let it out, burrowing back into him. "Fine," she muttered into his neck.

He dropped a kiss on the top of her head, next to her ponytail. "Thank you."

She let out a laugh full of sarcasm. "I'd invite you up to have some lunch, but since I'm busy running a bordello upstairs, I don't think I have room for another man."

"A what? Run that by me again, please?"

She stepped back and wiped a hand down her face, clearing the lingering emotion from her eyes as she did. Now she was back to Bar Owner Jo, tough as nails and nothing penetrated the shield. She explained about the city council, the mother taking her son's side, the hints and implications of some makeshift whorehouse upstairs above the bar. The idea that she wasn't a responsible business owner and shouldn't have a liquor license.

"That son of a bitch," he muttered, wanting to put his fist through a wall. But since he was surrounded by brick, he wisely decided not to try. "That slimy, underhanded, lying sack of—"

"Yes, yes. All that and more." Jo waved it away. "That's not the point. The point is, I need to figure out what to do to make this as uncomplicated as possible. The charges are false, and I know I won't lose my license over this. But it could get annoying very fast if I don't just head this off at the pass. Lock down the rumors once and for all."

It hurt her, he could see it. Despite the shield she'd put up, he could see the fact that she had to even bother defending herself stung. "I'm sorry, baby."

She stepped back from his comforting hand and shook her head. "It happens. And I'll make it go away. I just have to figure out how."

Knowing snuggle time was over, he stuck his hands in

his pockets to keep from instinctively reaching for her again. "Let me know if there's anything I can do to help. I know people . . ." Not many, not since he'd been gone almost a decade. But he knew who to ask to find out information. Get the names of more influential people.

"I'll let you know." She put on a smile, a little strained at the corners, but a smile nonetheless. "Did you come for lunch?"

He opened the door for her, and waited for her to walk in front of him. "I owe Emma a meal."

"We'll make it a good one."

Jo flipped the TV off, then turned and found Trace dead asleep beside her. He'd given her his baby-free night again, and instead of jumping on each other like wild monkeys, they'd lounged in bed and watched a movie. Lightly, she traced the planes of his face. He'd been so exhausted when he showed up on her doorstep. Not that he'd said a word. But when she suggested a movie, he'd jumped at the chance to slide horizontal and do nothing but veg.

He'd lasted ten minutes before she'd felt the deep, even breathing beneath her ear that signaled he was out cold. The man was working too hard. The ranch required so much of his time, energy, emotions. His connection to the place was intense. And though she didn't have personal experience with family, she'd watched her mother struggle to be a single parent . . . in between husbands, anyway. Even with the support of his family, she knew Trace took the brunt of the parenting himself. Which he should.

Not for the first time, Jo wondered where Seth's mother was. Single moms were a dime a dozen. But single fathers . . . a little more uncommon. Had the mother walked out on them? Had she broken Trace's heart when she left? Or maybe she'd left . . . permanently. An accident, or illness. Jo's heart clenched a little for Seth, thinking he might never know his mother.

Either way, she knew it added to Trace's overall appeal that he met the challenge of single fatherhood head on, with gusto, and even pleasure. That was the kicker. Nobody could say he regretted his son, or didn't enjoy being with him. Those two were peas in a pod. True love.

Love.

She rolled onto her back and stared at the ceiling. Love was such a complicated, messy thing. Attachments and relationships were bad enough, but love? No. Love meant permanency of a completely different kind. A kind she absolutely wasn't going to be talked into.

Trace straightened beside her, shifted, and then rolled over until his arm wrapped around her middle in an unconscious gesture of possession. She loved when he did that. As if his body knew they shouldn't be apart.

Okay, so it wasn't in keeping with her *no strings attached* motto. But every girl has a fantasy. And hers just happened to be . . . this.

Dangerous waters, girl. Jo had to tread carefully, or else she'd drown in a pool she'd never even intended to swim in.

Trace woke up to Jo's soft body curled up in the protective shell he'd unconsciously created in his sleep. He'd been so dead on his feet he hadn't let her even think about sex. But after a quick catnap, he was feeling just a little more in the mood. One hand snuck in the tight wedge she'd created of her body and found her breast, thumbing the nipple.

She stretched and yawned, twisting in the hollow of his body to face him. His hand cupped the heavy weight of her breast, kneading the flesh filling his hand.

"Mmm." She smiled with her eyes still closed. "Best way to wake up ever."

He said nothing, but played her body with hands that knew every inch of her. But as his fingers walked their way down to her stomach, she switched it up and flipped on top of him.

"My turn. You were beat. Let me play."

He might be a slow cowboy, but he wasn't an idiot. He propped himself back against the headboard, arms behind his head, and watched as she explored his chest with her hands, her lips, teeth. Every nip brought a restrained shiver down his spine, until she reached his hips. The pressure there had him fighting a buck.

And then she took his balls in her hand, working them gently, using just enough pressure to have him groaning. And when she took the head of his erection in her mouth, tongue swirling over the sensitive skin, he had to bite back a whimper that would have made Milton proud.

"God, Jo . . . oh, man." He couldn't resist any longer. As her mouth slowly advanced down the length of him, his hands cupped the back of her head. He could have directed her, chosen his pace. She was responsive in bed, receptive to what he needed, but he let her choose.

There was power in submission, he'd learned.

She worked him with her tongue, adding in her hand to cover more of him, squeezing in rhythm.

"Jo . . . close . . ."

She hummed in answer, and he lost any hope of holding out longer. He gave a short warning, then pulsed his release into the warmth of her mouth.

She pulled him back down from the high, staying with him until he tugged gently at her hair. Then she crawled up his body like a cat and collapsed beside him, one leg over his thigh, arm over his chest, head on his shoulder.

"When I can move again, your turn. 'Kay?" he asked, voice slurred. He couldn't gather the energy to enunciate.

"Deal." Jo shifted and smoothed a hand down Trace's chest. "I suppose while you're sleepy and satisfied, now would be a good time to get some intel on Seth's mother."

Trace stiffened, then forced himself to relax. "What intel?"

She laughed and rolled tighter into him. "No, I'm kidding. She seems to be a mystery to everyone. I assume your family knows about her but—"

"They don't."

"No?" The surprise in her voice shook off the last of the sexual cobwebs.

Be more open. Be honest. Last time he'd withheld info, he'd nearly lost her. Now was the time to give the story and let the chips fall. "I was too embarrassed to tell them, when I first got home. Now it's sort of a matter of pride to keep Peyton guessing."

"Sibling stuff," Jo scoffed.

"Partly. But mostly, I'm still embarrassed."

"You don't have to go into it. It doesn't matter."

"It does, and it doesn't. Let's try the honesty route this time." He grasped her hand over his chest and pressed it down. There was no way she could miss how his heart hammered in his chest, but he wasn't about to let go. "Seth's mom, Rose—"

"Rose," she said quietly.

"Yeah. Rose. She was married."

"And you were, what, her rebound? A divorce celebration?"

"Maybe I would have been, if she'd been divorced. She's still married now. Or at least, I assume she is."

Jo remained silent. He wanted so badly to tilt his head down and see what her face said, but he couldn't. He might not finish otherwise. So he plowed on, unknowing. Going on faith.

"I met her on the road. Liked her. She's a likable woman, not just a hot piece. Never thought it'd be anything permanent. Permanent wasn't really a word for me while I was moving from town to town, following the biggest prize money, you know?"

"Yeah, I know." The words were said simply, with no hint of her feelings.

"But I liked her. And so we spent time together. And then I found out she was married."

He knew where her mind was going. That Rose had already been pregnant when he found out.

"But I kept seeing her. I liked her. She wasn't happy with her marriage. He was an ass, and she'd left him and just hadn't gotten around to filing papers, whatever. Each day brought a new justification. All of them were bullshit. The minute I knew, I should have stopped. But we didn't."

Lonely. He'd been so lonely, so homesick, and she'd become a friendly face for him on the road. And he'd been weak enough to ignore everything he knew was right.

He breathed deep, and took a chance by lacing his fingers with hers. She allowed it.

"She ended it. I hate having to say that, too, since you'd think I'd have been man enough to walk away from the situation. But I wasn't. I let it ride until she said she and her husband were going to reconcile. It wasn't a hardship to let her go. I need you to know that. It wasn't like I loved her or anything."

Another black mark on his soul, but Jo said nothing.

"And then she found me a month later, saying she was pregnant and it was absolutely mine. Her husband was pissed, but maybe he wasn't quite the ass she'd led me to believe. He was ready to put the whole thing behind him if she was willing to give up the baby. Either adoption or abortion."

Jo's hand clenched a little around his, but she stayed quiet so he could finish.

"If I didn't want the baby, she was just going to abort. I didn't think twice before telling her no. But Jesus, after she left, I puked my guts out with nerves." He could smile a little now, at the memory of his pure panic. "I all but told her I was ready to tackle single fatherhood . . . and I'd never even held a baby in my adult life. Cradling Baby Bea when I was like five didn't count. I had no family nearby, no friends that were around for longer than a night or two before we went our separate ways again, and no home to call my own. Scared didn't even cover it."

"But you didn't call and take it back. You could have, and you didn't."

Her understanding, and even encouragement, pushed him on. "No. I didn't. And so, seven months later, I got the call to meet her at the hospital. I walked in, and there he was. Perfect."

He swallowed a little to keep from tearing up. "The most perfect thing I'd ever seen. And I knew, even though I'd been making a mess out of life when I made him, he was perfect and mine."

"You didn't get to see him being born?" Jo rubbed her cheek over his shoulder. "That's sad."

"Given the circumstances, I felt lucky she even went through with the whole pregnancy. She wasn't a monster. Rose, I mean. Neither was her husband, though she'd led me to believe it at first. Or maybe that's just how I painted him to justify my own actions. And I wasn't either. Just a handful of adults making bad choices, who were all fortunate enough to make the right ones so my son could have a chance."

"Do you ever wonder if she'll come back and try to get him? Get custody, or whatever?"

The idea had his blood pounding in an instinctive fight-or-flight response. But he breathed through that.

"She signed away her rights. I guess in this day and age, anyone can sue for rights again. You can sue someone because a candy bar made you fat. But instinct tells me she's not interested in remembering the affair—and consequence—that nearly ruined her marriage. I haven't heard from her since the day the final line was signed making me the sole parent. She's not a monster," he said again, reminding them both.

"Is that how you want it?" The question was cautious, though he wasn't sure whether the hesitation came from the question itself, or her fear of the answer.

"For now. Much as people like to talk about how a parenting duo is best, I know what my son needs is me. He's got a support dream team, a place to call his own, and he's got me. That's all he needs for the moment. I figure this parenting gig is sort of fluid. If something isn't working, we move on to try a new approach."

"Very scientific of you." Her voice held a touch of humor. "But why all the mystery?"

"I never want someone to look at my son and think *mistake*. He is blameless and amazing and I know that's what would happen if the story of his mother got out. So I just locked it all down."

She rolled until she was on top of him, her breasts pushing into his chest. "And the fact that people gossip and wonder doesn't bother you?"

"They can talk about me all they want," he said. He didn't care. They couldn't hurt him. "Doesn't matter. Seth is what matters. I can take it."

Jo kissed him lightly. "You're a good man, Trace."

He eyed her. "So you don't think less of me for it?"

"For what?" She seemed truly baffled.

"For having an affair with a married woman, knowing she was married."

Jo glanced over his head for a minute and chewed on her lip. But he knew she was trying to figure out how to word her response, not how to spin a lie.

"I think you made a mistake, which ended up reaping an unexpected reward. You obviously learned from it, since you're here beating yourself up about the whole thing. And in the end, when the chips were down, you had a choice, too."

"There was no choice." How could she think there was?

"There was," she argued softly. "So many men would have seen the out. She was fine with an abortion. Easy enough, and the problem goes away. You get to move on to the next woman, she gets her husband back, and nobody has to think about it again. You could have. But you didn't. You chose the hard route. The one that permanently tied you to another human being for the long haul. Not just eighteen years, but life."

"He's my son." That's all he could think. All he could say.

"Exactly." She kissed him again. "You're a good man. You made a mistake. Trust me, I've made a few myself. But you learned, and you can move on."

"With a kid."

"Yeah. With Seth." She nuzzled into the nook of his neck. "You're a cute pair."

"Why, thank you." He flipped her over onto her back and worked his way down her body to her breasts. "Now, I believe I had a turn coming to me."

Chapter Nineteen

Trace pulled up to the bar and parked. This was stupid. He shouldn't have come. But he just couldn't seem to stay away.

In the backseat of his extended cab, Seth whined and twisted in his seat. While the truck was in motion, his son never minded being buckled in. But when they pulled to a stop, it was game over. He wanted to go, or he wanted out. Trace felt the same way.

"Sorry, little man. Let's get you out of here." He hopped down and unbuckled Seth from the car seat, making up his mind then and there to stop by. "We're just going to pop in quickly and drop off the cookies from Emma. No pressure, right? We're not hanging around to make her nervous."

He knew Jo had the afternoon off; she'd texted him that much when he'd messaged her to say good morning. So he didn't even bother peeking in the bar doors, instead going straight up to her apartment. After a quick knock, he jostled Seth a little on his hip. "You're going to behave, right? All I need is for you to . . . hey."

Jo opened the door, watching them both warily. Her hair was up; she wore a faded scoop neck T-shirt and sweats with the elastic pushed up over her calves and bare feet. "Hey. What's up?"

He held up the hand with the bag. "Delivery from Emma."

"Oh." With another quick glance toward Seth, she opened the door farther and motioned. "Come on in."

"Thanks." He handed her the bag and set Seth on the floor with his stuffed dinosaur, Danny. The kid could crawl like hell on wheels, but the apartment was small enough—and Jo was tidy enough—there wasn't much for him to get into. "Emma wanted to thank you for lunch the other day."

Jo smirked. "You bought lunch downstairs. I didn't even make it. That would be Stu's domain."

"Well, he can have a cookie, too." He kissed her cheek, then breathed in. "You cleaning?"

"Yeah, how'd you know?"

"You smell like lemon," he said with a grin. It was such a homey, domestic picture, he couldn't help himself. He kissed her more fully on the lips, savoring the contact while still trying to keep one ear out for Seth and any possible mischief. This whole Dating Daddy thing was hell on his nerves.

"While you're here, you want one?" She pulled back and shook the bag. "I've got some milk up here, if you and Seth want some." She chewed her lip a little. "Can he have cookies yet?"

"Sure, one won't hurt the kid. And I'm always game for some milk and Emma's cookies." He found Seth pulling himself up to stand with the help of the edge of the coffee table. His newest favorite trick. Soon enough, the kid would be walking. The thought both thrilled him and terrified him. "Seth's not much for cups yet, though, so he'll just take the cookie." He went to pick up Seth for their snack.

"Oh, well . . ." Jo popped into the kitchen, then back out again, holding something. He walked over and took it.

It was a sippie cup, decorated with little cowboy boots and spurs and lassos. "What's this doing here?"

"I was going to give it to him next time I came over. Or just to you, to give to him." She snatched it back. "It was stupid. I saw it when I was grocery shopping this morning and I just bought it. It was an impulse purchase. Like a candy bar at the register. If you don't think he needs it, I can just—"

He kissed her again to stop the flow of words, arching his back in a complex pose to keep Seth from pulling Jo's hair.

She'd bought his son a sippie cup. A completely benign item, probably only a few bucks, and not altogether special on its own. But this was his Jo. And she'd done it all by herself. And now she was embarrassed by it.

This was a fantastic sign.

"It's perfect. He'll love it."

"I'll just go wash it," she mumbled and took off into the kitchen again.

Seth yanked on Trace's collar and he watched his son motion to the kitchen. "You want the cup back? She'll bring it. Let's sit down here a minute and wait our turn."

He sat, Seth on his knee, and angled the chair out to give them both room. With his legs as long as they were, both his and Seth's chubby thighs didn't fit under the table.

"Okay, so that's one milk for the little guy," Jo said, carrying in three glasses like a pro. She set the cup down in front of Seth, who grabbed it and started chugging. "Wow, thirsty, huh?"

"Kid likes his milk." Trace took the glass she offered him and smiled. "Thanks for letting us hang out. We weren't going to stay. . . ."

Jo smiled a little at Seth. "It's fine. He's cute. And much less crabby than last time, huh?" She reached out and traced one finger down the boy's cheek. Seth leaned into the touch and grunted excitedly.

Trace reached for the bag of cookies, but had to drop them to grab hold of Seth, who leaned over so far he almost fell from his perch. "Easy, son."

Seth swung his arms wildly and reached across the table.

"You'll get your cookie, calm down." He managed to keep one arm around Seth and reach in the bag for the other. "Kids are born knowing the difference between a carrot and a cookie, I swear it."

Jo broke one of the treats in half, chocolate chips melting and stretching between the two pieces. "Since my diet likely isn't much better than a toddler's, I have to agree with him on the eagerness."

Trace held out half a cookie, but Seth kept reaching across the table. Not at the bag, but at . . .

"Oh, no." Trace jiggled the boy a little on his knee. "She's busy eating her snack. You eat yours."

Jo's eyes widened. "Does he want my cookie? I thought they were all the same, but he can—"

"Not your cookie. You." He shrugged. "He likes people. You're still new. He wants to come over and say hi. He'll get over it."

Jo's hands froze, fingers almost to her mouth with a bite of cookie. "He wants me to hold him?"

"Probably, but don't worry about it. It's no big deal." He tried to distract Seth with the cup, but nothing doing. The kid kept reaching for Jo like she was a walking candy factory and he was a kid with a sweet tooth. "Or maybe we should just head out now, since he's a little anxious."

"Oh, well . . ." She put the cookie down and brushed her hands together, ridding them of crumbs. "If you don't mind, I could take him for a minute. I guess. . . ." She reached out, then pulled back. "I can't, like, hurt him or anything, can I?"

Trace chuckled, but swallowed it when he realized she was serious. "No, he's pretty well past the breakable stage. Kids are born with rubber in their bones anyway, Emma says. It's a survival thing. If you're sure."

"Yeah. I mean, he's a little kid. How hard could it be? You'll tell me if I do it wrong, right?" She reached out with more confidence now, and took Seth under the arms as Trace passed him over. His son cooed his happiness at the change of scenery and the new person to discover.

"Oh, hey." She gingerly removed one tiny fist from around her hoop earring. "Ouch. Okay, no more of that."

"Sorry." Trace stood, ready to take Seth back, but Jo motioned for him to sit back down.

"We're just getting to know each other. It's okay." She and Seth were nose to nose for a moment, and then Seth's chubby hands came out to palm her cheeks. He blew a spit bubble that nearly landed on her lips, and laughed hysterically.

"Apparently Muldoon men can't resist you."

Jo's smile was one of mild wonder. He recognized it easily. It was the same look he'd felt cross his face every time he snuck in to watch Seth sleeping in his crib the first few months of his life. He doubted it ever would completely fade away, the wonder and mystery that was watching your child grow up.

"Wanna try a cookie now?" She held out the snack, and Seth's hand shot out like a cannon to claim it. "I guess that's a yes."

Trace's cell phone buzzed in his pocket, and he stood to take it out and check the ID. "It's Bea." He slipped it back in his pocket. "She's probably got some stupid errand she wants me to run. Pass."

"So you're going to act like you didn't know." Jo's eyebrow rose in mock disapproval.

"Sure am. I'm surrounded by women in that house.

Seth's not a reliable partner in crime yet. I seize any life-line I can. God knows what she wants. Feminine hygiene products or something." He shuddered, and then frowned when his phone buzzed a second time. Bea again. "This is a little much, even for her. Just let me see what's up."

"Sure." Jo grabbed Seth's cup and set it in front of him, making it dance a little to his son's delight. "We're fine."

He stepped back toward the bedroom where Seth's squeals weren't so penetrating and answered the call. "What's up, Bea?"

"Trace?" Bea's voice was thin and shaky. An actress she might be, but even he recognized immediately this upset was real. "Can you come get me?"

"What happened? Where are you? Are you all right?"

Bea sniffled; then he could almost hear her sucking it up to get out the important facts. "I drove into town for some shopping."

"Where are you?"

"Not Marshall. I was heading to Pierre. I thought I could make a day of it. But then on my way a trucker ran me off the road and my car hit the guard rail and then another car hit me from behind and . . ." Despite her best efforts to continue the story, Trace lost her words from there in a sea of sobs and half-stutters and wails.

"Okay, Bea-Bea, okay. Calm down, now. We'll fix it. Where are you exactly?"

She named the small town where her car had been towed. Trace mentally calculated the distance. At least an hour out, maybe more depending on traffic.

"Okay. Someone will come—"

"No," she wailed. "You. Please, Trace. Peyton's not at the house, and neither is Emma, and Red is gone for the week. And I don't want any of the hands. I want my brother!" she ended on another sob.

"I'm coming. I'll come get you," he tried to soothe her. Inadequately, as it turned out, because she kept crying. "Are you sure you're okay? Should someone take you to a hospital just to check?"

"No, I'm fine. I'm just scared and I keep shaking."

"Try to find a blanket or something to stay warm in. That's shock. You'll be fine, Bea-Bea. I promise." He closed his phone and momentarily pressed his thumbs into his eyes.

If he drove all the way back home to drop Seth off—and with whom? Emma wasn't home now—he'd lose another hour or more, as Bea's location was in the other direction from the ranch. But there was nobody in town to take the boy.

Nothing he could do about it. He pocketed the phone and walked back to the living room. The sight that greeted him lifted his spirits momentarily, dragging him up from the trenches.

Seth had a hank of Jo's hair wrapped around his wrist. She was tugging on it playfully, whipping it around like a lasso and tickling his belly at the same time. Seth could barely keep upright, he was laughing so hard.

"We have to go."

Jo immediately recognized his tone and stood, shifting Seth to her hip in a natural motion that made Trace's chest squeeze. Did she even realize how good she could be with his son? "What happened?"

"Bea was in an accident, about an hour north of here." He reached for Seth, but the boy buried his face in Jo's neck. "Come on, kiddo, we've gotta go rescue your Auntie Bea."

Seth whimpered.

"Seth, little man, come on. I don't have time."

"I could keep him," Jo said, then her eyes widened as if she couldn't believe she'd said it.

Trace paused in the act of taking hold of Seth. "Seriously? You don't have to do that."

She watched Seth for a moment, then shrugged. "He's not even one yet. How hard could it be, right? You've got things for him?"

"In the truck. Are you sure? I don't want you to feel like you have to. I can figure something out. I can—"

"Go get the stuff, Trace." She rolled her eyes. "Offer closes in five minutes."

"Got it. Right." Not one to look a gift babysitter in the mouth, he hustled out the door to grab Seth's bag and prayed he wasn't making a huge mistake.

"How hard could it be, right?" Jo quietly mimicked herself as she paced the floor for the umpteenth time. "He's not even one yet."

Seth made a pathetic sort of sniffling sound and hiccuped. He was as fed up with the situation as she was.

At a loss, she rubbed his back a little and bounced. But the bouncing, which had worked twenty minutes ago, had lost its appeal with the little guy. He whimpered, so she stopped.

After a few moments, the sounds died down, and she walked past the hall mirror to check over her shoulder whether he was asleep.

Nope. Wide awake. But not crying. Yet. Taking a chance, she eased him to the floor, laying him on his back. "You've got the run of the place, dude. Explore."

Instead of rolling to his belly and taking off like a rocket as she expected, he stared up at her pitifully, as he had been doing the last hour.

"Go ahead. You can go," she said. Right, like that was going to make sense to him.

His lip quivered, and then the wailing started again.

Oh, God damn it.

"What?" She grabbed a handful of her own hair and tugged to relieve the tension in her skull. "What do you need? You're not dirty. You're not hungry. You're not cold, you're not hot. You don't want to be walked, you don't want to be put down, you don't want to be held. You're like an adult male, impossible to please. Let's cut the games and get to the good stuff. What do you need?"

The sarcastic outburst did nothing to improve the situation.

Of course, it didn't. What was she expecting? The kid to respond to adult humor? Unlikely. She let her head hit the table, and her phone rattled over the top. Phone. Who could she call?

She had the Muldoons' number . . . but that seemed like a cheat. Plus, wasn't that the reason she had Seth in the first place? Nobody was home.

Maybe she could go downstairs. Amanda was on morning shift. She had a niece . . . or was it a nephew? Oh, hell, who cared? She'd take experience with baby goats at this point.

She started to bend over to pick up the wailing child when it occurred to her, everyone would know whose baby it was. And everyone would be chatting it up about why she had the kid. And then would there be rumors that Trace was her star customer? Or maybe she was running a bordello and daycare. Two-for-one deal.

No. Better not to give people any reason to talk about her, good or bad.

With one last glance at Seth, his little face flushed with temper and confusion, she grabbed the phone and pushed speed dial three.

"Josephine!" her mother trilled in her ear. "Darling, I haven't heard from you for . . . sweetheart, what is that awful noise behind you?"

"Hi, Mother." She breathed a sigh of relief. Her mom

had experience with at least one baby. And since she was still alive, that had to prove something positive, right?

"Darling, are you in public transportation? There's a horrible sound—I can barely hear you. You know how icky public transportation is. Maybe you should call me back after—"

"No!" Jo all but screamed, then made herself take two deep breaths. "No, I'm actually babysitting." She said the words with a smile, but it felt more like a grimace.

"Oh, honey. Are you so hurting for money? That's awful. I could see if maybe your stepfather could lend you some cash."

"Okay, one? He's not my stepfather." None of them were. They were simply her mother's husbands. "And two, it's not for money. It's a favor for . . . a friend." She bent over and picked Seth up, rocking him side to side on the chair. "Nothing I'm doing is right. He's not dirty or hungry or anything you would normally think to check for. But he won't stop crying."

"Well, sweetie, maybe he just misses his parents. You should give him back now."

"I didn't take him out of a store. I have to wait until his father gets back." God, how had she made it past infancy with terrific parenting tips such as these?

"Then I'm not sure what to tell you. I'm sorry, that noise is too much for me. I've got to run. Ciao!"

"'Bye," Jo muttered to the dead connection, then tossed the phone on the table with a clunk. "Just you and me, little man. I think it's time we had a come to Jesus talk."

Seth blinked watery, owlish eyes.

"See, kids and I, we don't really get along together so well. But I don't want to admit that to anyone. I mean, I told your dad I don't do kids, and that's the truth, too. No offense, really."

Seth reached for one of her hoops, and she let him, because he was quiet.

"But I like for people to think it's my choice, you know?" She angled her head down as he tugged, trying to keep the pain to a minimum. "Not that I can't do it; I just don't want to. I'm a successful business owner, and manage a team of twenty employees daily, but I can't manage to keep one fifteen-pound baby in check for two hours? Not doing much for my image, if you know what I mean."

Seth blinked again, slower this time, as if he were becoming bored with the conversation.

That was fine with her. Bored kids fell asleep, didn't they? She could talk all night if that's what kept him quiet and, if not happy, at least not screaming his head off.

"It's just that, I like your dad. Oh, you can't tell him any of this last bit, okay?" When Seth didn't respond, she took that as an affirmative. "I like him a lot. More than I've liked any guy I've . . . dated before. And I want him to think I can do this. I don't even know why, since in theory, I don't want to be around kids anyway. Uh, no offense."

His head drooped a little to the left, which she took for *none taken*.

"I just need to figure out if this is what I really want. Because right now, I'm scared shitless. Don't repeat that word. And I'm pretty sure this family stuff isn't for me. I'm not exactly Mother Goose, you know?"

Seth blew a spit bubble. Clearly, they were on the same page.

"So maybe you're just reminding me why I never really wanted to do the kid thing. Maybe this is the sign to step back and evaluate again."

Seth blinked.

"In the end, I'm not good for you, either. I don't know

what I'm doing. I'm probably lucky I haven't dropped you yet. And what the hell am I going to teach you? How to open ten bottles in under ten seconds? How to flip vodka bottles? I'm just . . . not meant for this."

His face scrunched up, and she recognized—even from just the few hours' experience she had—his reaction meant nothing good. "Okay, all right, back up we go." She stood and hefted him to her hip and started to pace again. She'd made the fourth lap around the apartment, the last two with Seth's glass-shattering accompaniment, when Trace knocked and walked in.

"Hey, sorry . . . whoa, buddy." He immediately stepped in all the way and grabbed Seth. "What's wrong with you, huh?"

"If you find out, send up a smoke signal. Clearly, I had no clue how to fix it." Exhausted, Jo slid bonelessly to the couch. The position was uncomfortable, but she didn't have the energy to move. And yet, she had a shift starting in thirty minutes. Ha. "I couldn't make him happy."

"It happens. Hey, bud, let's talk, huh?" He made the same laps Jo just had completed around the apartment, only this time the pattern seemed to soothe Seth. After a moment, his tiny little head dropped to Daddy's shoulder, his thumb found his mouth, and his eyes started to droop.

"Right. Well, apparently he wanted Daddy." Who could blame him? She wanted his daddy, too. "I did my best."

"I know you did. Thanks for watching him."

"How's Bea?"

"Shaken, but safe and in one piece. Her little car can't say the same, unfortunately. But cars are replaceable." He rubbed his chin over Seth's hair a little. "Really, thanks for watching him. I could have taken him, but it woulda been hell for everyone."

"I know. I'd say I was glad to help, but I don't think I

was all that helpful." She checked the clock. Twenty-five minutes and counting. Hell. "I'm not sure how you do it."

"Do what?" His back was turned as he rocked on his heels a little.

The guy really had no clue. He just did his thing and kept on trucking. "The single parenting gig. I'm exhausted and it was only a couple hours."

"He's mine."

That was it. For Trace, that was enough. She saw the perfect love a parent had for a child in that moment, and wanted it so badly for herself. Not the parent-child love, but the deep, abiding love Trace so clearly had to give. And what she was about to say was going to ruin her chance of getting it.

"I think I'm not right for this."

"Right for what?" Trace bent down with innate grace and grabbed a stuffed animal from the bag to hand to Seth, who tucked the animal under his arm.

"Right for you both. You need someone who can take you on as a set. You're like salt and pepper. Even if you only like pepper, you can't just have a pepper shaker."

"What?" His brows knit together in confusion. "Why are we talking about shakers?"

"Never mind." She struggled to lift one hand to wave that away. After lugging the kid around for two hours straight, her arms felt like spaghetti. "I mean, it's occurred to me that some people are truly just not meant to do the kid thing. And no matter how slowly you approach it, that's never going to change. Like some people are cat people, and some aren't. I'm not a kid person." She watched as Seth's eyes finally closed completely. "Maybe a little part of me wishes I was, but I'm not."

"Jo," Trace warned quietly. "Don't."

"Facts are facts. I tried to go against instinct. And if it were just two adults in the mix, then it wouldn't be such a big deal. But there's a child who matters more here, and he'd take the brunt of whatever mistakes we made. So I think it's best to just give the whole relationship a pass now."

God, that hurt. If she'd had the energy, she'd have rubbed at the ache forming in her chest.

"Jo. Josephine Tallen, don't start." Trace shook his head. His voice was low, but determined. "You're thinking too far ahead. You don't know how things will work out in a few months."

"Kid person," she said, waving a hand out at him, then laying it flat against her chest. "Not a kid person. I can't do that to him." She smiled slightly, though it hurt. "Seth and I might not get along all that great, but I still think he's cute. Find someone who completes the set."

Trace stood, still and unmovable as an oak tree in the middle of her living room. "I'm not giving up. Not walking away from us. We're good. You know we are."

"We are, yeah. But the three of us? It's just hurt and pain waiting to happen, mostly for him." She leveraged herself up, feeling as unsteady as a drunk on the tail-end of a three-day bender. "I have a shift I need to get ready for."

He watched her silently, then nodded. The movement was curt, businesslike. "We'll get out of your way. Sorry we took up so much of your time. I didn't mean to inconvenience you."

"That's not what I—Trace." But he was gone, the door closing with a soft finality behind him. She leaned against it, forehead and palms pressing into the cool wood, listening to the sound of his boots going down the stairs. Listening for the sound of his truck doors closing, the engine starting, pulling away.

Oh, God, that hurt. Hurt more than she'd anticipated.

Sliding down, she sat on the floor and gave herself nineteen of the last twenty minutes she had to sulk.

Chapter Twenty

Salt and pepper shakers. What the hell was that woman talking about? Jesus.

Trace ran a hand over his hair and pulled hard. Infuriating. The entire gender was completely infuriating. Why the hell would she think she wasn't right for them? Why would she think she was wrong for Seth? She'd done her best watching him; he was still in one piece. Half the time, that's all Trace ever hoped for on the days when things weren't meshing. Had she expected him to come back and be pissed off she hadn't taught his son the alphabet yet?

Seth snorted and shifted positions in the car seat behind him. Trace smiled in spite of his annoyance. The kid was quite the charmer, clearly, if a few hours with Jo sent her running for the hills.

Maybe he should have been more annoyed. Pissed, even. But he couldn't work up the head of steam to get there. Probably because, despite it all, he knew better. Jo was it for him. He didn't know quite yet how to convince her of that fact, but they'd get there.

He didn't need a nanny, didn't want a stepmom for his son. He wanted a woman for himself. Yeah, she had to be good with Seth, overall. A good person, a mature influence. But she didn't need to bake bread or know exactly what Seth needed at all times. He didn't expect her to drop her life and stay home with the kid. He didn't even expect her to have more babies.

He loved Seth, with all his heart. But he was perfectly fine making Seth his only shot at fatherhood.

So, he'd bide his time. Give her some space. And then he'd calculate the next move.

Jo Tallen was it for him. And whether she wanted to believe it or not right now, she felt the same way about him.

Like hell was he gonna give that up.

Hours later, after he'd put Seth to bed and knew Emma was tucked in for the night, he wandered the house. But it wasn't enough space. The walls of the big house were closing in on him, like hot breath on the back of his neck. He grabbed his boots by the front door and stepped into them barefooted on the front porch. Just the quick change of atmosphere released a small amount of pressure. So he'd take a quick walk around the property and let loose some steam.

Maybe a long grooming session with Lad would work out some of the kinks in his mind. As he headed in that direction, a figure stepped out of the shadows of the garage and headed with a determined, long-legged stride toward the stable. Trace froze, his mind flashing back to months ago when they'd had break-ins and near-sabotage on their hands, perpetrated by their previous trainer, Sam Nylen.

But there was no way that figure was male. In fact . . .

He nearly bit his tongue. That was Bea. He'd bet his favorite boots on it. What the hell was his sister doing, walking around in the dark?

He stayed in the shadows. She didn't even notice him as she crept into the barn and down the long corridor. He risked a peek around the door and saw her handling his tack. What the hell! But instead of Lad, she chose another horse—Lover Boy—to saddle. He'd figured Bea couldn't saddle a horse if someone ordered her to at gunpoint, but she was proving him wrong. Her hands worked quickly and efficiently, and she didn't flinch at the weight of the heavy saddle.

He didn't question why she chose his tack. Peyton's would be way too short, and she'd have reservations about using one of the hands' things. So, by default, his won out. He ducked out moments before she turned to lead Lover Boy out the wide double doors. She paused long enough to swing easily into the saddle, no grunts or whining or moaning about chipped nails. And she was off, setting a natural pace and moving in the saddle like she was born to it.

He stared, slack-jawed, after her for a minute. How the hell had that happened? When had his Bea-Bea, the self-proclaimed indoor, city girl who hated dirt and thought horses were big, filthy beasts learned to ride?

Not just ride, he corrected. But ride like she'd been doing it for years. No hand had taught her to do all that as fast and efficiently as she had in the few months she'd been back.

Beatrice had been holding out on them. He mused over that—and why she might want to keep her riding a secret—as he walked toward her garage apartment. So maybe he'd wait for her, surprise her when she came back from her ride.

As his boots thundered up the stairs outside the trainer's apartment she'd taken over, he could hear a whine start. Damn dog. He opened the unlocked door and stepped inside to find the thing wearing . . .

Oh, hell no. Was that dog wearing a robe? Jesus. Trace plopped down on the floor and called the dog over. Milton walked gingerly toward him, as if not sure why a man was in his mother's apartment.

"I'm not going to hurt you." He patted his thigh gently. Milton shook and wouldn't approach. "Fine, I was gonna take that stupid robe off of you but—"

As if he understood, Milton was over by his side in a second, nudging his hand with his nose and silently begging to be released. Trace picked him up and set him on his legs while he unwrapped the robe's tiny sash and pulled it off the dog's front two legs.

"A robe," he muttered, and tossed it at the bed. "There. You're free. Off you go."

Milton hopped down and went to lap up some water from his baby blue water bowl. A bowl, he noted, that had crowns all over it. The dog had no chance.

He ignored the soft sounds of Milton's snort-breathing and heavy lapping and tried to figure out how to get through to Jo. She was freaked out, that was clear enough. And she wasn't the type to play games. It wasn't one of those I'm breaking up with you to see if you'll chase me games some females played. She honestly thought she was a bad deal for Seth.

In his mind, the fact that she considered what was best for Seth at all made her better than most. The sippie cup danced through his thoughts again, and he smiled. He didn't even mind when Milton's dripping wet muzzle pushed at his hand to make room for his squat body on his lap. Absently, Trace scratched the dog between his soft, floppy ears.

So he'd give her time. She wasn't the type to hop from man to man. He had time to make sure the next move he made was the right move.

He was all but asleep on the floor, sitting up, a twenty-pound mutt in his lap, when Bea walked through the door and screamed like someone had stabbed her in the chest.

He jolted awake and sprang to his feet, Milton scrambling under the kitchen table for safety. "What? What the fuck?"

Bea fell back against the door and held a hand over her heart. "Oh, my God. Trace. What the hell are you doing here? You scared me to death."

Trace ran a hand down his face. "I think the feeling is mutual there. I was just out for a walk, thought I'd stop by and . . . check on you." He watched her face for any hint of guilt.

She smiled. "That was sweet. But we're doing fine, aren't we, Milton? Come here, boy. Come . . . hey. Where'd your robe go?" She searched the floor before she caught sight of it on the bed. "We always wear our robes before bed, Milton."

Milton flattened himself on the floor, as if trying to sink through it.

"You're not in your robe," Trace pointed out. "Hey, where've you been, anyway? Are those actually your clothes?"

She looked down at her outfit. Simple brown boots, faded jeans, and a shirt that looked like she'd pilfered it from Peyton's closet, except it would be too small if that were the case. Which meant it was actually hers. She actually owned clothes that were meant to be worked in, ridden in, dirtied up. The world got stranger and stranger. "Just, you know. Out." She ignored the second question.

"Out," he repeated, biting the inside of his cheek to keep from grinning. "Walking around?"

"Yeah. You know, fresh air and all that. I forgot what clean air smelled like." She reached under the table and dragged Milton from his opossum position. The dog's toes dragged across the linoleum in defiance.

"Need to talk anything out?" he asked. "You know, anything weighing on your mind? Maybe a secret or two you've got pent up, want to get off your chest?"

"Of course not. Secrets are so not my thing." She huffed and looked offended. Damn, she was a good little actress.

"And I'll beg you to remember you're the one with the secrets, Mister Who's the Baby's Mama?"

Point taken. "How are you feeling? Any stiffness?"

Bea rolled her neck to the side. "Not really. I think I'm supposed to feel it tomorrow, or something. I'll just use it as an excuse to go get a massage."

He smiled at that. Riding might not have been the best choice the evening after an impressive car wreck. But then again, it was Bea. "You need to make sure to lock your door."

"You could have stayed out, since I clearly wasn't here to answer it."

"But then I wouldn't have been able to rescue the dog from his fabric prison."

"Right. My head's clear now, so we're ready for bed." She stared at him, then the door, then back at him again with a raised brow.

"Uh-huh." He walked over and knuckled the top of Milton's head. "Keep it real, dude. No more robes."

"He likes it," Bea protested, but Trace was already moving down the stairs, head shaking in denial.

As he passed the stable, he slowed and debated stopping in. Then he kept walking, back to the big house and his son. He'd check on his tack in the morning. But he had a feeling it'd be right back where it started, in good working order. Bea was more of a puzzle than he'd originally thought.

But then again, what woman wasn't?

Stu followed Jo out the door after her shift. "Mail came while you were dealing with the beer rep."

"Put it in my office, I'll deal with it tomorrow." She wanted a hot shower and bed, just like she had the last few days since Trace and Seth had walked out her apartment door. She wasn't interested in being a Chatty Cathy today. Or any other day in the near future.

If the thought of taking on both father and son scared her so much, and she was past wanting to be with them, why was the opposite hurting just as much? Not being with Trace?

Ignore the pain. It will pass.

She unlocked her door, then turned. "You're stalking me because . . ."

"Hey, just 'cause you're in a breakup funk, don't crawl up my ass." Stu held out the stack of mail. "You're gonna wanna read that one on top."

The letter looked completely innocuous, with a return address in Marshall, but no name or business to identify it. "Why?"

"I expected it."

Jo walked in, and Stu followed without invitation, closing the door behind him. She ripped open the envelope and pulled out the sheet of official-looking paper. She scanned it and then her head snapped up. "I have a hearing with the city council next week?"

"Yeah." Stu, making himself at home, wandered into her kitchen and grabbed himself a Coke. "I knew it was coming, so I've been watching for it to make sure it didn't get buried."

Jo's hands tightened around the edge of the letter. She managed to relax her grip slightly as she heard the crinkle of paper. "If you knew it was coming, why didn't you say something?"

"When? As you served customers? Or while you were stomping up to your place after shift? You've had the *talk to me and die* look on your face all week. So, I waited until there was more concrete evidence."

She couldn't argue there. Her mood had been foul, and

she knew it. Fingering the studs in her right lobe, she examined the page again. "What the hell do I do about this? Do I need a lawyer?"

"For a city council meeting?" Stu laughed and took a swig. "Nah. You're not in Dallas anymore, remember?"

"I never lived in Dallas," she murmured, reading the sheet for the third time.

"Whatever. You just show up and plead your case. Bring in people to stand up for you. It's real informal around here. I mean, shit can get ugly. Don't mention anything to anyone about the Founder's Day float incident of '96."

Jo stared at him. "You're kidding, right?"

"Nope. That one drew some blood, and I don't even mean metaphorically." Stu killed the can and headed for the kitchen sink and the trash can under the counter. He started out, then doubled back and came out holding the sippie cup she'd bought for Seth. "What's this still doing sitting around?"

Her heart kicked up a notch, but she shrugged. "Just keep forgetting to toss it."

"Oh, well, here." He made to step back to the trash can, but she lunged.

"No!" As her hand closed around the thick plastic, she realized just how pathetic she looked. "I mean, that's wasteful. It was barely used, you know? I'm sure someone would want it."

"Uh-huh." Stu waited while she put the cup back in the kitchen, next to the stove, where she mentally punished herself by seeing it twenty times a day. She was sick. "Maybe you shouldn't give up on things so easily."

Jo snorted. "I don't think it's giving up to know what you're good at and what you're not. It's called knowing your strengths and running with them."

"Your parents teach you that?"

"My father, whoever the hell he is, has taught me nothing. My mom, yeah." Jo sat and started opening mail at
random, not even looking at each piece before moving on
to the next envelope. "If a marriage wasn't working out
for her, she was gone. New city not turning up any
wealthy prospects? Try something else. Why stick with
what isn't working?"

"What'd she do with you?"

"I got dragged along sometimes." Rip. Tear. Open.
Push aside. "Sometimes I ended up in decent boarding
schools or private schools or whatever."

"And you liked that, as a kid?"

"Hated it," she answered automatically, then cursed herself. "It doesn't matter. We're not talking about husband
hopping here. This isn't about my mom. We're talking
about a kid who needs adults in his life who can be there
for him and handle childrearing. Who won't one day
wake up and regret having him in their life because they're
over being a parent and want to try some . . . thing . . .
new. . . ."

Stu smiled smugly. "This isn't about your mom, huh?
Sounds like you just lapsed there. Mixing up your past and
your present."

"Shut up," she muttered, then realized she was wrin-
kling the electric bill. Smoothing it back down, she nodded to the door. "Don't you have a grill to man?"

"Yeah, yeah." He stopped by and kissed the top of her
forehead. "You know, you've got more people in your life
you can count on now. People who give a damn and don't
see you as inconvenient. Who want to watch you move
up in the world and are willing to give you a boost to get
there."

"Thanks." She watched him walk out the door, then
stood and took the sippie cup from the kitchen. "This is
stupid. Why am I keeping this?"

The sippie cup, predictably, didn't answer.

"You're not some magical talisman binding me to them. I'm not going to die if I throw you away. They're not going to die. It's not like I'll never see them again, right? Small town. I'll catch glimpses now and then. And the gossip . . . well, maybe I'll have to start paying attention. Why am I talking to you again?"

She wasn't sure, but she thought one of the cowboy boots might have mocked her.

"Whatever." She slammed the cup back down on the counter and headed for the bathroom. She was losing her mind, all over a fucking cup.

As she ripped off layer after layer of clothing, she acknowledged Stu had a point. Maybe her lack of a normal, steady childhood had something to do with her inability to see herself having a typical, Cleaver-style family. Or some variation thereof. But again, it wasn't just her who would be screwed if she didn't listen to her instincts. It was Seth.

Were her selfish desires worth possibly throwing him in the middle of a clusterfuck?

Chapter Twenty-one

Trace brushed over Lad's coat in slow, even strokes, front to back, following the lines of the horse's muscle. He'd been doing this far too long, but as if Lad understood he needed the time, the horse patiently stood, leaning into each brushstroke and letting him think.

He'd checked the tack every morning since discovering Bea's little secret. He'd asked once, just to test her, if she wanted to go riding with him one afternoon. She'd stared at him as if he'd grown two extra heads. So she was sticking to her act. He could do the same. At least for now.

Lad snuffled and shuffled his feet. Trace soothed with some cooing and a few clucks of his tongue. Much as his touch calmed Lad, the rhythmic motions soothed Trace's chaotic mind enough to let thoughts truly connect and form more coherent ideas.

He needed to try again. Bringing Seth over to Jo's apartment had been a mistake, one he should have anticipated. Though he had meant it to be just a short visit, and they'd been getting along so well. She'd bought Seth a sippie cup to keep at her place. That meant something.

Bea's accident was ill-timed, but just because Seth had had a crabby afternoon, that didn't mean Jo was doing anything wrong. She needed to see that. Needed to get it through her mind that Trace wasn't in this for a nanny.

That he wanted her. Just her. He could get his own flipping nanny if he needed to. But he had a feeling that wouldn't be necessary. He'd watched Seth's face, entranced with Jo's attention. And her own eyes lit when she made Seth smile. They were crazy about each other . . . she just wasn't ready to admit it yet. Wasn't ready to look past her own fears to see it.

But how the hell did he prove to her he wanted her, bar and all?

"Trace?"

"Yeah, hey, Morgan." He sighed quietly and kissed his introspective time good-bye.

Their vet, and Trace's childhood friend, walked over to Lad's stall and rested his elbows on the door. "How are things?"

"You know, trucking along." He let the brush fall into the bucket by the door and stepped out. Over the door he handed Lad a carrot and rubbed the animal's nose in silent thanks for giving him some alone time. "What are you up to? Red call you over?"

"Nah." Morgan pushed at his glasses, smudging the lenses a little. It was a habit from childhood he'd never grown out of. "I actually came by to see if Bea was okay. And Ma wanted me to bring something over. I've got the basket in my car."

Poor guy. Smitten. That would lead nowhere good. "She's at the house, milking the accident for all it's worth. The day after, she suddenly developed a sore neck." Sore neck, his foot.

"She wasn't hurt too badly, was she? Rumors have her with everything from a concussion to broken ribs."

Of course. The Marshall grapevine hard at work. "Nothing more than a sore neck for a few days. It's likely fine by now, but you couldn't tell by the sounds she makes.

Girl's got the pathetic whine down to a science. She probably taught it to that rat she calls a dog."

"She was in a car accident, Trace," Morgan scolded. "She's entitled to rest a little."

"Rest, sure. No problem there. But she's a very loud . . . rester." He nodded to the house. "I need to grab lunch myself. I'll walk up with you." He waited while Morgan retrieved the basket his mother had sent over from the back of his truck. "What'd your mom pack?"

"Nothing for you. It's for Bea."

Trace sighed and walked on. "So how are things coming along with your practice? Take on any help yet?"

"No, but I need to." He shrugged. "I've got an interview with a woman next month. She's finishing up her current contract, then wants to try country life for a while. Livestock and all that."

"She's nuts. Who would trade petting pampered pooches in the city for getting a hoof to the balls?"

"Someone without balls?" Morgan shrugged and slowed his pace a little. With legs like his, he was constantly outpacing others. "I need another receptionist, too, since mine wants to train up to become a vet tech. Which is great, but annoying to have yet another person to find."

"Easier position to fill," Trace pointed out. "Fewer requirements."

"True there. So anyway, if you hear of anyone looking for a job, and you think they'd fit in, let me know."

"Sure thing." They walked in silence a few more feet.

"Was over at Jo's Place the other day. Talked to Stu, the cook."

"Yeah?" Trace stuck his hands in his pockets and slowed down a little more, hoping to drag out any mention of Jo without being too obvious.

"Apparently, Jo has a hearing with the city council at

the end of the week. She has to basically give her account of the facts with that whole drunk driving situation, and hope they don't launch a further investigation that might result in her business license being revoked. Or liquor license, which is almost as bad, given the nature of her business."

"Damn." He rubbed the back of his neck. "How did I not know about that?"

"I dunno. You guys are kinda removed from town, unless you need something. And since I'm guessing you haven't been in to the bar lately . . ." He gave Trace a pointed look. Damn grapevine. "I just assumed you didn't know."

He hadn't. And he might have missed it had Morgan not swung by to talk. "Is she planning to go and fight?"

"Of course. She's not backing down. Pissed, from what it seems, but coldly so. Ready to kick ass and take names, according to Stu."

That was his Jo. "I hate that she has to go through this." It hurt her, he knew. She wanted to belong, be a part of the community, and having unfounded accusations tossed so easily at her was a stab to her heart. A heart that was far more tender than she ever wanted anyone to know.

"Well, between us, and everyone else I've heard from, they all think it's bull. Jo might be new, but plenty of people love what she's done with the place, and they respect the hell out of her." Morgan reached to open the front door, waited while Trace headed in, then took off his boots. He knew the drill as well as anyone.

"I wish there was something I could do."

"Maybe there is." Morgan shrugged and set the basket on the table. "All I know is, there's gonna be plenty of people who will be pissed if Jo's Place shuts down."

Trace considered that while Morgan followed the

sounds of TV to the living room to check on Bea. If everyone else in the town wanted Jo to stay, maybe he had a shot at doing something productive.

Sometimes the grapevine had its advantages.

Jo straightened her suit jacket—the only one she owned—and tried to keep her hands from shaking. This was just a simple council meeting. Nothing would actually happen today. She just had the opportunity to go in there and explain what had happened.

So why did her body tremble at the thought of the possible outcome?

"Let's get this over with," Stu grumbled behind her. At her request, he'd agreed to come with her. But he'd balked at putting on a suit. His concession had been a simple polo shirt and his best jeans.

She'd take it.

They walked into the meeting room together and looked around. A long table sat up front, with seven people behind it talking amongst themselves. They had the air of being more important than they needed to be.

Not the time to crack jokes, Tallen. These people might decide your fate later.

In the rows of chairs facing the table, only four others were seated.

"This is it?" she mouthed to Stu.

"What were you expecting, a prom?" He shrugged. "It's a city council meeting for a small town in the middle of nowhere. Biggest issue that gets brought up here is likely some neighbor complaining about dog crap on their lawn."

She stifled a laugh, then swallowed impulsive giggles. Okay, so she had nerves. Nerves could be a good thing. They kept you on your toes. But as she nearly hiccupped with the effort to keep the giggles at bay, she knew these were not helpful nerves. "At least there won't be many witnesses to my humiliation."

They took seats in the middle row, off to the left. Jeff wasn't there yet. Or maybe he wouldn't show up at all. Would that work in her favor, or against her?

The cold metal of the folding chair was uncomfortable, and she couldn't get settled. Did they have to crank the AC in this place? Why was it so cold? And why was it bothering her that there were no friendly faces? She hadn't issued engraved invitations, for cripes sake. So it shouldn't settle so sourly on her that she was fighting this one alone.

Alone. On her own. The way she wanted it, right? Shouldn't count on anyone else.

The council members straightened to face forward, and something about the woman in the middle looked familiar. But it didn't click right away, so she brushed it off. Right as the woman in the middle started to speak, Officers White and Nelson entered. They took seats a few rows in front of her and Stu. Nelson turned to give her a smile, and she felt her whole body relax in response. How bad could this be, anyway? It appeared the law—at least—was on her side.

"We call this meeting to order. My name is Judy Plumber, and I am the chairwoman."

Judy Plumber. The woman who'd caught her and Trace in a standoff in the frozen foods aisle the day she first saw Seth. Right . . . great.

Good old Judy called attendance for those at the table, and started to read the minutes of the last meeting. Jo felt her eyelids droop and she bit back a yawn. Stu elbowed her in the side.

"We're getting to the good stuff."

"—brought to our attention that Jo's Place, a bar and restaurant, illegally over-served a driver and failed to offer

him alternative transportation, i.e., calling a taxi service."
She paused, then sneered, as if hating to say, "Allegedly.
Said driver was then in a car accident, which caused sub-
stantial property damage, though no extensive injuries."

No question which side of the fault line the chairwoman sat on. Jo bit her lip and clenched her hands
around the metal of the chair seat. Jumping up to shout,
"It's all a pack of crap!" probably wouldn't go over so well.

"We have an investigation pending by Officers White
and Nelson. Are they present?"

Officer White stood. "Yes, we are. The investigation is
still pending. However, there is no evidence to suggest
Ms. Tallen, or any of her employees, over-served the
driver, or that she refused to call him a cab."

Jo released the breath she'd been holding.

Judy the Righteous checked her notes over the rims of
her glasses. "But there is no evidence fully disproving this
same fact, am I correct?"

"Ms. Tallen produced the receipt, which does show the
driver only purchased a single beer, along with his meal."

"But does this prove he was not given complimentary
alcohol?"

Nelson cleared his throat. "No, that's not possible to see
on the receipt."

"So it seems, as far as evidence is concerned, we are at
square one. Nothing proves, nor disproves, the claim."

White nodded, then sat down, looking like a chastised
child rather than an upholder of the law.

Jo couldn't blame him. He'd tried, and he'd been honest. How do you produce evidence of something that
didn't exist?

The chairwoman checked her notes again. "I see here
Miranda Effingham has asked to speak."

"Yes, I'm here, thank you." A woman with a pinched
face and impossibly straight posture stood, facing forward.

"Miranda, hello!" The man on the end of the table beamed. "How's Jeffrey? I haven't seen him on the course lately."

"He's fine, Bill." She smiled. "Busy. How are the kids and Nancy?"

"Oh, you know. Nancy's got that Christmas board thing coming up. You're on that, aren't you? She's dying for some grandbabies but so far—"

"Ahem." Judy coughed. "Can we proceed?"

The man—Bill—flushed straight to the top of his bald head. "Sorry," he mumbled and bent over his paper as if he were writing something. Jo would bet he wasn't.

Miranda stiffened, poker face back on. "As most of you know, I am J. J.'s mother."

Jo's mind echoed the words Jeff had mentioned about his mother. Community leader. Charity board member, on every committee known to man.

She was so screwed.

"J. J. wanted to be here, but he had to be back at school. He's in law school, you know." She said it with an odd mixture of pure maternal pride and snotty one-upmanship. "I think we all know J. J. made a mistake. One he regrets most deeply." Miranda fluttered a hand over her heart for emphasis. "But he was led down the path of bad choices by someone older, one who had a responsibility she chose to ignore. My son trusted Josephine Tallen and he was let down. For that, I think the blame lies solely on the bar owner's shoulders."

"Breathe," Stu muttered. "You're turning blue."

She tried—really, she did—but it hurt too much.

"I think we all know . . ." Miranda's gaze finally moved from the front of the room toward the door seconds before it opened. Trace Muldoon strode in, a little extra swagger to his hips Jo hadn't seen before.

Jo's breath caught again, but for a different reason this

time. He'd come. Without being asked, he'd come to support her. And he'd brought the cavalry. Peyton, followed by Red and Emma, walked in behind him. Her chest ached with gratefulness.

"Sorry we're late," he announced to the room at large. "Got the times mixed up." He winked to her, then took a seat two rows behind. His family followed.

"Continue, Miranda," Judy encouraged.

"Right, yes." Flustered, she went on. "I think we all know this is a case of he-said, she-said, with little evidence. And that means . . ."

The doors opened again, and several servers from the bar, along with a few lunchtime regulars, poured in like water through a funnel. Amanda waved cheerfully and pointed to a few seats in the back.

"Please be seated," the chairwoman droned.

They hushed and quickly settled. But before Miranda could continue, a new flood of people showed up. Some she recognized—the local vet, more regulars from the bar, even Mr. Meldon, who owned soon-to-be-closed Gimmie's. She recognized others, but couldn't place names with faces.

The noise echoed off the tall ceilings in the open room. Feet shuffled over the stained linoleum, chairs squeaked as they were pulled out or pushed forward, bags plopped to the floor, voices were not-so-very hushed as they whispered to save a seat or scoot over.

"This is ridiculous," Miranda protested.

The chairwoman pounded her palm on the table rapidly. "Quiet. Quiet down now!" But even with the admonishment, it took several minutes before everyone settled down.

Jo surveyed the faces sitting around her, behind her, in front of her. And her throat closed up at the obvious support these people were lending her.

"As I was saying," Miranda bit out. "It seems to be a little unfair—dare I say, presumptuous—to believe the word of a veritable stranger over the son of a pillar of the community. Jeffrey's family has lived here for generations, as has mine. You all know us. I think that should carry some weight."

"Who cares?" someone called out from the back of the room, and waves of laughter erupted.

Judy banged her hand again. Jo's own palm stung from the sound alone. Man, that had to hurt. "If you don't quiet down, we'll limit this meeting to necessary personnel only."

That worked. Immediately, it was as quiet as a church on Sunday with half the congregation asleep. Jo wondered if she should start sweating like a sinner now, or wait until later.

Miranda threw up her hands. "I'm done, I suppose." She sat with a thump.

Jo raised her hand. "Am I allowed to defend myself here?"

Miranda shot her a steely look. "Why bother?"

"Don't hit her. Don't hit her," Stu muttered.

Judy motioned for her to stand. "Name, occupation, and business here for the record please."

Lord, these people were high on power. "Jo—Josephine—Tallen, owner of Jo's Place, and I'm here to, uh, argue the case against me?"

The woman rolled her eyes, but waved a hand to indicate she should go on.

Okay then. The town wanted a little show . . . she'd give them a show.

Chapter Twenty-two

"There's not much to say, really. I served Jeff one beer, which he drank. That's on the receipt. I didn't hand him another one. He was gone quickly. He didn't even eat his dinner. I'm not sure where he got the alcohol, or what he did after he left the restaurant. But it wasn't from me."

Good old Bill on the end motioned for her attention. "If you have no proof, such as security footage or witnesses—"

"I'm a witness." Stu stood, imposing and, okay, a little bit scary, in his height and girth.

"You're an employee," Bill said. "You don't exactly count as an impartial witness."

Stu grumbled, but sat back down.

"If you have no other witnesses," Judy put in, "ones that can clearly agree you didn't over-serve J. J. Effingham, then I'm afraid we have no choice but to investigate further. I move to suspend her liquor license until we have completely investigated the entire matter."

Jo dared a quick glance at Miranda, who was all but bouncing in her seat with glee.

"You can't do that. I've done nothing wrong. There's no proof to go on."

"I'd like to speak."

Jo turned and saw Mr. Meldon walking to the middle

of the aisle. Oh, God. Was he going to blame her for all this? A parting shot at the competition?

"This young lady runs a nice establishment. Her bar's been a good thing for the community. God knows that building was torn up before she got here. And I think many of the others here would agree she's done a good job with the place. I've never seen anything get too out of hand over there before."

"There've been a few bar fights," Judy argued.

"There will always be fights where liquor is concerned. If fights are the problem, you should yank the liquor license of everyone who serves in this town. And none of them have resulted in anything—or anyone—being seriously injured or broken."

Judy settled back in her chair, not pleased with being shot down.

"Jo Tallen is a sweet girl."

Sweet girl? Stu mouthed to her with a grin. She kicked him in the foot.

"She brought me a potted plant when she heard I was leaving. Stayed to chat with me, ask my advice on things, really listened to what I had to say. Can't say the same for other people in this room." His eyes, still sharp and steely, cut through the people at the front table. "If nothing else, her efforts to bring more business to downtown should be recognized and acknowledged. She's been here a year now. She's not some fly-by-night operator."

The back of Jo's eyes burned, but she blinked rapidly.

"That's about all I have to say."

Soft, polite applause ushered him back to his seat one slow, careful step at a time. As he sat, he caught her eye and nodded. She mouthed her thanks.

Jo slipped her professional, impersonal mask back on and turned to the council. "I'm not sure what I've done to warrant such a reaction to a single unfounded accusation, but I'm telling you, I'm innocent and I'm not going to stop saying it. And you'll have the fight of your life if you try to yank my license."

More applause echoed off the ceilings.

The chairwoman scooted her chair back and the other six followed her into some sort of pseudo-huddle, like a peewee football game.

"I'm sorry." Miranda stood again, a look of disgust covering her face. "What about her . . . illicit actions above the bar?"

"Are you kidding—?"

"I'd like to say something about that."

Jo froze. Trace. There was no mistaking his voice. She turned to the right and caught him standing out of the corner of her eye. And in that moment, she realized something she'd been trying to circle around, step over, and ignore for weeks.

She loved him. He'd done this—brought these people together—for her. Even after she'd turned him away, he'd done it for her.

"I hardly think anyone believes Jo is running an old-fashioned bordello here. This isn't 1890. Plus, I'm not sure how she'd manage it, since she spends about ninety percent of her time behind the bar anyway."

Murmurs of agreement sounded in soft waves.

"I have witnesses that place men in her apartment."

"What, one snot-nosed kid trying to get out of trouble by spewing lies?" Trace bit out.

"I'm allowed to have a personal life!" Jo called at the same time. They looked at each other and smiled.

Miranda's mouth set in a firm line. "How inappropriate."

"To have a love life?" Jo asked. "Tell me where in the town by-laws that little gem is."

The crowd went silent. The council looked . . . she

wasn't sure. Some of them looked almost sick, others uncertain or confused. And then she realized she'd all but
admitted to an entire town—give or take a few hundred—
she was having sex.

Which would lead to speculation about who she was
having said sex with . . . those who hadn't already figured
it out, anyway.

Which would lead to rumors, gossip, maybe more damaging lies. So why not cut to the chase?

She glanced at Trace. It was his business, too. His permission came in the form of a slight nod, and a wink.

Deep breath. "I can't believe I'm about to do this," she
muttered.

"What's the alternative?" Stu asked.

"Good point. Okay, so I have a love life. I'm not sleeping with a married man, not screwing in the bar, not doing anything illegal. I really don't see how the rest of this
is anyone's—"

"Who's the lucky guy?"

Jo shot Mr. Meldon a threatening look. He merely
smiled and shrugged. "I'm an old, curious man. Sue me."

God help her, she smiled back. What the hell else could
she do? She'd wanted small town life, and here it was. After
a moment's hesitation, she knew what she needed to do.

"I'm not spending time with multiple men. I've been
spending time with Trace Muldoon. Just him."

More silence, but for the hum of the AC. No gasps of
shock, no looks of horror, no applause. What, was this really old news to everyone?

"I'm new here. That has been made abundantly clear."
She resisted sticking her tongue out at Miranda's back . . .
barely. "But I want roots. I plan to plant them here. And
if I have to fight every step of the way, battle for every
inch, I'll do it. I've made up my mind, and that's not
something that can be easily changed."

Judy Plumber looked at her fellow high-horsers and once again they huddled together.

"Time to pray," Stu warned her.

"I've never been much on prayer." But she could sure start now. As she started to formulate her opening to God, the council finished their mini-huddle and straightened.

"It appears to us," Judy said in a tight voice, "there is no further action needed at this time."

The room erupted into applause. Jo grabbed the back of the chair in front of her to keep her legs from buckling with relief.

"Is it over?"

Stu put a hand on her shoulder and squeezed. "Yeah, it's over. I'm heading back to the bar. Not sure why, but I have a feeling we're about to get the bum rush for a late lunch."

"Yeah." She grinned. "I think you might be right."

The next ten minutes were a blur of congratulations, staggering backslaps and handshakes. She smiled so much her cheeks hurt, but she couldn't help it.

From the corner of her eye, she caught Miranda Effingham slip out the side door. Let her sulk. Maybe she'd think twice about picking on the new guy from now on.

A spike of awareness lifted the hairs on the back of her neck. And she knew he was behind her.

"Hey."

Her body shivered in response to Trace's voice. She turned, and stared up into his eyes, and smiled.

She was smiling. That had to be a good thing.

"Hey, yourself, cowboy." She looked past his arm to the trickle of people who had yet to exit the building. "Interesting meeting."

"Yeah, well. I heard these things were a real riot. Couldn't pass up a chance to see for myself. Community outreach, and all that." She said nothing, and he started to feel like an idiot. Rather than reach for her and pull her into his arms for a hug, he stuffed his hands in his pockets. "So, you must be relieved."

"I'm a lot of things." She ran a hand over her eyes, as if wiping away the stress of the day. "Relieved is a biggie."

"And?"

"Grateful, for another." She reached for him, and the skin of his forearm sizzled where she touched. "Thank you. I know it was you who brought all these people out here."

"I just told them when and where. They made up their minds to come on their own. You might be the new guy, Jo, but you're far from unwanted." He hoped she understood that he meant that in more ways than one.

But he'd promised not to push.

"Where's Seth?"

Not a question he'd expected. "At home with Bea. I'm sure they're catching up on the week's soaps. When I get home, he'll likely think he's his own evil twin, bent on revenge for one of his stuffed animals ruining his life."

She laughed. "She's just keeping up on—"

"Industry news," they finished together, and chuckled.

"Yeah, well, anyway. You heading back to the bar? I think you're going to have a standing room only situation on your hands tonight."

"Eventually." She smiled a little, the gesture confusing him. Normally, she smiled at him like that right before she would jump him in bed.

"Then I should let you go."

"Don't." Her other arm wrapped around him, pulling them together. "Don't let me go."

"Jo," he warned.

"I screwed up. Full disclosure, I do that sometimes. Maybe more than sometimes."

The words, almost a mirror of what he'd told her before, made him smile. "People are watching," he said without moving his mouth.

"Let them." She didn't look around, just kept eye contact. "I freaked out. You've had like a year to handle being a dad. I had a few days with the little guy, and only a couple of hours alone. I still need time to get there, feel comfortable with Seth. But that doesn't mean I don't like him."

"I know that." Taking a chance, he stroked one hand down her ponytail, gripping the end at the small of her back. "I do. And he likes you, too."

"And I like his dad." She took a deep breath, pressing her breasts into his chest. "Maybe I even more than like his dad."

"More than like, huh?" He grinned at that. "How about I take the first step? I love you, Jo."

She let her forehead fall to his sternum. "Why is it so easy for you to say? Isn't the girl supposed to be all in touch with her emotions and the guy all hung up on using words like that?"

"So we've got a little role reversal. No big. I'm man enough to know when I'm in love. And I still get to wear the chaps."

She laughed. Laughed so hard tears started to roll down her cheeks. "Okay. Take me home to my bordello."

The minute her apartment door closed behind them, Jo tore at his shirt. Her hands slid over warm skin, sleek hard muscles. Oh, God, she'd missed him.

"Oh!" She startled as he lifted her up with both hands under her ass. On cue, she wrapped her legs around his waist and let him carry her the rest of the way to the bed.

"Don't push me away again." His lips moved over her face. Up the bridge of her nose, over her eyelids, her temple, down to nuzzle below her ear. "Kick me out for the night if you're pissed at me. But don't push me away."

"No." She could barely breathe the word through the tightness in her chest.

He lowered them both to the bed and undressed her slowly, pulling her nice jacket off and tossing it to the floor. She had a fleeting thought that it'd have to be hung up, but then he managed to tug the supportive chemise top down over her breast and latch his mouth on her nipple and she didn't care about laundry. Her hands cupped the back of his head, fingers scratching. Her head dug into the pillow as she arched into him.

And then she was cold. Or cooler than she'd been before. Somehow he'd managed to divest her of her pants while she'd been enjoying his attentions up top. Smooth operator, this cowboy. Smoother still, as he slid down her body and put that sweet-talking mouth to good use. His shoulders propped her thighs wider and one hand rested over her stomach, keeping her from moving too much while he licked through her warmth.

Her stomach tightened under his touch, but he rubbed until she relaxed. At least, relaxed her torso. Her hands fisted in the comforter and she resisted the urge to scream. What with a full house downstairs, she figured that wouldn't exactly be good for business. Or the rumors about her running a brothel . . .

"Oh, God. Trace . . ." Her hands found his head and she stroked until she couldn't wait any longer. "Stop, please stop."

He lifted his head, and she smiled. "With me."

He broke land records for removing his clothes—if such records existed—and was with her in an instant, pushing inside her, moving with her until they were both sweating from the exertion to hold back. Without saying it, they both wanted to make it last.

"I love you," he whispered, kissing her neck. "I love you."

She wanted to say something, anything. But her climax caught her off guard and she cried out. He muffled her sounds with a deep kiss, back tightening under her hands, as he came.

Five minutes later, Jo was still struggling to regulate her breathing.

"That was some ride."

"Mmphfeed."

"Either that's a cowboy term I haven't learned yet, or you have to take your face out of the pillow first."

He lifted his grinning face. "I said, 'indeed.' Some ride."

Jo stroked one hand over his face, the hair that missed a cut a week ago, the scruff he ignored so often. "I love you."

His eyes lit, and she realized he hadn't expected her to say it back. Hadn't assumed. Hadn't been ready to pressure her into it, make her feel guilty about it. He'd just been prepared to wait. Which only made her love him more?

"I love you," she said again, the words bringing a lightness to her breathing, to her life. "Wow. I can't remember the last time I said that."

"About two seconds ago. But say it again, so you can remember how."

"I love y—" She broke off when he kissed her. "You," she finished.

"No pressure."

She closed her eyes a moment. "I can't promise I'm what's best for Seth."

"I'm what's best for Seth. And you're what's best for me. So, ipso facto . . ."

One brow arched. "Did you say 'ipso facto' to me while you're still inside me?"

"Whoops." He pulled out and gave her a serious look. "Ipso facto. Better?"

"Smart ass," she said, slapping him playfully on the thigh as he got up to head to the bathroom.

"But I'm your smart ass." His face sobered a little. "We take it slow, for real this time. We hang together, you promise not to freak out when he cries—which he will, because he's a baby. And we go from there. You've got a lot of love built up in you, Jo. You just weren't ready to open the floodgates yet."

"Oh, you know that for a fact, do you?" She pinched his butt.

"Yeah, I do. If you aren't worried about us cramping your style—"

Her mouth dropped open. "What? Why would I worry about that?"

"Super hot bar owner suddenly takes on boring father and son?" He shrugged. "It could drag a person down."

"Hardly." She blew out a breath and nodded. "Fine. You don't worry about cramping my style, and I won't worry about screwing up with Seth daily."

"It's a deal." He kissed her to seal it.

"Love you," she sighed. She couldn't stop saying it, hearing her own voice give power to the words.

"Love you, too."

They'd be good. The two, and then the three of them. She could believe it now.

If you love contemporary Western romance, be sure to check out Cat Johnson's Oklahoma Nights series.

ONE NIGHT WITH A COWBOY
On sale now

One Sweet Ride . . .
Oh, yeah. A single look at the leggy blonde in the stands and Tucker Jenkins is ready to buck all night long. It's time to forget all about his cheating ex and his usual hands off policy.

One Hot Night . . .
Becca Hart is an East Coast professor. Not a buckle bunny. But no degree can prepare her for the moves of the sexy bull rider she hooks up with at her first rodeo . . . or the shock of finding him at her first Oklahoma State University staff meeting.

One Happy Ending . . .
Tuck knows it's all about holding on, no matter how wild the ride. Now he just has to convince Becca that a rough start out of the chute doesn't mean they aren't a smokin' combination . . .

"Cat Johnson continues to be one of my favorite authors. Whether it is in military, contemporary or the cowboy arena she definitely knows her alpha males."
—Joyfully Reviewed

"One sexy romp with a sweet and hot hero you'll want to keep around for longer than one night!"
—Lorelei James, *New York Times* bestselling author

The Oklahoma Nights series continues in *Two Times as Hot,* coming this October. Read on for an excerpt from Chapter One, as plans for Becca and Tuck's wedding get underway.

"This'll be your first time meeting Bec's sister, won't it?" Logan dipped his head in a nod. "Yes, sir. It sure will be."

"I'm not worried about Emma fitting in. Everyone loves her. It's the rest of the relatives I'm concerned about." Becca screwed up her face into a scowl. "My father, Mr. Punctuality, is beside himself they're not here an hour early and it sounded like my mother was already well into her sherry. She bought a bottle at the duty-free shop at the airport."

"Sounds like a hell of a start to a party." Jace walked through the door and scooped Becca into a hug that lifted her feet right off the ground. "Hey there, darlin'. You look great, as usual."

Speak of the devil . . . Jace gave Becca a kiss and set her on the ground.

Becca laughed. "Save some of those compliments for later when my relatives from New York are here and I'm tearing my hair out. I may need to hear them."

"You got it. And just send me the signal and I'll sneak you some booze too, if you want it." Jace winked at her and slid a flask out of his pocket.

"I'll keep that in mind. A visit with my parents might

require some alcohol." Becca glanced at Tuck. "I'm going to go see if your mom needs any help in the kitchen."

"Sounds good, baby." Tuck nodded.

Jace watched Becca leave as he walked over to Tuck. He stuck out one arm to shake the groom's hand. "Hey, man. How you holding up? I got the truck filled up with diesel and coolers full of ice-cold beer. It's parked right outside, just in case. You ready to bolt yet?"

Logan shook his head. Typical Jace. As changeable as the wind. Sucking up to the bride with one breath, and offering to help the groom escape with the other.

Tuck's gaze cut to the doorway Becca had left through before he answered, "Not at all. I'm loving every minute of it. Nothing more fun than planning a big ol' wedding. You want a beer? I'm getting myself another one."

Logan glanced at his own bottle. He wasn't even half way done with his own beer yet but Tuck's was empty. Tuck might pretend he was calm, cool and collected about the wedding and all it entailed, but the empty bottle told another story.

Out of town relatives. Nervous brides. Rentals. Last minute errands. Saying *I do* for the rest of your life . . . Yup, Logan sure was happy he'd be on the ushers' side of the altar rather than directly in the line of fire like the groom.

"Definite yes on the beer." Jace answered Tuck and turned to extend a hand toward Logan. "Lieutenant Colonel Hunt, sir. What's the status of the Oklahoma State ROTC program?"

Logan laughed as Jace lowered his tone of voice and spoke more like a battalion commander than a bull rider. "A little slow right now since we're between semesters for the summer, but thanks for asking. How you been, Jace?"

"Good. Rodeoing quite a bit now that it's summer.

Dragging Tuck with me when I can convince him to ride."

"Just don't break him, please. Tuck may be a bull rider part time, but full time he's one of my soldiers, and one of my department's best military science instructors. I need him with two good working legs for when we go back to working out with the cadets. Got it?"

"Sure thing. Let's just hope Becca doesn't break him during the honeymoon." Jace waggled his eyebrows. "As for rodeo, he usually ends up getting his ribs broken when he wrecks, not his legs, so we're good. Broke ribs hurt like a son of a bitch, but he can still run with 'em."

Jace grinned and accepted the beer Tuck handed him. "Thanks for the vote of confidence, Jace. And I only broke my ribs once or twice, thank you very much."

"Once or twice, my sweet ass. You can't seem to keep yourself out from under hoof. You're too tall for a bull rider, if you ask me. You need to be small and quick like me. You should have stuck with team roping."

Watching the two men bicker, Logan sipped his beer and stayed out of the fray. He wasn't about to enter that debate. Bull riders were crazy.

Sure, Logan had joined the Army knowing there'd be times during his career he was going to be up against an enemy who wanted him dead, but to get on the back of a bucking bull knowing you were going to be thrown in the dirt every damn time? Nope. Not for him.

While Jace and Tuck continued to banter—something about which bull Jace drew last time he rode—motion out in the driveway caught Logan's eye. He turned to watch through the window as a hot as hell woman in a short, black dress reached one long, bare leg out of the car. She stepped out of the open passenger door and even doing nothing but standing in the driveway, she was sexy enough to make a man take notice. Her blond hair and resemblance to Becca told him this must be her sister Emma.

Logan glanced at Tuck and wondered how bad of a friend he was that Tuck's soon to be sister-in-law was giving him a hard-on. Just from his thinking about what the curves that dress accentuated so nicely would feel like beneath his touch.

Imagine if he ever actually got his hands on her?

An older woman and man got out of the front doors of the sedan and joined the blonde. They had to be Tuck's new in-laws. Their presence should have diminished Logan's amorous fantasies about Emma. It didn't. It seemed Emma had captured his attention and she wasn't letting go. He managed to block her parents right out as he wondered what her hair would feel like against his cheek while he ran his tongue down her throat.

"Hey, Tuck. It looks like Emma's here." Jace came to stand next to Logan at the window. He let out a slow whistle. "Boy oh boy, is she looking good."

The tone of Jace's voice made Logan turn to get a good look at him. The man had a knowing expression on his face that didn't sit well at all. "You know her?"

"Ohhh, yeah." Jace dragged the two short words out to be obscenely long. What the hell was that about? Logan's brows rose. He turned to glance at Tuck.

"Emma was here with Becca the first time she came to Oklahoma for the job interview at OSU. You know, the night she and I met at the rodeo," Tuck had answered without Logan having to ask, but that sure as hell didn't explain the rest. Such as why Jace was acting as if he and Emma had done more than just meet that night?

Those were details Logan was more than interested in having. "Yeah, I remember you telling me about the rodeo."

But not that Jace and Becca's hot sister from New York had had a little one night rodeo of their own.

Of course, Jace liked to exaggerate. It didn't matter if it was about conquering a bull or a woman. Logan had known the man for years through Tuck. Since the two had ridden on the rodeo circuit together before Tuck had enlisted in the Army. If nothing else, he knew Jace could throw the shit with the best of them. It was very possible nothing at all had happened between Jace and Emma, except in Jace's own overactive imagination.

He decided to run with that theory and see how things progressed. It was far better than the alternative—assuming Jace had a prior claim and having to back off. A lot could happen over a short period of time. Look at how one night between Tuck and Becca had changed both of their lives. Logan had an entire weekend and a wedding reception to work with. There'd be sentimental speeches and tears, music and a fully stocked bar. Everything to put the partygoers—and Emma—in the mood for romance.

Not to mention Logan had Tuck on his side, pulling for him, putting in a good word. At least Tuck had better be on his side. Jace was Tuck's friend, yes, but Logan was like a brother. Not to mention his boss and a superior officer. If it came right down to it, Logan would pull rank. Hell, he could order Tuck to put in a good word for him with Emma or else.

When it involved leggy blondes with curves like Emma's, a man had to bend the rules a little sometimes.

Don't miss the next in Kat Murray's Roped and Wrangled series. *Busting Loose* is coming next January.

Morgan Browning, DVM, stared his arch-nemesis down.

"You can't beat me."

His enemy blinked.

"I'm smarter. I'm stronger. And I can think."

Blink. Blink.

"I will take you down."

The phone blinked again, signaling that this little intimidation exercise had not, in fact, helped solve the problem of how to get the voicemail off the machine to make the light go off.

"Damn it." He pushed away from the desk in disgust. Why had Jaycee left for the day already? It was just three. She was the only one who knew how to make the stupid machine behave.

She'd given him a month to find a replacement for her as she trained to be his new vet tech. Despite the inconvenience of having to hire someone new, he agreed with her choice to become a tech. And Jaycee had been pulling double duty, answering phones between patients.

But why, God why, had she left him alone for the afternoon without teaching him how to make the ugly thing stop blinking?

The bell above the door swung open, and Morgan

pasted on his friendly, paying-customer smile. But as he turned and caught sight of his patient, the smile broadened naturally.

"Bea, hey. What's going on?"

"I—" She glanced at the phone as it rang, then at the empty chair. "Do you need to get that?"

"No, it's fine." He reached for Bea's Boston terrier, Milton, which she'd adopted a few months ago. "Do you have an appointment?" The dog licked his face, smudging one lens of his glasses even more than it already had been.

The phone stopped ringing, and blissful silence—except for the dog's snuffled breathing—filled the waiting area. He sighed in relief; then his body clenched again when the phone rang once more.

"No appointment. I just . . . okay, are you sure you don't want to get that?" She pointed a finger at The Devil. "We can wait a few minutes."

"Ignore it." He was. Morgan held the Boston up to eye level. "Hey, dude. What's up?"

"He keeps scratching." Bea puffed and blew out some baby-fine white-blond hair from her eyes. Her hair reminded him of a pile of feathers, it looked so lightweight.

"Dogs scratch, Bea." He hid a smile behind Milton's back. To Bea's mind, every whimper and whine was a new health scare for her pup. "But let's go take a look at—"

"That's it!" Bea swerved around the desk on heels so high they had to be a danger to her health and plopped down in Jacyee's chair. Picking up the phone and pressing two buttons he never would have considered pressing together, she chirped, "Morgan Browning's office, how can I help you?"

Morgan's eyes nearly bugged out as far as Milton's. The flighty, sometimes-ditzy Beatrice Muldoon had just sounded like a true professional. Fascinated, he leaned over the desk to observe.

"Yes, of course. Oh, the poor thing," she cooed. "Let me check for you; please hold just one moment." Pressing another two buttons, she glanced over at him quickly. "Appointments this evening?"

He shook his head. "None so far. Who is it?"

"The Peckinpaughs. Their family dog is throwing up. Do you want to . . ." She motioned to the phone.

"Yeah, just a minute."

He picked up the receiver, then stared helplessly at The Devil. "Help."

"Men," she muttered, then pressed a few buttons and waved for him to continue.

"Thank you," he mouthed and pointed toward the open exam room behind him, holding up a finger to indicate he'd be there in a moment.

She nodded and scooped Milton up, walking to the room and closing the door behind her.

God almighty, those legs of hers made his mouth water more than any rare steak ever could. The things he would give up in life to be able to watch her kick off her shoes under his exam table and crawl up there for—

"Hello?"

Shit. "Yes, hello, Mrs. Peckinpaugh. I hear Toby's having some trouble."

Legs could wait. At least for now.

"No, Milton, stop that." She bent down and placed her fingers between his scratching paw and his neck, earning an unintentional swipe over her knuckles for her trouble. "Ow, that hurt."

"Did he get ya?"

Morgan's voice from behind startled her, and she straightened so fast, blood rushed from her head. His hands went around her biceps to steady her and ease her into a chair.

"Whoa, now. Didn't mean to scare you. Just sit a second. Standing up at that altitude might really get ya."

"Altitude?" she asked, bringing her hand up to inspect the scratch. Just a red scrape, no broken skin. She eyed the dog, who looked innocent. A look he'd been perfecting for a few months now.

"The heels," he said with a smile. "Need me to check your pulse?" He was watching her eyes from behind hopelessly smudged glasses, and she knew he was taking stock of whether her pupils were dilated. Or not dilated. Whatever it was those medical types were looking for.

Cutie. Dr. Cutie. Wanting to save the world one forlorn case at a time.

"I'm fine. But Milton needs help."

Morgan looked skeptical at that, but he hunkered down and called the dog, who trotted toward him with ease. Morgan removed his collar to inspect the skin underneath. "Where is he scratching?"

"His shoulders and neck, mostly. Sometimes at his ears."

"You're using a flea and tick prevention?"

"The one you recommended, yes."

"Bathed him in anything new?"

"No. Same stuff since I got him."

"Hmm." Morgan picked up the dog and checked under one leg, then the other. "Any other problems? Not eating, not drinking?"

"He's fine, other than the scratching."

"Well, then I think you're gonna make it, my man." He roughed up the top of Milton's head with two knuckles in a gesture of manly affection for the small dog. "I think he's got allergies."

"Allergies? The dog?" She rolled her eyes. "It would figure I'd get a high maintenance dog. Allergies."

He refrained from making any sort of joke about a high maintenance dog for a high maintenance woman. She appreciated the restraint. But he did smile and hold out a hand to help her up.

"I'll get some samples of allergy meds. But really, you can give him the human stuff. I've got a paper around here somewhere that gives you the dosing instructions based on his weight."

He walked back out to the front desk and started opening file cabinets at random, peering in, and slamming them shut again quickly. Milton escaped deep under the desk, in a dark corner, as if sensing something bad was coming.

The phone rang again, and Morgan completely ignored it.

After the third ring, she asked, "Should I get that again?"

"No, I can do it." His voice was muffled in a drawer.

Uh huh. Right. Since he didn't know how to take a call off hold, he could obviously answer the complex office phone system. "You look like you're busy—I'll just answer this one." She slid around him, her thigh brushing against his shoulder.

And okay, wow, her nerve endings stood up on point for that one. Clearly, if she was getting hot for the vet, she'd been in Marshall too long. Finding him adorable in a distant, *sure, he's cute* sort of way was one thing. Getting hot for the good animal doctor was another thing entirely.

"Morgan Browning's office, how can I help you?" She listened, scribbling the message down on a pad of paper to pass him when he was through. "That's wonderful, I'm so glad you're considering a dog from the shelter. I have to tell you, I just got my Milton from there a few months ago."

Morgan turned to watch her, but she shrugged. How hard could this be?

"What kind of dog are you looking for? Mm hmm, yes, okay . . ." She scribbled down the traits the family was hoping for on a pad of paper. "I'll have Dr. Browning give you a call back in a bit, after he's had a chance to think about it. How does that sound? In the meantime, there's a form online you can print off and fill out to bring in with you. That would save you some time when you come Yes, just go to the vet website, then click on the tab up above for the shelter. Yes, that's right. Well, thanks to you, too. I hope you find what you're looking for!"

She hung up and smiled, then caught Morgan's stare. "What?"

"How did you do that?"

"What?" She looked at the phone. "Answer it?"

"No, know how to do all that . . ." He waved a hand around like he was swatting flies. "All that talking crap."

Bea rolled her eyes and patted his cheek . . . which was easy to reach since he was squatting by another file cabinet. "Sweetie, talking is what I do for a living. Acting on a soap is ninety percent talking. And plus, I just went through this process a few months ago. It's fresh in my mind. They're looking for a small dog, more of a lap dog than anything. No kids, just the wife and her husband. Empty nesters." She pushed the pad toward him and stood. "That's their number. I told them you'd check what's available now and get back to them."

He grabbed her arms again, the way he had in the exam room, but it had nothing to do with catching her before she fainted. His hands were warm against her chilled, bare skin, the pressure just a little insistent.

"You can answer the phones."

She nodded slowly at his wild-eyed gaze. "Yes."

"You can talk to people."

"I manage to use real words and everything," she bit off.

"Can you use e-mail and figure out a calendar program?"

"Morgan, who the hell doesn't know how to use e-mail anymore? What's this all about?"

"You're hired."

"I'm what?"